ROBERT B. PARKER'S

# Blackjack

## THE SPENSER NOVELS

*Robert B. Parker's Kickback*
(by Ace Atkins)
*Robert B. Parker's Cheap Shot*
(by Ace Atkins)
*Silent Night*
(with Helen Brann)
*Robert B. Parker's Wonderland*
(by Ace Atkins)
*Robert B. Parker's Lullaby*
(by Ace Atkins)
*Sixkill*
*Painted Ladies*
*The Professional*
*Rough Weather*
*Now & Then*
*Hundred-Dollar Baby*
*School Days*
*Cold Service*
*Bad Business*
*Back Story*
*Widow's Walk*
*Potshot*
*Hugger Mugger*
*Hush Money*
*Sudden Mischief*
*Small Vices*
*Chance*
*Thin Air*
*Walking Shadow*

*Paper Doll*
*Double Deuce*
*Pastime*
*Stardust*
*Playmates*
*Crimson Joy*
*Pale Kings and Princes*
*Taming a Sea-Horse*
*A Catskill Eagle*
*Valediction*
*The Widening Gyre*
*Ceremony*
*A Savage Place*
*Early Autumn*
*Looking for Rachel Wallace*
*The Judas Goat*
*Promised Land*
*Mortal Stakes*
*God Save the Child*
*The Godwulf Manuscript*

## THE JESSE STONE NOVELS

*Robert B. Parker's The Devil Wins*
(by Reed Farrel Coleman)
*Robert B. Parker's Blind Spot*
(by Reed Farrel Coleman)
*Robert B. Parker's Damned If You Do*
(by Michael Brandman)

*Robert B. Parker's Fool Me Twice*
(by Michael Brandman)
*Robert B. Parker's Killing the Blues*
(by Michael Brandman)
*Split Image*
*Night and Day*
*Stranger in Paradise*
*High Profile*
*Sea Change*
*Stone Cold*
*Death in Paradise*
*Trouble in Paradise*
*Night Passage*

## THE SUNNY RANDALL NOVELS

*Spare Change*
*Blue Screen*
*Melancholy Baby*
*Shrink Rap*
*Perish Twice*
*Family Honor*

## THE COLE/HITCH WESTERNS

*Robert B. Parker's The Bridge*
(by Robert Knott)
*Robert B. Parker's Bull River*
(by Robert Knott)

*Robert B. Parker's Ironhorse*
(by Robert Knott)
*Blue-Eyed Devil*
*Brimstone*
*Resolution*
*Appaloosa*

## ALSO BY ROBERT B. PARKER

*Double Play*
*Gunman's Rhapsody*
*All Our Yesterdays*
*A Year at the Races*
(with Joan H. Parker)
*Perchance to Dream*
*Poodle Springs*
(with Raymond Chandler)
*Love and Glory*
*Wilderness*
*Three Weeks in Spring*
(with Joan H. Parker)
*Training with Weights*
(with John R. Marsh)

ROBERT B. PARKER'S

# Blackjack

Robert Knott

G. P. PUTNAM'S SONS
*New York*

G. P. PUTNAM'S SONS
*Publishers Since 1838*
An imprint of Penguin Random House LLC
375 Hudson Street
New York, New York 10014

Copyright © 2016 by The Estate of Robert B. Parker
Penguin supports copyright. Copyright fuels creativity, encourages diverse voices,
promotes free speech, and creates a vibrant culture. Thank you for buying an authorized
edition of this book and for complying with copyright laws by not reproducing, scanning,
or distributing any part of it in any form without permission. You are supporting writers
and allowing Penguin to continue to publish books for every reader.

ISBN 978-1-101-98253-2

Printed in the United States of America
1   3   5   7   9   10   8   6   4   2

BOOK DESIGN BY AMANDA DEWEY

*For Julie*

# 1.

R uth Ann was running now, moving as fast as she could through the dense forest. The Comanche moon hanging directly above dimly lit her way through thick timber of pine, blackjack, birch, and maple.

There were no shoes on her bloody feet and what was left of her dress was ripped, soiled, and hanging off her bare shoulders. She was dirty, with leaves and sticks tangled in her auburn hair. She glanced back as she ran. She was terrified, her face tearstained, scratched, and bleeding, and her eyes were wide with fear and . . . then he awoke. It was not the first time Roger Wayne Messenger awoke from this vision, this nightmare of Ruth Ann running through the woods, and he was fairly certain it would not be his last.

Roger sat up a little and worked the ache from his back. His mouth was dry and his head was pounding. With the exception of the dampness he found in the corners of his eyes, the rye whiskey he consumed on the journey sucked his body of all its moisture. His mouth was so parched his lips were stuck together. He sat up and looked around at the dark landscape passing by. All of the other passengers were asleep. He wished he, too, was asleep, but sleep was something he had not been accustomed to for some time. He dug into his knapsack and found his canteen and drank and drank.

Roger was a big, lean, and strong man with thick, dark hair that was three inches long on the top and cropped tight to the sides of his head. He was normally clean-shaven around his sweeping thick mustache, but at the moment he was sporting three days of whiskers. He wore a brown herringbone suit that was usually pressed over a starched white shirt, but currently his attire was crumpled from days of neglect.

When Roger stepped off the morning train in Appaloosa, he snugged his brown wide-brim with rolled edges over his square forehead and walked into town. He stopped at S. Q. Johnson's Grocery and bought a can of beans. He sat under the shade of the store's overhang, opened the can with his army knife, and ate the beans using the blade. When he finished he went about the task he'd come to Appaloosa to accomplish.

He poked his head in the door of Cheever's Saddle shop and asked the old-timer tanning a large hide for directions to his destination. Then he walked seven blocks, turned south on Main Street, and went two more blocks to the construction site.

It was an impressive building. Three stories tall and at least seventy-five feet wide, with a second-story covered porch that had five sets of glassed double doors across the balcony. To Roger's untrained eye the structure appeared to be nearly complete, but the building was busy with construction workers.

Roger thought about just walking into the place, but decided he would watch for a while, watch and wait. He was good at watching and waiting; it was part of his job, and now that he was here, he was not in any hurry. Better to be patient. Better to wait.

He stood across the street, watching all the laborers going about their business. There were painters on scaffoldings painting a second coat of white and carpenters on the boardwalk, assembling wood pieces and going about other various tasks of measuring and sawing, remeasuring and resawing.

A team of mules pulling a flatbed stopped in front of the stairs leading up to the entrance with a load of hardwood. Roger rolled and lit a cigarette as he watched a few of the teamsters unload the flatbed and stack the shiny planks neatly on the boardwalk under a wide leaded-glass window.

He thought about the amount of money it must take for an impressive undertaking such as this. He had no idea, but then again, this line of business was something that Roger was just not all that familiar with.

Roger watched and waited. He moved off the boardwalk and found a comfortable spot in the narrow alley between an upholstery shop and a dry-goods store, where he had a good view of the goings-on across the street. His head was still throbbing and he felt a little dozy, but he remained alert by nipping on the second bottle of rye he had in his knapsack and rolling and smoking cigarettes. He had plenty of both.

At nearly ten-thirty a slender sorrel pulling a two-seater buggy with a covered backseat rounded the corner and stopped in front of the building. An older, portly man with bushy white muttonchops and wearing a flattop brushed beaver hat sat in the backseat. Next to him was an attractive young woman wearing a plum-colored dress with a high collar.

They remained under the shaded cover, looking at the building for a long while. Then the man worked his way butt first out of the buggy's backseat.

Roger smiled to himself as he watched the round man struggle to get his chubby frame out of the backseat. When he was out of the buggy and standing, supporting his stance with the aid of a polished black cane, he removed his hat and wiped sweat from his forehead with a handkerchief. The young woman remained in the buggy. She leaned out and her eyes caught a little sunlight before she sat back in the shade of the buggy.

"Come back, pick me up by two o'clock," he said to the driver, "two o'clock sharp."

"Sir," the driver said with a tip of his brim, and then clucked the sorrel and moved off down the street, with the young woman still aboard and leaving the portly man looking up to the building. He turned, walked a few steps toward the middle of the wide street, stopped, then turned and looked back up at the building.

It was obvious to Roger the man wanted to have a full view of the building, wanted to take in all its grandness. The way the man moved and held his chin high reminded Roger of his own grandfather's survey after a day of stacking hay in the barn. But this man was no farmer. Roger thought by the way he stood with his fists on his hips holding back the sides of his coat, watching the workers with an appraising eye, that he must be the man with the money, the man in charge or the banker that loaned the business the money.

Then Roger saw him, the man that he had traveled two days on the train to locate. The man known in gambling parlors from New Orleans to San Francisco as Boston Bill Black.

Boston Bill came walking out of the building flanked by two smaller men. It's not that the men by his side were in any way short or even below average in size, it was simply that Boston Bill was unusually tall. Not unlike Roger—Roger was tall, too—but he was a good hand shorter than Boston Bill. Boston Bill's head barely cleared the top of the door as he walked out. He was wearing a fancy suit with a green vest that was adorned with a draping gold watch fob.

# 2.

The tall gambling man that Roger had come searching for in Appaloosa was right here in front of him now. He was a strong, handsome-looking man with silver-streaked black hair and a black-as-coal mustache.

At the moment he had a huge smile on his face as he walked down the steps with his hand extended toward the portly man in the street. The two men with him stayed back behind him a few steps. They both wore dark suits, but they weren't refined in any way, not like Boston Bill.

Roger could certainly determine that detail about the two men. It was part of his job to quickly assess people and he was good at assessing. He figured if it wasn't for their long, dirty hair, they might pass for guardsmen, like Dickerson men or Pinkertons or Denver police, even. But hell, they were nothing, no-accounts. One of them was blond and pretty like a woman, Roger thought. The other had deep-set eyes with a scraggly beard. He was skinny and younger than the blond man and a little smaller.

They both were heeled and looked like capable customers to Roger, but he was unconcerned with them. It was the tall man, it was Boston Bill, that Roger was interested in.

Roger knew how to do his job. He'd been at it for a long while, and even

*though this time the job was personal, he still operated as he had always oper-*
*ated, with ease and friendliness. No need to get all rigged up or emotionally*
*boiling.*

"Mr. Pritchard," Boston Bill said. "Good to see you. How was your trip?"

*Before Mr. Pritchard could answer, Roger moved out of the narrow alley*
*and spoke with some volume.*

"Mr. Black."

*Roger stepped off the boardwalk and took a few steps into the street. He*
*took a step back and waited as a horse and buggy passed, then continued to*
*walk toward Boston Bill.* It's okay, *Roger thought.* It is okay.

"I'd like to have a word or two with you," *Roger said.* "Just a moment of
your time."

*Roger always worked like this. He was as smooth as butter, everyone*
*would say. Boston Bill glanced back at his two seconds, then looked back at*
*Roger. Roger had to slow up again as a horse and rider hurried by.*

"I'm sorry," *Boston Bill said.* "If you are looking for work, I'm afraid
there are no positions available at this time."

"Oh, no, no," *he said.* "Not looking for any position."

"Well, what can I help you with, then?"

*Roger thought to himself,* Just keep it simple; just keep it calm. *Roger*
*had done this sort of thing at least one hundred times. And like mother*
*always said,* "An ounce of kindness Roger, an ounce of kindness is worth,
worth . . . something about gold . . . the weight in gold?"

"Just a little business matter," *Roger said.*

*Boston Bill's second, the one with the blond hair, stepped forward with a*
*stance that suggested to Roger he thought he was much tougher than he looked.*

"That's far enough," *the blond man said.*

*Roger smiled.*

"There's no need to concern yourself, young man. This isn't any of your
business."

*The other of Boston Bill's seconds, the smaller man with the dark beard,* took a stance and spoke up with speech that seemed to Roger to be impaired by what looked to be a swollen jaw.

"It is our business," the man with the dark beard said, and then spit in the street.

Most of the workers stopped what they were doing and turned their attention to Roger.

Boston Bill looked to Mr. Pritchard and nodded toward the entrance of the building.

"Let's step inside," he said. "After you, Mr. Pritchard."

"Just hold on," Roger said. "Just a moment, I have something you need to see."

Roger put his hand into his knapsack, and when he did the blond man quickly pulled a butt-forward Colt.

"No," Roger said. "Just . . ."

Roger had underestimated the essence of the men. He did not expect this, not at all.

There were two quick shots. Gun smoke kicked from the barrel of the blond man's Colt. Roger was stunned. He stood looking at the smoke that hung almost motionless in the stillness of the late morning.

One of the shots went through the side of Roger's jacket, missing his torso, but one shot hit him dead center in his midsection. Roger looked down to where the bullet had entered. His hand came out of the knapsack clenching a scrolled paper.

"Oh, lordy," Roger said.

Roger staggered, falling on his backside on the hard packed dirt, and when he did his jacket opened up to reveal a shiny silver star pinned just over his heart on his gingham vest.

Somebody shouted, "He's a lawman."

"Goddamn it," Roger said. "Can't anybody do anything right?"

Roger managed to get back up on his feet, but he did not go for his pistol. He turned away and stepped up onto the boardwalk.

*"You have gone and done it now," Roger said. "And here I was trying to be proper and trying to keep this very . . ."*

*Roger took a few steps and thought about the fact that besides that damn can of beans he'd eaten earlier, he had not consumed much of anything substantial in the last few days, nothing at all. Then he thought maybe he should have gone about this little matter of business involving Boston Bill Black in a different way.*

*He took a few more steps. They were wobbly and awkward. Then he stumbled a bit and fell headfirst through a window of the upholstery shop.*

# 3.

Virgil bought Allie a new Chickering and Sons piano for Christmas, and she played it most every evening after dinner and sometimes after lunch, as she was doing this particular afternoon. Virgil and I both thought it curious that she wasn't getting any better, but she was trying and practicing and we were always offering our appreciation, encouragement, and support.

Currently Allie was playing a waltz and it was fairly smooth, but it wasn't helping Virgil's concentration. We were sitting on the back porch playing a game of chess, and Virgil had been taking his sweet time contemplating his next move.

It was a beautiful day in Appaloosa and there was not a cloud in the sky. The air was warm and there was just enough of a gentle breeze coming out of the north to keep the temperature from climbing up to discomfort. When Allie finished the tune, Virgil moved his rook and then sat back with some relief and a hint of strategic pride.

I studied the board and was waiting for another selection from Allie, but there was a knock at the front door instead.

"Oh, hey, there, Skinny Jack," we heard Allie say.

I leaned back in my chair and could see through the open rear door to the open front door, where Deputy Skinny Jack stood with his well-worn derby in his hand.

"Afternoon, Mrs. French. Sorry to interrupt. I'm looking for Marshal Cole and—"

"Not at all, come in, come in, they're out back."

"Thank you, ma'am."

"Good to see you," she said.

Allie put her hand on his shoulder and they walked down the hall toward the back porch.

"You have been on my mind," she said. "I think about your mother often . . . How have you been getting by?"

"Doing pretty okay," he said. "Coming up on the one-year anniversary of Mom's passing."

"My God, really?" Allie said. "Seems like yesterday. I sure miss her."

"Thank you, Mrs. French," he said. "Me, too . . . I appreciate your thoughts."

"Company," Allie said as they arrived at the back door.

Allie normally wore her long auburn hair up, but at the moment it was down. It was parted in the middle and fell well past her breasts and was pulled back behind one ear. She had on a light blue cotton dress that was loose and open around her neck, and her walnut tan skin made her blue eyes seem even bluer. She stood to the side, next to the doorjamb, with her shoulders back so Skinny Jack could step out onto the porch.

"Howdy, Marshal," he said. "Everett."

"Hey, Skinny Jack," I said.

Then I moved my bishop. Virgil met my eye with a tinge of dislike regarding my strategy. I smiled and leaned back, looking up at the young deputy.

"What is it, Jack?" I said.

He glanced at Allie, then back to me.

"Sheriff wanted me to fetch y'all."

Virgil looked from the board to Skinny Jack.

"For?" I said.

Skinny Jack pulled at the whiskers of his scruffy goatee as he smiled at Allie a little.

"Oh," she said, smiling back at Skinny Jack. "Excuse me, I've got dishes to wash anyway."

Virgil grinned at Allie.

"What?" Allie said.

"Nothing, Allie."

"Oh, Virgil," she said.

Skinny Jack watched as Allie walked off down the hall, then looked to Virgil.

"Been a shooting," Skinny Jack said.

"Who?" Virgil said.

"A policeman."

"Policeman?" I said.

"None of us," Skinny Jack said. "Thank God."

"What policeman?" Virgil said.

"He's from Denver."

"A Denver policeman shot here in Appaloosa?" I said.

"Seems so."

"Dead?" Virgil said.

"Not at the moment. Don't know if he'll make it, though."

"Who did it?" Virgil said.

"Truitt Shirley."

Virgil's eyes narrowed.

"You remember him?" I said.

Virgil held his squint a bit.

"Do," he said. "Bad seed."

I nodded.

"We had a run-in with him and some of his toughs," Virgil said.

"We did. You convinced him, the lot of 'em, to sleep it off."

"How do you know it was Truitt that did the shooting?" Virgil said.

"Witnesses," Skinny Jack said.

"Truitt been arrested?" I said.

"No."

"What's a Denver policeman doing here?" I said. "And why has he been shot by Truitt?"

"We don't know all the particulars," Skinny Jack said. "Know his name is Roger Messenger."

"Messenger?" Virgil said.

"You know him?" I said.

Virgil thought for a moment, then shook his head.

"Name is familiar," he said.

"He had a knapsack with a ticket receipt of travel from Denver and we found his name in his pocketbook. He showed up here in Appaloosa on the morning train. That's what we know about him."

"Have you wired the Denver authorities?" I said.

"No, sir. Sheriff wanted y'all to know."

"When was this?"

"'Bout an hour ago," Skinny Jack said.

"Where is the Denver fella now?" I said.

"Hospital. Doc said besides his condition being not so good, said he was drunk as hell, too. He had an empty bottle of rye in his knapsack."

"Where was this?" Virgil said

"In front of the new gambling-parlor building. But that's not all. This here is the reason Sheriff especially wanted me to find you two."

Skinny Jack pulled a rolled-up paper from his coat pocket and laid it on the table in front of us.

"This Roger fella had this here warrant for the gambling man, Boston Bill Black, in his possession. Matter of detail, he had it in his hand when he was shot."

I read it and then handed it to Virgil.

Virgil read it. Stared at it some.

"I'll be damn," he said.

"You called it," I said.

"Suspected it," he said.

"I was not far off your mark, Virgil."

Virgil nodded a little.

"Boston Bill Black wanted for murder," I said. "Ever since he showed up, acting special . . . you damn sure called it."

"Where is Sheriff Chastain?" Virgil said.

"Book, the sheriff, and the other deputies are out looking for Truitt and Bill Black."

Virgil turned to the open, curtain-covered window to his left.

"You hear everything okay, Allie?" he said.

Allie spoke from behind the curtains.

"Don't mean it's true."

"No, Allie, it don't, but there is this warrant here."

"Just a piece of paper," she said.

"No," Virgil said. "It's not just a piece of paper. A warrant is issued when there is proof and evidence."

Allie pulled back the curtains.

"Well, I don't believe it, Virgil."

Virgil turned to me then back to Allie.

"What?" he said with a shake of his head. "Why?"

"Not one word of it."

"Well, why would you not, Allie?"

"He's a fine upstanding gentleman."

Virgil rested both of his hands on the table, cocked his head, looking at Allie, then narrowed his brow.

"How would you know?"

"I just do," she said. "Call it woman's intuition."

Virgil smiled at me and shook his head a little, then looked back to Allie.

"Woman's intuition?" he said.

"Yes."

Virgil shook his head again.

"The man has been in town here for a short while and you're vouching for him."

"I'm not vouching for him, Virgil. I just heard from some of the ladies that he was a good fella."

"That so?"

"Yes," she said.

"Some of the ladies?"

"Yes," she said. "I even said hello to him at the town hall, and he was perfectly nice and upstanding."

"Well, hell," Virgil said. "That'd be for the judge to decide."

# 4.

I had first laid eyes on Boston Bill Black on a dark rainy night not long after he showed up in Appaloosa. I'd heard about his arrival and I knew he was an imposing character. His reputation as a gun hand, rounder, and raconteur preceded him, too, but then again, there are always two sides to a coin.

It was late in the evening when I stopped in for a whiskey at the Boston House that I saw the big man. I thought it was amusing or half interesting that a man named Boston Bill Black was in the Boston House Hotel Saloon. There he was, bigger than life, dealing cards in the gambling parlor just off the main barroom. He was seated at a corner table with three other fellas, dapper mining executives. I could tell by the stacks of the chips they were playing a high-stakes game of ventiuna; that was the common name for the game in the southwestern parts of the country. Some people called it twenty-one. Others . . . most . . . called it blackjack.

Boston Bill was an impressive-looking gent, no doubt. He was as big and strong as any man I ever saw. His neck, forearms, and wrists pushed outward on the fine fabric of his long jacket like the cylinders that drove and powered the wheels of a locomotive. I got myself a whiskey and took a seat at the end of the bar next to Pearl, a half-Cherokee, half-black whore from the Indian Territory. We had a connection, Pearl and me. Her father was a marshal, killed in the line of duty when he was working for hanging Judge Isaac Parker. Pearl was good at her profession and very nice to look at in her silky dresses that always exposed her strong, bare shoulders, but she was also unusual for a working woman. She was college-educated, smooth with conversation, political, and unafraid to speak her mind. She lived with another woman named Bernice and had only one main interest in men, and that was their money. Pearl was a friend, and as friends often do, she felt inclined to fill me in on some details she'd personally gathered regarding Boston Bill Black and his proclivities.

She glanced back over her brown shoulder at him sitting at the table, telling tall tales to his flip-card partners, and told me she had given him a ride two nights previous. She said that besides the fact he liked to gab a bit and was full of shit, he was rough with her.

"How so?" I said.

"Oh, he needed to turn me every which way," she said. "Like a damn origami or some such, Everett. Like he was trying to fix me into something I wasn't, and in the process he needed to whip me, spank me, like a cow . . . I didn't mind it, though. Some men are that way. Not you, of course, Everett, you are a gentleman. I believe it has to do with them being pulled from the teat too soon. Malnourishment obviously does not always have an effect on physical growth, but it most certainly affects the brain. The premature lack of nutrition causes them to feel the need to take out their aggression on the weaker sex, a manifestation of their need to be dominant though they are really just lacking in solid character. . . . Something you know nothing about, Everett."

She laughed, looked back at him, and studied him for a moment.

"Boston goddamn Bill," she said, shaking her head as she turned back to me. "I don't think that is where he is from, either, Boston. I think he is from the West, someplace."

Pearl smiled at Wallis as he strolled up behind the bar, cleaning a glass with a cotton towel.

"Wallis, my dear," Pearl said, "may I have some of that fine brandy?"

"You know it," Wallis said as he picked up a fancy bottle that was displayed in front of the silver-backed mirror behind the bar.

"I'm telling Everett about the molehill that comes in the form of a mountain."

Wallis smiled and set the clean glass in front of Pearl and poured her a shot of brandy, then rested both his hands out wide on the bar, facing Pearl and me.

"I told Boston Bill," she said, "that he reminded me of an Oregon man and it made him mad . . . I kind of knew it would make him mad, but I don't really care."

She laughed and spoke as if she were imitating him. "I am not from softwood country, you should know that, be able to tell that about me, darlin'. I'm from eastern, hardwood country, east of the mighty Mississippi, where hickories, gums, maples, oaks, and walnuts grow, and not from the western softwood country of cedars, hemlocks, pines, spruces, and firs."

She shook her head.

"Pat Cromwell said he's known him for a long time," Wallis said. "Pat said he put eight notches on the handle of his Colt while he worked the big boats up and down the Missouri, Ohio, Arkansas, and Mississippi."

"Well," I said, "I've not had the pleasure."

An older gentlemanly-looking man in a natty gray suit came in from the hotel and peered into the bar. Wallis nodded to Pearl; she turned, seeing him at the same time he saw her. She turned back to Wallis and me, then slipped off the stool.

"Time for a bedtime story," she said, and moved away to greet him.

I looked back to Boston Bill, whose chips appeared to be growing.

"Dyes the gray out of that mustache," Wallis said, eyeing Boston Bill.

"No doubt," I said.

Virgil had seen Boston Bill up close when he purchased a big buckskin geld from Salt at the livery. He introduced himself to Virgil, and it was then that Virgil grew suspicious and cautious of him. Virgil said Black proudly opened his long jacket to show he was not heeled. Said he was no longer a man that carried a gun. Said he'd been on both sides of the law and shot a good number of men in his time, but that those days were behind him now.

Regardless of who Boston Bill Black was or was not or where he was from or where he currently was located, he was now in our jurisdiction and was most assuredly wanted for murder.

# 5.

When Virgil and I walked to the hospital with Skinny Jack, the streets were busy with activity. Fact was, Appaloosa was always bustling these days, and every day it seemed the population was continuing to grow.

With the growth, the police force had tripled; Senior Deputy Clay Chastain was now Sheriff and deputies Skinny Jack Newton and Lloyd "Book" Daniels were no longer the inexperienced greenhorns they once were. Skinny Jack had grown from scrawny and skinny to lanky and lean, and Book, once just a hefty bookworm kid with rosy cheeks and spectacles, was now a grown man with a good head on his shoulders. Skinny Jack and Book taught, managed, and wrangled the group of deputies Sheriff Chastain hired to keep the peace, and every month it seemed a new deputy was in training.

Appaloosa was not hell-bent and rowdy like Muskogee, Deadwood, or Abilene, but Chastain's force was always busy handling one kind of situation or another.

When we got to the end of 5th Street we walked up the hill to the recently reconstructed, bigger, cleaner hospital and saw Sheriff

Chastain and Deputy Book sitting in the shade under the porch over-hang.

"What's the situation?" Virgil said.

"Well," Chastain said with his Texas drawl as he got to his feet, "last we heard from Doc Burris, he's still alive. Doc's in there with him now."

Chastain was a tough, rawboned man from Dallas with a scar from eyebrow to jawbone that supported his no-bullshit manner.

"Were you able to talk with him?" I said.

"No."

"What about Boston Bill Black and Truitt Shirley?"

Chastain shook his head.

"Not to be found."

"Big Boston Bill Black is hard to miss," I said.

"I know," Chastain said, "but we looked all over, so far nothing. I got pretty much everybody looking for him. So far all we got is the sonofabitch is gone."

"Anyone, seen him?" I said.

Deputy Book pointed up the street.

"Mrs. Bowen, over at the front desk of the Colcord, where he stays, said she saw him. Said he came in, went up to his room, was there a few minutes, then left."

"What about Truitt Shirley?" I said.

"Him, too," Chastain said.

"Gone?" Virgil said.

"Yep," Chastain said. "No sign of him and that other fella that was with him."

"Somebody has had to seen them," I said.

Chastain nodded.

"They could be around someplace," he said. "Most likely we'll find someone that can point us in the right direction or at least tell us the direction they left, but we have yet to do so."

"What was Truitt doing there," Virgil said, "with Bill Black?"

"Not real sure, but we think he was working for Boston Bill," Book said.

"Doing what?" I said.

"Truitt has not done an honest day's work in his life," Skinny Jack said.

"I don't know," Book said. "What one of the workers told me is all, and he was the one standing next to Boston Bill that shot the Denver policeman."

"I have not seen him in town, didn't know he was around till this," Skinny Jack said. "But Truitt has always run with a bunch of no-goods. Hell, I knew him as a kid. His old man was the same way. Both them apples got worms. Don't do much but connive folks and gamble."

Book said, "Didn't you tell me that Truitt and his bunch held up some westerners on the trail?"

Skinny Jack nodded.

"That's what I heard," he said.

"Whatever he is," Chastain said, "he's up till this moment not to be found, and now he's a wanted man himself, for killing this Denver policeman."

"He's not dead yet," Doc Burris said as he walked out the door, wiping his hands on a white cloth, then slapped the cloth to rest over his shoulder. He struck a match on the porch post and lit the pipe he had wedged in the corner of his mouth.

"Doubtful he'll pull through," he said, puffing on his pipe. "But he's still breathing."

"Is he alert, Doc?" I said.

"No," he said. "He's not."

Chastain looked to Virgil.

"You want me to round up a posse," he said.

Virgil shook his head.

"Right now," he said, "let's get out there and find someone that has laid eyes on Boston Bill, go from there. Truitt, too . . ."

"Witnesses said Messenger had a Colt in a belt holster when Truitt shot him," Book said. "But Messenger never went for it. They said he put his hand in his knapsack and that is when he got shot."

"What witnesses?" I said. "Who have you talked to, who was there when it happened?"

"Construction workers, mostly," Chastain said. "There was also Mr. Pritchard."

"Hollis Pritchard?" I said. "He was there?"

"He was."

Virgil looked at me.

"The owner of the gambling hall?"

"He is," I said.

"You talk to him?" Virgil said.

"A little bit," Chastain said. "He seemed upset and confused by what happened."

"So what the hell did happen?" I said.

"Workers I talked with said the Denver fella walked out from the boardwalk across the street," Book said. "He had a few words with Boston Bill and then come out of his knapsack holding that warrant you got in your hand."

I held up my hand with the rolled-up warrant Skinny Jack had handed to us on Virgil's back porch.

"Did Boston Bill see this," I said. "Know about this?"

"Don't know," Chastain said. "We don't have any idea about that."

Chastain looked to Virgil. Virgil was looking off as if he were thinking about something else.

"What now, Virgil?"

Virgil waited a moment as he thought, then looked back to Chastain.

"Contact Denver," he said. "See what you can find out about Roger Messenger, about the warrant, about who was murdered."

Chastain nodded.

"Book, you and Skinny Jack and the rest of your hands keep looking around, see if anyone knows anything," Virgil said. "Don't approach, just find out. Got one lawman shot, I damn sure don't want another."

Book and Skinny Jack nodded.

"Everett, let's you and me go have us a visit with Pritchard."

"Murdered?" Doc Burris said.

Doc Burris looked back and forth between Virgil and me.

"What, may I ask," he said, pointing to the warrant with his pipe, "is the nature of all this dismay, what's this drama?"

I held up the note. Doc leaned in and read it, then leaned back.

"So rolls the tumble of the dice," he said.

# 6.

Virgil and I walked up the steps of the gambling parlor, and when we left the bright light of outdoors, crossed the lobby, and stepped into the dark main room of the parlor we heard the distinct sound of a Winchester being cocked. The clicks of the lever action were followed by a deep voice. "That's far enough."

We quickly stepped back into the lobby. Virgil readied his Colt and I slid back the hammers of my eight-gauge.

"Who's there?" the deep voice said.

We said nothing for a moment and listened. Then Virgil answered.

"Marshals Virgil Cole and Everett Hitch," he said.

We heard some muffled talking from above.

"Whoever you are," Virgil said. "Put down what you picked up." Virgil looked to me.

"I'm Charles Lemley," the voice said. "I'm up here with Hollis Pritchard."

"Know who Pritchard is," I said. "Who are you?"

"I'm Mr. Pritchard's building foreman here. I manage the construction of this place."

"Who else is up there with you?" I said.

"No one."

"Just the two of you up there?" Virgil said.

"It is."

"Bill Black?"

"Not up here," Charles said.

"Truitt Shirley?"

"Just us two up here," Charles said. "Fact."

"Mr. Pritchard?" Virgil said as he looked up.

"Yes," the voice responded.

The voice was noticeably older and raspy.

"It that you, Mr. Pritchard?" Virgil said.

"It most certainly is," he said.

"And it's just the two of you?" Virgil said.

"Yes," Pritchard said.

"Where are your workers?" I said.

Silence. Then.

"After what happened here today, I sent them home," Charles said. "Told them to take the rest of the day off."

"Unload that rifle you got in your hand," Virgil said, "and drop it down here, over the edge."

He did as he was told. We listened as the bullets were ejected, then the Winchester was tossed from above. It landed flat on a table we could see clearly at the bottom of the stairs that was covered with drawings and construction plans.

"Come down," Virgil said. "Hands up and away."

After a moment we heard the floorboards creak upstairs. We moved into the main room and saw coming down the wide sweeping staircase Hollis Pritchard followed by a slender older man with leathery dark skin and short-cropped white hair.

"You need not be concerned with us," Pritchard said. "We have no intention of malice whatsoever."

When they got to the bottom of the staircase Pritchard wasted no time taking a seat where the Winchester lay atop the table.

We'd seen Hollis Pritchard before, when he visited months earlier to speak with the city elders about bringing business to Appaloosa.

"I would not have had the rifle at the ready, Marshal, I assure you, not my protocol," Charles said. "But we were unsure what the hell was happening here with this shooting, so I thought it best to err on the side of caution."

Pritchard nodded a little. His eyes had a leering, judgelike quality as they shifted back and forth between us. He remained seated, slumped forward in his chair with one hand resting on his knee and the other hand on the top of his cane.

"Like to ask you a few questions," Virgil said.

"Let me ask you first," Pritchard said.

He pointed to the street.

"The man that was shot out there a while ago, is he dead or alive?"

"At the moment," I said, "alive."

He shook his head.

"My word," he said.

Charles Lemley extended his hand and introduced himself.

I shook his hand; Virgil did not.

"You know the man that was shot?" Virgil said.

"No," Charles said.

"You, Mr. Pritchard?"

"I do not."

"Who was he?" Charles said.

"He was wearing a badge," Pritchard said. "But he seemed odd, acted rather unstable, inebriated, I think, perhaps."

"Either of you ever see him around here before?" Virgil said.

Charles shook his head.

"I never saw him at all," he said.

"No," Pritchard said. "I just arrived, been to town less than a few hours. I checked into my hotel, then came straight here, and before I could even set foot into this place, this man steps out from across the street there, and in a matter of moments, shots are fired."

"Me neither," Charles said. "I've just been in town with this job and I'm not too acquainted."

"As Charles said . . . he works for me, in all my construction business. Wherever and whenever."

Charles nodded.

"Going on fifteen years now," Pritchard said.

"Any idea where to find Bill Black?" Virgil said.

Mr. Pritchard sat back with a concerned look on his face.

"I've not seen him since the shooting," Pritchard said.

Virgil looked to Charles.

"Me neither," Charles said.

"Know where he is?" Virgil said.

They both said no.

"He just walked away?" I said.

Pritchard nodded.

"Apparently," he said. "After the man was shot I was ushered into the building here by Bill, then he said he was going to see about the man across the street, and I've not seen him since."

"What about Truitt Shirley?"

Mr. Pritchard looked to Charles.

"He's the one who shot the officer?" Pritchard said.

"I was not a witness, but that is what I understand," Charles said.

"I know nothing about this man," Pritchard said. "First time I ever laid eyes on him or the other man he was with."

"What about you?" I said.

Charles's eyes narrowed as he shook his head slightly.

"Mr. Black hired them," Charles said.

"Hired them to do what?" Virgil said.

"Good question," he said. "And I asked Mr. Black that very question. What they did and about their pay and all, and Mr. Black told me to mind my own goddamn business. I don't know the other man's name even, the one with the dark hair and beard, but I can tell you this, he is as mean as a rattlesnake."

"What'd he do for you to think that?" I said.

"Damn near shot me."

"What happened?"

"I walked out the back door here, he had his back to me. He was relieving himself there in the alley. He turned on me with his pistol. But when he saw it was me, he still kept it pointing at me and said don't ever walk up behind him again. He said next time I won't be so lucky."

Virgil looked at Charles a long bit. Then cut his eyes to Pritchard.

"Did you know Black was wanted for murder?" Virgil said.

# 7.

What?" Pritchard said.

Virgil did not say anything.

"My God," Charles said.

"Murder of who?" Pritchard said.

"What do you know about that, Mr. Pritchard?" Virgil said.

"Well, I am shocked," he said.

I looked to Charles.

"That it, Mr. Pritchard?" Virgil said.

"Well, yes," Pritchard said. "This comes as a complete shock."

"And you?" Virgil said to Charles.

"Had no idea," he said.

"How long have Truitt and the other man been around here with Black?" I said.

"They showed up here about a week ago," Charles said.

"And what do you speculate is the nature of their relationship?" I said.

"I can't really say," Charles said.

"Hands?" Virgil said. "Or friends?"

"Well, what I saw of them, they were not overly friendly or really communicative with Bill . . . they were, I don't know, subordinate, it seemed. But I don't know. I was not around them that much, and, well, Bill was not around a great deal, either."

"Where was he?" Virgil said.

"Not sure, really."

"Leave town?" Virgil said.

"Could have," Charles said. "I have no idea."

"How long gone?" I said.

"I can't say, really. I mean, he would be here and then he'd be gone. I have my job to do here and he had his. Mine is the construction side and his is to oversee, and with me doing the work there is not much to oversee, frankly."

"He your boss?"

Charles looked to Pritchard, then back to me.

"To some degree he is," Charles said. "Though there was not much for him to do."

"Charles has been working with the same workers for a long time and they know what they are doing," Pritchard said.

"Bill basically stayed out of my way," Charles said. "And I stayed out of his."

"So I guess you'd say you guys aren't friends?" I said.

"We're not enemies."

"You build the hall in Denver?" Virgil said.

Charles glanced at Pritchard again.

"He did," Pritchard said.

"One thing I can say about Bill of late," Charles said, "is he's been, I don't know, *on edge* might be the right words. Not pleasant, I don't know. Normally he was always kind of pretty even-tempered, but there were a few occasions where he was angry."

"Like when you asked him what Truitt and the other man with him were doing?" I said.

"Yes," Charles said.

"What about them, Truitt and the other fella, you know where they reside?" I said.

"I don't know," Charles said.

"No idea?"

"Not at all."

"You did not see the shooting?" I said.

Charles shook his head.

"No, I was inside, upstairs in the back above us here, and didn't see what happened. By the time I was out, the owners, the man and wife of the upholstery shop there across the street, were tending to him, there was a crowd of people around, but there was no sign of Mr. Black or Truitt or the other sonofabitch that pulled a gun on me."

"And you never learned that other fella's name?" I said.

Charles shook his head.

"Was not introduced."

Virgil turned, surveying the big open room a moment, then leveled a look at Mr. Pritchard.

"Tell me about Bill Black, Mr. Pritchard," Virgil said.

"What do you want to know?"

"He works for you?"

"He does."

"What does he do?"

"Well, he handles my gambling operations."

"Doing what, exactly?" Virgil said.

Pritchard's eyes narrowed a little.

"Everything," he said.

"You want to tell me what you know about the murder?" Virgil said.

# 8.

W hat?" Pritchard said with a perturbed expression on his face. "The murder," Virgil said.

"I goddamn do not know anything about anyone being murdered," he said. "Listen, this is a shock to me. Bill works for me, same as Charles. I have many employees, many enterprises, Marshal. All sorts: cotton, coal, a hotel here and there, Western Union offices, banks, and I hire individuals, experts in their particular fields, to help me run my enterprises. I have over a hundred people working for me. Bill Black is just one of them. He's an expert in the business of gambling. He knows gambling inside and out and he has worked for me for nearly three years. Ever since I got into the business of the gambling trade, but I goddamn know nothing of this business of murder and who was murdered."

"How does Black knowing gambling inside and out help you, exactly?" Virgil said.

"Just like you knowing law work, Marshal," he said. "You've clearly had many occasions to hone your craft. Same as Charles, same as me, same as Bill."

"How did you meet him?" Virgil said.

Pritchard focused his look to the floor as he twirled the lion head of his cane around and around.

"He operated a fine gambling parlor in San Francisco, that's where I met him, there. I bought out the owner of that operation, and with that purchase I got Mr. Black. Much to my liking, I might add."

"You own him?" Virgil said.

"Own?" he said. "No, of course not. He has helped me build two other halls besides this one, one in Saint Louis and one in Denver."

"Denver?"

"Yes, Denver," Pritchard said. "He's been a loyal and trusted employee and I do not own him."

"You said you just got here this morning," I said. "You just come in from Denver, on the morning train?"

"Why, yes," he said.

"And you didn't know about this?" I said.

"What do you mean?" he said. "Know about what?"

"The man that was shot arrived on the same train with you this morning."

"With me?"

Mr. Pritchard leaned back in his chair, looking up at us.

"What are you saying?"

"Just that," Virgil said.

"Marshal, you would think as old and beat-up as I am that I'd be familiar with all kinds of subterfuge, including when someone doesn't hear or chooses not to believe what I say."

"Tell us what you know," Virgil said.

"I told you," he said.

Pritchard's face flushed red.

"I did not know the man," he said. "But by the nature of this inquiry, I can only assume you are suggesting that I am in some way connected to this altercation and that I must be propagating deceitfulness."

"We are not suggesting anything," I said.

"Goddamn sure sounds like it," he said.

"Just trying to put together the comings and goings of all this, Mr. Pritchard," I said.

"You might not know," Virgil said, "but at this point in time you know more than we do, and until we know more than you do we will keep asking questions of you or anybody else until we get to the bottom of this."

"It's what we do," I said.

"I was not in Denver," Pritchard said.

His face flushed even more and his eyes were now bulging.

"I was through Denver on my way to here. I subsequently changed trains there, passing through there is all, but did not stay over. I was planning on actually stopping by, spend a few days there at my gambling establishment on my return."

"To?" Virgil said.

"Saint Louis," he said. "Where I live."

"When were you last in Denver?"

"A few months ago, Marshal Cole."

"What about Bill Black?" Virgil said. "When was he last in Denver?"

"He was there with me," he said. "Same time."

Pritchard pulled his watch from his vest pocket, checked the time. Then, with the support of his glossy brass-topped lion-head cane he slowly lifted himself from his chair.

"Now," he said, "if you will excuse me, I have someone coming to collect me about now. If you need anything else from me you can find me at the Colcord Hotel, room twelve. But right now, I'm tired and unwilling to chew any more of this cud."

"We'll knock on your door," Virgil said.

# 9.

What was left of the day, Virgil and I spent searching Appaloosa and its outskirts for Truitt Shirley and Boston Bill, but there was no sign of either one of them. After dark, Virgil and I made our way back to the sheriff's office, and when we arrived Chastain was sitting on the porch.

A sconce on the wall above him was engulfed with a swarm of moths and early-summer bugs. When we neared, Chastain got to his feet. He was chewing a huge plug of tobacco. He moved to the edge of the porch and spit.

"Find anything?" Virgil said.

Chastain shook his head.

"Hard to say," he said.

He pointed south.

"Skinny Jack said he talked to a ranch hand near the river yonder that was putting out salt for his cattle. Hand said he saw some riders in the early afternoon, caught a quick glimpse of them riding off down toward the hard rock ford, said they was far off, riding close together, and couldn't tell how many exactly, that's all we know . . ."

"Nothing else?" Virgil said.

"Nope, not a goddamn thing," he said. "Y'all?"

"No," I said.

"You'd think they'd not have been able to just up and get gone like they done," Chastain said.

"You would," I said.

"Might well be them the ranch hand saw," he said.

Chastain spit.

"Other than that, none of us found any other sign . . ." he said. "Did, though, get word back from Denver."

Chastain fished the telegram from his vest pocket, unfolded it, and held it out.

"Not sure what to make of it," he said, shaking his head. "Hell of a deal. Take a look."

He waved the telegram a little, holding it a bit outright some more.

I stepped out of the saddle, took the note from Chastain, then moved under the sconce, where I could read it.

"I told everybody to keep at it, keep looking," Chastain said. "Until I talked to you, Virgil. See what you wanted to do. Also I told them if they so much as even get a whiff of Boston Bill or Truitt Shirley to just let me know, so nothing else happens. I told them if they had nothing by nine, to come back here."

Virgil remained mounted as I sat on the bench under the light and read the telegram.

"What about Messenger," Virgil said. "You check on him?"

"I did. I just talked to the doc and he said his condition was the same. Was surprised he was still holding on, figured he'd have died by now, but evidently he ain't."

"Well, I'll be damn," I said, looking up from the note. "Is a hell of a deal."

"What?" Virgil said.

"Boston Bill Black is damn sure wanted for murder," I said. "He's wanted for the murder of a woman named Ruth Ann Messenger."

Chastain nodded.

"How about that shit?" Chastain said. "Figure that has to be Roger Messenger's sister or maybe his wife."

"Yep," I said. "No coincidence."

"There's more there, too, about the goddamn money," Chastain said. "Says there is a hefty bounty on his head, too."

"How much?" Virgil said.

Chastain spit.

"Three thousand," I said.

"How about that shit?" Chastain said. "Hefty."

"Who's that wire from?" Virgil said.

"Police Captain G. W. McPherson," I said. "The Department of Law Enforcement, Denver, Colorado."

"That it?" Virgil said.

Chastain shook his head.

"Not quite," I said. "Says here the department is appreciative of the information and the communication, and that they will be subsequently dispatching a unit to follow up."

"Unit to follow up?" Virgil said.

"That's the shit I don't understand," Chastain said. "Follow up with what, exactly?"

"I would imagine they want to make certain Boston Bill Black is either arrested or killed."

"Or collect their own money," Virgil said.

Chastain pulled his watch and looked at it.

"It's almost nine now," he said. "You want me to get a posse together?"

Virgil thought for a moment and shook his head.

"No, lot of places they could be, and for all we know they could still be right here. What do you think, Everett?"

"I doubt it, but it's not out of the question."

Chastain agreed.

"Unless we find them tonight," I said, "or get some other sign as to their direction, I'd say we will go with the notion the riders that the ranch hand saw heading toward the ford have to be Truitt and Boston Bill and the other fella."

Virgil looked to Chastain.

"Let's stay after it tonight, keep looking, and come morning if we've found no sign, Everett and me will go with Skinny Jack, ride to the rancher's place, get a direction on where the riders were headed."

"All we can do," I said.

"Is," Virgil said.

# 10.

After an extensive search and finding no sign of Boston Bill or Truitt Shirley or the third man, Virgil and I sat on the front porch of his house and drank some whiskey before turning in. It was after two o'clock in the morning, and with the exception of the saloons on the north end of town that stayed open twenty-four hours a day, the whole of Appaloosa, including Allie, was fast asleep.

"Lot of money on Boston Bill's head," I said.

"Damn sure is," Virgil said.

"Not good," I said.

"Not," Virgil said.

"Been our experience," I said. "Comes the money, comes the trouble."

"Yep," Virgil said.

"I guess killing a lawman's family member had to raise the ante," I said.

"They obviously got some kind of strong proof," Virgil said. "Some evidence on Boston Bill."

"Why now?" I said.

"I was wondering the same thing," Virgil said.

"Boston Bill has been here in Appaloosa for, hell, a good damn while," I said. "I mean, we've not been keeping a tab on him or anything, even though you had your suspicions about him, he's given no cause, no reason, but the thought of him catching a train back to Denver, killing a woman named Ruth Ann Messenger, and then returning to Appaloosa to get back to work at building a goddamn gambling parlor sounds suspect at best."

"Does," Virgil said.

"Maybe someone just came forward of recent with evidence," I said.

"Maybe," Virgil said.

"This shit with Roger Messenger don't make good sense, either," I said.

"No," Virgil said. "It don't."

"One thing we do know with Messenger is it was personal."

"Drunk and personal," Virgil said.

"If he doesn't live," I said. "I don't imagine we'll figure out the answer to all of what Roger Messenger is about."

Virgil and I sat for a while in silence. After I polished off my whiskey I bid Virgil good night and left him on the porch to finish his cigar. I walked back in the cool of the summer evening to my room above the survey office, and within a half-hour was fast asleep.


At daybreak, Skinny Jack was waiting for Virgil and me at the office with a fresh pot of coffee and hot-out-of-the-oven biscuits he'd picked up from Hal's Café.

Skinny Jack had quickly advanced as Chastain's top deputy in Appaloosa, and Virgil and I had a fond appreciation for him, mainly because he was friendly, well liked by the townspeople, and a good role model for the younger deputies.

He had a way of going about his job as a peace officer without the gruff or self-styled importance that was most always evident with young law enforcement officers. He had a reputation as a young man with an easy disposition who was not an adversary quick to point out what was wrong or hobble the folks of Appaloosa, but rather an ally, ready and willing to assist those in need.

After we drank some coffee and ate a few biscuits, we rode out to meet with the ranch hand that had told Skinny Jack he'd seen the riders headed toward the river.

By seven o'clock we'd met the ranch hand and followed his point in the direction he'd previously seen the riders the day before, and with little effort we found on the river's edge fresh tracks of three horses disappearing into the water.

"Got to be them," Virgil said.

Virgil rode into the water, heading for the opposite side, and Skinny Jack and I followed.

We easily found the tracks coming out of the water's eastern edge fifty yards downriver. The soft ground rising up from the bottomland made for favorable tracking conditions, and for the moment we were able to follow them without trouble.

When we got to the top of the rise the land stretched out for miles in front of us. I took the lead, following the tracks, and we were able to keep a steady pace.

"As long as the wind don't pick up any more than it is," I said. "Long as it stays like this, we got a good chance to be knocking at their back door."

We moved across the dry shrubland with rolling vast swards of yellow short-grass prairie. In between the swards there were long stretches of sandy loam that was laced with clusters of summer coat mesquite and purple sage.

Around noon we came to a spot where the riders had made camp within a spread of dry thickets surrounded by a stand of weeping acacias that lined an empty creek bed.

Left were remains of a fire, some dead ends of cigarettes, and an empty half-pint bottle lying in the ashes. When I got off my horse to check the expired fire I noticed the wind had changed direction and was getting a little stronger.

I leaned down and felt through the ashes.

"They rode to here from midday when they left yesterday, I'd say. Stopped likely when they got dark bit."

Virgil nodded.

I looked in the direction the breeze was coming, and in the far distance there was darkness.

I nodded to it, and Virgil and Skinny Jack followed my look.

"Wind," I said.

"Headed this way," Skinny Jack said.

"Sure enough," Virgil said.

"Goddamn," Skinny Jack said. "Wouldn't you know it?"

I mounted up.

"Ashes are cold," I said. "Hard to say when they took off."

"You'd think daylight, wouldn't you, Everett?" Skinny Jack said.

"Maybe. Maybe not."

"Men on the run," Virgil said, "run."

We kept on the move, and within an hour's time the wind had picked up, and not far behind there was a wall of dust that was headed our way.

Skinny Jack looked back.

"This don't look so good," he said.

"Road," I said.

Ahead, less than a half-mile on the downslope before us, was a north-south road.

"Be better than a good idea," Virgil said, "to get over there. Don't want this wind coming in and cover things up, and we lose the direction they chose."

# 11.

The three of us galloped over to the road, stopping twenty yards shy so not to put our own tracks in the mix. We dismounted and walked up. It was a well-traveled road with fairly fresh wagon ruts.

"Here they are," Skinny Jack said, pointing to the ground in front of him. "Tracks here."

Virgil and I moved to Skinny Jack's trail. The grass was bent and broken over from where the three horses made it up to the road. We followed the single-file path, and when we got on the road it was clear which way they were traveling.

"There they go," Skinny Jack said. "South."

"Pretty sure this is the stage route between Benson City and Lamar," I said.

"I think that is right," Skinny Jack said. "That way; would be Benson City. Not sure how far."

"We'll know when we get there," I said.

"Four-way stage route," Virgil said.

"Is," I said.

"We been through there," Virgil said. "Benson City?"

"We have," I said. "More than once, but not from this road."

"No," Virgil said. "The other road through there. Goes to Clemmings west and Yaqui the other way."

"That's right," I said.

Since Virgil and I had been living and working out of Appaloosa, we'd at one point or another visited every city within two days' ride that was connected to Appaloosa by road and rail.

The dust was rolling in, so the three of us untied our slickers from our saddles and put them on. After Virgil got his buttoned he stepped up in the saddle, turned his horse, and moved off the road. He galloped north a ways, then turned and looked closely at the road as he walked his horse back in our direction.

"What now?" Skinny Jack said.

"Just making sure it is Benson City and they didn't make some effort to double back on us," I said.

"Think they know of us?" Skinny Jack said. "Know we are after them?"

"Got a suspicion, I'd say," I said. "They damn sure got out of town and on the move."

"Where do men run to, Everett?" Skinny Jack said.

I looked at Skinny Jack. He was looking at me with an expectant gaze, and his question had the same quality to it as if he were a little boy asking what's above the sky or where do we go when we die and what's Heaven like.

"Good question," I said.

"I suppose to a better place," Skinny Jack said. "A better place than where they would be if they were caught."

"I suppose that's right, Skinny Jack."

Virgil walked his horse slowly, looking at the ground, and when he got back to us, he shook his head and pointed south.

"Benson City it is," I said.

The wind and dust kept coming as we rode. It was not as heavy as I'd expected, but it was steady and it remained with us throughout the afternoon. We stopped a few times to rest our horses and have some hard tack, and by the time we got to Benson City the wind had lightened up as the sun was going down.

"Let's move off," Virgil said. "Come in from the back and see what we can see."

Skinny Jack and I followed Virgil off the road. We circled around, came up on the back of the town, and dismounted behind some outlaying barns. We tied off behind one of the structures. Virgil and Skinny Jack got their Winchesters and I removed my eight-gauge from its scabbard.

We moved off on foot toward the main street. For the moment we saw no one moving about, and with the fading light we could walk about ourselves with a sense of ease that we were not being too obvious.

Benson City was not much of a city. It had a small population and a handful of businesses that catered to the four-way stage route. There were some barns and corrals scattered around the outskirts and a few houses sitting back from the road, but that was the sum of the place.

We came up behind a general store with a loading dock and crouched down behind a row of chicken coops. From where we were we could see a two-story hotel next to the store, with an open back door on the first floor. Next to that, about fifty yards away, was a stage stop building with a connecting corral. A group of mules and horses stood munching on hay that was being pitched to them from someone we could not see in the shadows under a lean-to.

Across from the stage stop was a small travelers' café, and next to that was a tall windmill that was providing a squeaking cadence.

"Think this hotel here has the only saloon," I said.

"Could be more, or another by now," Virgil said.

"Let me walk over there to the other side of that store and have a look, see what I can see on the street, horsewise and whatnot."

Virgil nodded.

I leaned my eight-gauge up against the coops and walked off through the opening between the store and saloon.

I came to the road between the buildings and eased out, looking up and down the short street. There were two horses in front of the hotel saloon, but there was nobody moving about. Down the road on the opposite side I could see two women wearing white sitting on the porch under the overhang of a small shack.

I returned between the buildings and walked back to Virgil and Skinny Jack. I picked up my eight-gauge and cradled it in the crook of my arm.

"There are two horses in front of the saloon here," I said. "But that is it. Don't see any other watering holes or anybody about. Across the road, down that way, there's a whoring joint with couple of gals sitting on the porch out of work, but no horses."

Virgil nodded a little, looking at the backside of the hotel saloon.

"Reckon we get in there and see what is what?" I said.

Virgil nodded.

"Why don't Skinny Jack and me come in the back here," he said. "We'll give you a minute, Everett. Come in from the front."

I cocked my eight-gauge and started off.

"See you in a minute," I said.

# 12.

I walked around to the entrance. The horses out front were working cow ponies with well-used ropes and weathered saddles.

A sign above the door said *Hotel Revelation and Saloon*. I entered just as Virgil and Skinny Jack walked in from the back. We had our guns raised.

The bottom floor had a bar on my left, and at the far end of the room, a staircase. There were three men in the room, but they were not the three men we were looking for, and there was one woman. All of them turned to look at us. They first saw Virgil and Skinny Jack, and then me. One was clearly the bartender, a short fellow wearing a clean white shirt and standing behind the bar. He had his hands raised in the air and backed up until his butt hit the backside of the bar, making bottles rattle.

The woman looked to be about forty. She was attractive for her age, and though she was sitting down she looked to be very tall. She had broad shoulders, blue eyes, high cheekbones, and silver-blond hair. She wore a black dress and was sitting in a corner between the bar and the staircase, with a collection of books and papers stacked in front of her. She was reading a newspaper that she lowered and peered over the top of when we walked in. The other two men were young, skinny cowhands that hadn't yet had the opportunity or necessity to put a razor to their face. They were playing cards at a table up against the wall opposite the bar.

The woman calmly lowered the newspaper on the table and looked back and forth between Virgil and me.

"I'd say come on in and relax," she said, "but I have a feeling that you gentlemen have something else on your minds."

I was pretty sure her accent was German. There was a precise manner of her chosen words that suggested she was most likely an educated woman.

The bartender looked back and forth among Virgil, Skinny Jack, and me.

Virgil moved his lapel to the side.

"I'm Marshal Virgil Cole. These men here with me are also lawmen."

"Well, if it is not my fortunate day," she said. "There is nothing about the law that I do not appreciate, Marshal Cole."

She swiveled in her chair, looking Virgil up and down, then turned her attention to me.

"He has already unfortunately left," she said.

"Ma'am?" I said.

"There is no need to stand on ceremony here, gentlemen," she said.

I didn't say anything.

She stood slowly, then took a step to get a better look at us.

"The man you are looking for, of course," she said. "He has unfortunately left."

"When?"

She walked slowly around the table. Her tall figure was slender and her demeanor was elegant as she moved to the center of the room between Virgil and me.

"He has been gone for a while," she said.

Virgil looked to the bartender.

"You," he said.

"Marshal, sir?" he said.

"What do you know?"

The bartender looked to the woman, and she nodded, as if giving him permission to speak.

"There were three fellas here last night for a bit, but far as I know, they are long gone."

The woman smiled and looked back and forth between Virgil and me.

"With that being said, what can I do for you gentlemen?" she said, directing the question to me. "If you are weary and in need of rest we have rooms, drinks, and food available."

"How long has he been gone?" Virgil said.

She turned and looked to Virgil and crossed her arms.

"How long," he said, "and where to?"

"No need to be insensitive, Marshal."

Virgil moved a step but didn't say anything. He looked to the two young cowboys sitting at the table by the wall.

"We ain't seen nobody, don't know nothin'," one of the boys said, shaking his head. "We just got here, sir, Marshal, sir. We just come over after work for a drink or two."

Virgil looked back to the woman.

"Where is he?" Virgil said.

She shook her head.

"You have plenty of time. He has a good day on you. So. Take a moment, why don't you," the woman said. "Please, and I will tell you what else comes to my mind. Some of which may surprise you."

She looked to me, smiled, then looked back to Virgil. She was poised and gentle for such a tall woman.

"Perhaps have a drink or two yourself, why don't you?" she said. "On me. I do not normally drink, especially in the transition of day to night, but today I have been rather fraught for one reason or another, so I will even join you."

Virgil looked to me. He released the hammer on his Winchester and took a step into the room.

"I will tell you everything you want to know and then some," she said. "I am in the mood, so you should take my offer before I decide to keep my thoughts to myself."

Virgil looked around the room for a moment, then nodded slightly.

"Grand," she said, then looked to the bartender. "Set them up, Timothy."

"You bet," he said. "Whiskey?"

Virgil nodded and moved toward the bar.

Skinny Jack followed him and I did the same.

Timothy got a bottle and four glasses and poured. The woman moved to the bar between Virgil and me. She turned around, facing away from the bar, and leaned back a little on the counter; the move made her seem even taller than she was.

Virgil handed one of the whiskeys to the woman.

"What's your name?" Virgil said.

"Mike," she said. "The proprietress."

Virgil glanced to me, then looked at her, but said nothing.

"You own the place?" I said.

"As a matter of fact I do," she said. "Lovely, don't you think, Revelation Hotel?"

She held out her whiskey to toast. We toasted and she took a small sip.

"What can you tell us, Mike?" he said.

"I am not certain he killed her," she said.

# 13.

H e may have," she said. "I know he is capable."

"Who are you talking about?" Virgil said.

"I thought it important to impart this to you before you unscrupulously hunt him down," she said. "And unceremoniously kill him. But then again, he may have done it, he might deserve the medicine, I don't know."

"Who?" I said.

She looked back to me, then to Virgil.

"Bill, of course," she said. "Boston Bill Black. The man you are looking for."

"Who did he or didn't he kill?" Virgil said.

"The woman in Denver," she said.

Virgil looked to me, then back to her.

"What woman in Denver?" Virgil said.

"I didn't get her name," she said.

"No?" I said.

"No."

She looked me in the eye, then looked to the two cowboys that were gawking up at her like kids mesmerized watching a puppet show.

"You two," she said. "Leave."

The two cowhands looked at each other, wondering what they did wrong.

"Now," she said, and clapped her hands. "Before I come over there and drag you out by your ears."

They got up and walked out like they actually did do something wrong.

"Why don't you tell us what you know," Virgil said.

She looked back to Timothy and tipped her head to the door.

"You, too," she said.

"Oh, you bet, Mike," Timothy said.

Timothy moved from behind the bar and hurried out the front door. Then she took the bottle from the bar and moved to a close-by table.

"Please," she said.

We sat with her at the table.

She looked back and forth between Virgil and me for a moment, never looking at Skinny Jack. He scooted away from the table a bit and slumped in his chair, doing his best to act like he wasn't there.

"You may wonder what a woman of my stature is doing in a place like this," she said.

Virgil solemnly gazed at her with his hands resting on the table.

"I am no whore," she said.

"Didn't say you were," Virgil said.

"No, but you were thinking it."

"Just tell us what you know."

"You do not think he showed up here in beautiful Benson City by choice, do you?"

"You know him?" Virgil said.

She nodded. Virgil looked to me, then back to her.

"How?" Virgil said.

"He knew my husband . . ." she said. "And he . . . knew me, too, I suppose you can say."

She looked at Virgil for a long moment, then nodded toward the front window.

"Out there, just over that rise beyond that noisy windmill," she said. "There is a grave. And in the grave there is a man that at one point in time was my husband. Two winters ago, we came this way from Santa Fe, heading for Yaqui, where we were planning to catch the train that was meant to take us all the way to Philadelphia, where my husband, George, was hired as an engineer for a new steam company. He was determined to work hard and change his ways and I believed him, but he was shot and killed."

She pointed to a spot on the floor.

"Shot and killed right here in this very saloon. He died right over there. That is what is left of him, his dried blood there. I keep thinking that one day, after enough traffic from sodbusters, drifters, cowboys, drunks, and weary travelers moves across that stain, that it will eventually disappear and I will forget about him. But of course forgetting is hard and, well, memory can sometimes be tricky business."

"Was it Black?" Virgil said. "Black shoot him?"

She shook her head.

"No," she said.

"Who?"

"It does not matter," she said.

"No?" I said.

She shook her head.

"No," she said. "Not anymore. It does not."

"And you stayed here?" I said.

She nodded.

"The stage that brought me here left that day without me."

# 14.

I buried my husband and have been in this place ever since. I don't completely remember just why I stayed really, I just had no place to go. Two years now. I bought this saloon with the last money we had, and currently I just watch all the travelers come and go with their dreams. I think of this place as somewhere between Heaven and Hell, a halfway stop of sorts. A reckoning happens here, it's a way station of Revelation."

She smiled a wistful, reflective smile.

"I'm a midwife, you could say. Truths are conveyed here and I know whose dreams will come true and whose won't. I know what truths travelers carry with them . . . One day, when the blood is gone, I will move on."

"It wasn't Black who killed your husband?" Virgil said.

"I told you he did not."

"You telling the truth?" Virgil said.

She looked at Virgil without blinking . . .

"No."

"So he did?" Virgil said.

"My husband had it coming," she said. "He pulled on him."

"You also told us memory can be tricky business," Virgil said. "So what is the real story?"

"Bill Black's horse went lame. He shot his horse and he got on the same stage I was on with George. They became quick friends, and to my disliking, they gambled together on the trip. My husband liked to gamble. For the most part he was good at it, unless he was gambling against Bill. He found that out rather fast."

"And the two of you?" I said. "Bill and you?"

"What about us?"

She looked at me for a steady moment, then smiled some and nodded.

"Yes . . . as I mentioned, I knew him, too, you see. I got to know him, too . . . and I liked him, very much . . ."

She paused, looked away, then said, "He is a dangerous sort."

Virgil looked at me.

"Since he has been near here, over in Appaloosa, he has been here to see me on occasion. More than once . . . always thrilling, we have a special friendship."

She took a drink of whiskey, set the glass back on the table, and glided her finger around the rim.

"I sleep with who or whom I want to sleep with, when I want to sleep with them," she said.

She looked up and smiled at Virgil.

"But of course him coming here this time was very different," she said.

"Different how?" Virgil said.

"Well, that is obvious, is it not, Marshal?" she said. "He showed up here with other men, some no-good men, and with you after him, hunting him down to kill him."

"Not hunting him down to kill him," I said.

"He know we are after him?" Virgil said.

"Suspected," she said with a nod.

Skinny Jack looked up at me a little, then lowered his eyes.

"And I personally abide by that impression as to why he was here for such a short while," she said with a smile. "I would hate to think I was the reason for him moving on in haste . . . I would say it concerns me that he is on the run, but frankly nothing truly concerns me anymore. I will also say, since he was in Appaloosa, so near, I was hopeful that he might come back over here someday and perhaps stay awhile. Or take me away, save me, and help me to forget. But that is, or was, wishful thinking, and now there is every reason to believe he will die. Just like my husband. He will be killed."

"When the time comes he will have a choice," Virgil said.

"Providing he makes the right choice?" she said.

"Where is he?" Virgil said.

She looked down to her hands resting on the table. She smiled a little and then looked back up at Virgil's eyes.

"I've told you," she said. "Gone, just gone."

"And the other two," I said. "What about them?"

She shook her head.

"I do not know about them. Gone, too, I assume," she said. "I saw them for a brief time. Bill told them to leave here and he would collect them when he was ready to leave. They went over to the girls across the way and thankfully stayed there . . . I assume."

"When did Bill leave?" I said.

"Early this morning. I awoke and he was gone."

Virgil nodded and flatly stared at her for a long moment, then shifted in his chair and placed his elbow on the table and leveled his eyes at her.

"He didn't mention the Denver woman's name to you?"

"No."

"What else can you tell us?" Virgil said.

She shook her head.

"Nothing," she said.

"I don't suppose you'd be too inclined to share where he might be headed?"

"Inclination aside," she said, "I have no idea, Marshal."

Virgil looked at her, steady.

She looked back at him, a little steadier.

"What, and why did he mention anything to you about a woman in Denver at all?" he said.

She shrugged.

"I don't know."

"Why do you think?" I said.

"I don't think and I don't know."

"You have to have some kind of idea?" I said.

"No," she said, "I don't . . . He is an anomaly. In actuality, he functions pretty much like a hole card."

"How so?" Virgil said.

She shrugged a little.

"He keeps himself facedown, never obliged to reveal what he's about until it is time for the showdown."

Virgil looked at her for an extended moment, then looked to me.

"Do you think he killed her?" I said.

"Perhaps his reasoning for bringing up this business of murdering the woman in Denver was an attempt to simply madden me, to put me in my place. Then again, perhaps it was his celestial epitaph of finality. Regardless, as I told you, this is a place of reckoning. And Boston Bill Black was . . . is no fool, but he is also no exception."

# 15.

When we left Mike in her saloon it was good and dark out. The night air was pleasant and the wind had died down to a gentle breeze.

"Tangled goddamn web," I said.

"Is," Virgil said.

"I'll say," Skinny Jack said. "She's . . . well, I don't know, strange, I guess."

We got our horses and rode off down the street to pay the whores a visit. We wanted to see if they might be able to offer up any news regarding the intended whereabouts of Truitt Shirley, his buddy, and Boston Bill.

The working girls were sitting on the porch in two weathered armchairs when we rode up. A lamp hung from a rope draped over the porch's eave beam made it possible to see them clearly. One of the women lifted out of her chair when we came to a stop.

"Good evening, gentlemen," she said. "Welcome. I am Irena."

"I am Ursula," the seated woman said.

They were fairly young, and it was obvious by their accents that they were Polish.

Irena leaned on the porch post and showed us the flesh of her thigh.

"You like?" she said.

She smiled a wide smile.

"Tell me if you like?"

"Very nice," I said. "But . . ."

"Me love good," Ursula said as she, too, got to her feet.

Though I'm sure they were good at their trade, their English was limited. Irena was slightly older than Ursula and seemed able to manage words a little better.

"Tonight," Irena said, "we can make you feel really so very good, you will see."

She turned around and showed us her backside.

"You will feel better," Irena said, looking back over her shoulder.

"No," Virgil said. "Just want to talk."

She remained looking at us over her shoulder for a moment, then slowly turned to face us.

"Talk about what?" Irena said.

"The men you were with last night," I said.

Irena put a hand to her hip.

"What men?"

"The blond fella, long hair, and the other man, young, dark hair, beard. They were with another man, an older tall fella."

Irena looked to Ursula. Ursula shook her head and Irena looked to me, shaking her head.

I moved close to the porch, pulled a dollar from my vest, leaned out, and handed it to Irena. She looked at the dollar in the palm of her hand, then back at me.

"What about them?" Irena said.

"Do you know where they are?"

Irena looked to Ursula, then to me, and shook her head.

"No."

"When did they leave?" Virgil said.

"Last night," Irena said. "Very late. They left in the middle of the night."

"You sure?" I said.

"Yes," Irena said. "The big man came in here and told the other two they had to leave. They left."

"Any idea which way they rode away?"

"No," she said.

Virgil looked to me, nodded a bit, then backed his horse up.

"Appreciate it," I said.

Ursula said something in Polish that made Irena laugh.

"What's that?" I said

"The one man," Irena said, "the young man. He could not do fun with Ursula, he was very sick with tooth."

"Yes," Ursula said, then rattled off something in Polish and pointed to her temple.

Irena nodded.

"Yes, his tooth was very bad, he was in much pain," she said as she pointed two fingers to her eyes. "He was crazy."

Ursula nodded.

"Blood . . ." Irena said. "He was spitting much blood like he was the devil."

Ursula nodded her head in agreement and said something in Polish again.

"Yes, he drank a lot of whiskey," Irena said, "to, you know, to help with pain, but it did little good. And he was mad at the other man."

"Mad?" I said. "Why?"

Irena shook her head.

"I do not know, they just complain about each other, like little boys fighting over candy."

Virgil looked to me, then looked back to the women and nodded.

"All right, then," he said.

Virgil tipped his hat and reined his horse away from the women a little.

"Special," Ursula said as she moved to the door.

She held back the tarp that covered the door and pointed to Skinny Jack and then pointed in the room.

"For you," she said. "Special."

Skinny Jack looked to me, then to Virgil, and pointed to himself. "Me?"

"Yes. Special," she said, nodding. "Ursula show you and I will make very good for you."

"Um, gosh, thank you," Skinny Jack said, "but no, thank you, ma'am."

"No, you come," she said.

"No," he said. "I . . . I won't come, ma'am."

"Yes," she said.

She pointed to Skinny Jack, then pointed into the room like she was angry, and she spoke to Skinny Jack in a scolding tone.

"Special, Ursula will show you."

Skinny Jack backed his horse up and shook his head.

"Got to go, ma'am," Skinny Jack said.

"Ursula do extra-special for you."

"Sorry, ma'am," Skinny Jack said.

Ursula laughed and pulled down one side of her loose-fitting cotton dress and showed one of her breasts. I couldn't see Skinny Jack in the dark, but I was pretty sure he was blushing.

Virgil smiled and turned his horse.

"Good evening, ladies," he said, and moved on.

"You sure you do not want some love?" Ursula said again to Skinny Jack.

"Maybe next time," I said, speaking for Skinny Jack. "Maybe next time."

"There is no better time than now," Irena said as we rode off in the dark. "No better time."

She laughed and Ursula joined her. Their laughter cut through the otherwise still evening. We could hear them jabbering in Polish as Skinny Jack and I caught up with Virgil. The three of us rode abreast for a moment before Virgil spoke up.

"Well, there you have it."

"Yep," I said.

"That Polish lady has a sure enough hankering for you, Skinny Jack," Virgil said.

"Sure enough," I said. "Special."

"Extra-special," Virgil said.

# 16.

We rode to the corral behind the stage stop, where an elderly black fellow we'd seen pitching hay earlier gladly gave us some feed for our animals.

His name was Louis. He was a tall, lanky man hunched over from years of hard work, friendly but not at all talkative. He said he'd seen Black and the other two ride in but never talked with them or saw them after they rode by.

Louis shared with us some food he cooked. It was a good-tasting red broth stew made of pork, corn, rice, and beans. We sat under the lean-to behind the stop and ate with the animals.

"They damn sure keeping on the move," I said.

"They are," Virgil said.

"Sounds like the one fella is in some pain," Skinny Jack said.

"Does," I said.

"We getting on the road tonight?" Skinny Jack said. "Stay after them?"

Virgil nodded.

"Don't you think, Everett?"

"I do, especially since they took off last night and not this morning. I don't think it a good idea to rest up too long and give them the whole of the evening."

Louis walked out with the kettle of stew and without saying a word he ladled each of us another scoop.

Virgil nodded.

"Thank you, Louis," Virgil said.

Louis nodded and started back inside.

"Louis," Virgil said.

He turned back.

"Yes, sir."

"Like to find a lamp or two," he said. "We got to get us some light before we get on the road."

Louis pointed us to a small house behind the general store and told us to wake up the old man that runs the store. He let us know that he didn't much care for the old sonofabitch and was happy for lawmen to make him have to open up after hours.

After we ate and got our horses ready to ride, we rousted the store's owner. There was most certainly something about him that made us feel comfortable with the opinion Louis had of the old fellow. He was grumpy and unfriendly, but he did have what we needed.

He didn't have any lamps to spare, but we made ourselves some good stave torches of Hessian and paraffin he had available. Then we rode out to the crossroads, lit the torches, and searched the ground for fresh tracks. In no time we located the trio's hoofprints.

"South it is," Virgil said.

We walked slowly on the road at first, keeping the tracks visible, making sure they had not veered off in a different direction, and once we were convinced they stayed to the road, we put out the light and kept traveling.

The night was clear and full of stars. We had a bit of light from the low-slung moon as we rode. Every few miles we fired the torches, making sure we still had track.

"I been thinking," Skinny Jack said. "There's a good chance they might ride for La Verne."

"What makes you think that?" I said.

"Well, I don't know for sure, but down there Truitt knows his way around those parts," Skinny Jack said. "I mean, it's a long damn ways to La Verne, but, um, that is where Truitt's from."

"Got to be a good hundred and fifty miles," I said.

"We know it," Virgil said. "La Verne."

"We do," I said.

"You think they'd go there?" Skinny Jack said.

"Hard to say about Black and the other fella, but for Truitt it wouldn't be unlikely," Virgil said.

"When things are uncertain," I said, "a place that is known gives a fella some security and comfort to uncertainty. Like you were saying, Skinny Jack. A better place than where they were."

"That's right," Virgil said.

"Then again, Yaqui is the train," I said.

"Is," Virgil said.

"Well, La Verne's damn sure Truitt's home place," Skinny Jack said. "I was raised just east of there at the fort. I got a lot of family down that way myself. That's how I know about Truitt and his family. My dad knew his pa from the fort. Truitt's got kin all through there that could and would lie for him, hide him and protect him."

We rode solid through the night and into the morning hours. We continued to follow the tracks and just before noon we came upon a sign: *Ray Opelka's—Way Station & Supply Depot—3 miles ahead.*

The road between the sign and the way station worked its way back and forth through rocky terrain and was uphill. After we topped the long rise we came to the depot on the other side of the crest.

The way station was built on the west side of the road in front of a bluff that protected the place from the late afternoon sun. The main building had a wide porch that fronted the road. Behind that was a living quarters structure surrounded by smaller outbuildings, a small barn, and empty corrals, and behind that there was a pen with a big hog standing stock-still.

There was nobody moving about. Other than the hog, the only sign of life was a trickle of smoke rising from a single chimney in the storefront.

As we rode closer there was a flash from a north-facing window followed by a rifle report. A bullet ricocheted off the road just behind us. A quick second shot was fired and it hit Skinny Jack, knocking him to the ground and sending his horse running off back the way we came.

# 17.

More gunshots followed, one after another, after another. The shots appeared to all come from one rifle, from the north-facing window.

Virgil moved off the road quick to the right. I turned in the opposite direction. The shooter was focused, aiming on me as I moved quickly. The shots were coming in close, but I managed to get behind an outcropping of low rock near the side of the road.

I slid from my horse and tied off on a thick juniper and pulled my Winchester from the scabbard.

From where I was positioned, I could see Virgil; he was still riding off at a fast pace behind a rise that separated him from direct sight of the way station. When he dropped to the other side he pulled up and dismounted.

I stayed low to the ground, where I had protection from low boulders and brush, as I inched back out toward the road and Skinny Jack. I could see the way station's window through the brush, and for a moment the shooting subsided.

Skinny Jack lay facedown, motionless in the middle of the rutted thoroughfare, with both of his arms under his body.

"Skinny Jack," I said.

Skinny Jack moaned.

"Where are you hit?"

"Everett?"

"I'm here."

He moaned again but did not move.

"Everett?"

"Just stay put, I'm coming to get you."

He moaned again.

"Where are you hit?"

There was no reply.

"Skinny Jack?" I said.

Again, there was no reply.

I turned my focus back to the way station's window and saw movement and a hint of light reflect from the barrel of the rifle in the window. Then it was gone.

I looked over and could see Virgil. He was crouched low to the ground and moving up the rise in front of him with his rifle.

"Virgil," I called out.

He looked in my direction.

I pointed to Skinny Jack down in the road, then pointed to myself and back to Skinny Jack.

Virgil nodded.

"Coming to get you, Skinny Jack," I said.

Virgil positioned himself with his rifle ready.

"Just hang on, Skinny Jack. Hang on."

Virgil held up his hand, and when he dropped it he began firing on the way station's window.

I crawled out quickly and pulled Skinny Jack off to the side of the road and behind the rocks. Once Virgil saw we were off the road he quit firing, sat back, and reloaded.

I turned Skinny Jack over. He was staring up at me. He grabbed my arm and squeezed. He looked down to his chest, where there was blood.

I took out my knife and split open the front of his shirt and found the bullet had entered just to the side of his heart.

"Everett?"

"I'm here."

"Everett?"

"Yes, Skinny Jack."

"I'm sorry."

"Just hold on, Skinny Jack, hold on . . ."

He looked down at the blood, then laid his head back, looking up at me. He lifted his head off the ground.

"Everett?" he said.

"Yeah, Skinny Jack?"

He spit blood and then squeezed my arm.

"Do me a favor."

"Sure."

"Kill the sonofabitch that killed me."

His head dropped back in the dirt, and he breathed in his last breath and died staring up at me.

I looked up at Virgil across the road and he was looking at me. I shook my head.

Virgil lowered his chin to his chest.

I closed Skinny Jack's eyes and sat back on my boots and looked at his young face for a long moment.

"Goddamn it . . ." I said. "Goddamn it."

I rested Skinny Jack's hat across his face, then moved toward the bush at the edge of the large rock that separated me from the way station. I got flat on the ground with my Winchester and leveled it through the scrub bush toward the station window. I rested the rifle's barrel through the bush on a solid piece of branch in front of me, giving me a steady bead, and flipped up my back sight.

I figured I was about a hundred and twenty-five yards out, and for some reason, besides being very angry, I was feeling lucky.

# 18.

I aimed my Winchester at the center of the window and waited. Then I waited some more. With my cheek to the stock and my eye looking down the barrel, I was waiting and ready.

"Come on, you no-good sonofabitch," I said quietly to myself. "Surely you're not done. Show yourself; show your no-good goddamn sonofabitch coward self. Just show me a piece, the smallest piece, and . . ."

There he was. I squeezed off one shot. Then I heard screaming from inside, followed by a woman running out the front door.

She ran across the road and up a slight embankment. She was a short, heavy woman wearing a dark dress that she held up as she ran. She slipped trying to get up the embankment but kept churning and churning her feet until she was upright, over the rise and running away from the way station.

I cocked the rifle and waited for another shot, but there was no movement and no more sound from within the way station.

I looked over to Virgil. He was making his way back to his horse.

I watched the window for a moment longer, then pulled my rifle from the bush, got to my feet, and made my way back to my horse.

I mounted up but did not move out onto the road. I rode off farther from the road and angled my way toward the direction in which the woman was running.

I rode a ways and then I saw her. She was in the bottom of a dry wash, no longer running, but was bent over with her hands on her knees, trying to catch her breath.

She looked up as I rode closer. Her round face was tearstained and her chest was heaving as she continued to try to catch her breath.

I dismounted and walked toward her.

She was frightened and tried to back away.

I showed her my badge.

"I'm Deputy Marshal Everett Hitch, ma'am," I said. "I'm here now. You'll be okay."

She looked at me, chest still heaving, and dropped to her knees.

I moved to her. She looked up at me and shook her head.

"Who are you?" I said.

"This . . . here," she said, trying to breathe and shaking her head, "is . . . our place. Me . . . and my husband, Ray."

She started crying.

"What's happened here?"

"He's dead," she said. "Big Ray is dead."

"Just try and tell me what we're dealing with here."

"Three men come here," she said.

She dropped to her bottom and leaned back to the side of the wash, shaking her head slowly.

"Me and Ray been out here eighteen years. Never had a problem, raised two boys here, now he's dead, just like that. He's lying out there in the field behind the house, dead."

"What about the three men?"

"Two of them left. They left the third man and he shot and killed my Ray this morning. He would have killed me, too, but I took care of him, I pulled two of his teeth. Then you come riding up and shot him. Thank God in Heaven. Thank God."

"What caused him to shoot your husband?"

"I do not think that man needs a reason. Besides being a goddamn miscreant," she said. "He's completely out of his mind, delirious and sick with the fever."

"Is he dead?"

"I don't know," she said. "I sure hope so . . . oh, God, I hope so. He screamed and fell back, holding his bloody face. Then I got up, opened the door, and ran."

"The other two men, when did they leave?"

"This morning," she said. "While the other fella was asleep. He woke up mad as hell and with no horse. Them other two took his horse. Wished my boys would had been here. This would have never have happened."

"Where are they," I said. "Your boys."

"They made a supply run and took all the horses to get re-shod over in Pilgrim's Corner," she said. "Be back anytime. Ray told the sonofabitch to wait and he'd have a fresh horse, but no, he was angry and . . . Oh, God, I don't know, this is, oh, God . . ."

"How many of them, your boys?"

"Two boys. Ray Junior and Carl."

She lowered her head and sobbed.

"Stay right here," I said. "Don't move."

I moved to tie off my horse as Virgil came riding up the wash with his Winchester in hand.

"What do we got?" he said.

"Shot him," I said. "Not sure if he's dead or alive. Neither is she."

"This woman, this is her place here, hers and her husband. She said her husband was killed this morning by the one man that was left here, the sick one. Guess Truitt and Black left him here, left him to his damnable fate."

"Who else here, besides her?"

"Nobody. She said her two sons were expected back here soon."

"Ray told him he could have a horse just as soon as my boys returned," she said. "But he shot Ray anyway."

Virgil nodded, then dismounted.

I exchanged my Winchester for my eight-gauge, and once Virgil got tied off we moved off, following the wash south.

# 19.

Virgil and I followed the rock-bottom wash for about a hundred yards, and then it curved back toward the road. We crossed the road out of sight of the way station. Then we made our way back toward the building. Once we had it in sight we cut back to the west, walked another couple hundred yards, and came up on the depot from the back side.

We split up and moved up on opposite sides of the living quarters. After a time of waiting, hearing nothing and not seeing movement, we crossed swiftly up to the back of the way station.

The back door was cracked open, and Virgil moved up to one side of the door and I positioned myself on the other side.

I pushed on the door with the barrel of my eight-gauge and it swung open. There were no shots fired. I took off my hat and moved it just past the doorjamb, soliciting fire, but again there was nothing, and within an instant I moved in and Virgil followed.

The interior was a simple storeroom with supplies for sale and a kitchen with a counter for eating and drinking.

Lying flat on his back in the center of the room was the man with the dark scraggly beard we'd heard about. It was obvious by his size and shape he was young, but how young exactly was hard to tell because his face was covered with blood. He was very much alive and it was clear to see the result of my single shot was at least for the moment not fatal, but the bullet had clipped off his nose. The combination of his missing nose and swollen jaw from where Mrs. Opelka removed two teeth made for a grotesque image.

He turned his head ever so slightly, looking blankly at Virgil and me, and then looked back up at the ceiling. Every labored breath he took made a bubble of blood where his nose used to be.

The rifle he killed Skinny Jack with was lying in front of the north window where he dropped it when I shot him. He made no effort to go for the rifle or the pistol he had on his hip.

I moved to him and removed the pistol from his hip and snugged it behind my belt.

"Where are the other two?" Virgil said.

He choked on his blood, then spit.

"Fuck them," he said. "They . . . they left me here . . ."

His voice was muffled and muted from a swollen mouth and a missing nose. He turned his head a little and spit a large gob of blood across the floor, and when he did we could see the bullet not only took off his nose but took a hunk of flesh from his cheek as well.

"They . . . they . . . took my horse," he said.

"Truitt and Bill got your nose shot off, too," I said.

He looked at me wide-eyed as tears welled up.

"Fu . . . fuck them," he said again, then moaned.

"Where are they?"

He didn't answer. He lay motionless, staring at the ceiling.

"How about we help you," I said. "Give you an ounce of satisfaction."

He stared at the ceiling for a long moment.

"Wh . . . what?" he said, then spit another stream of blood. "How the fuck are you gonna give me satisfaction?"

"By you telling us where they took off to," I said. "That would have to give you some satisfaction."

He raised his hand up to his face where his nose used to be. Then he shook his head from side to side and spoke through clenched teeth.

"Oh, God," he said. "Fuck . . ."

"Yeah, you don't look so good," I said. "Don't imagine you feel too good, either."

"Seeing how they left you here to fend for yourself," Virgil said. "And got your nose shot off and took your horse to boot, I think the quicker you let us know where Truitt and Bill went, the better things might go for you."

"Fuck," he said.

He looked at the ceiling and shook his head from side to side and mumbled as if he were having a conversation with himself.

"They . . ." he said.

"They what?" I said.

A bubble of blood swelled up as he exhaled, and then it popped. He gasped, choked on more blood, then coughed and spit. He tried to talk, but blood filled his mouth and he gagged. I pulled a chair from the counter and grabbed him with one hand by the collar and lifted him.

"Up," I said.

He managed to rise. He leaned over and spit. I slid the chair under him and he sat. He lowered his head as if he were about to black out.

"I got little concern for you," I said. "Where?"

He looked worse sitting up than he did lying down. In my time fighting the Comanche I'd seen plenty of people live with faces disfigured like this, missing lips and noses and ears and scalps. He lowered his chin to his chest.

"Do not pass out on us," I said.

"Tell us what you know," Virgil said.

He lifted his head a little.

"You're . . . you're Hitch . . . and Cole," he said.

# 20.

"Bill knew you'd be after us," he said. "Knew you was marshals in Appaloosa and that it would not be long until you was on his trail."

He leaned over and spit blood on the floor.

"Oh . . . goddamn . . ."

"Go on," Virgil said.

He lowered his head again.

"Why'd you shoot at us?" I said.

"He told Truitt and me you'd be coming. Figured you to be a few days back . . . I figured different. I'm smart like that."

"Black's long gone and then you poked that Winchester out that window and killed one of us," I said. "Why?"

He didn't answer.

"There is a good man out there dead 'cause of you," I said. "He was younger than you. You killed him."

"I'm sorry, goddamn it," he said.

"You're sorry?" I said.

It was all I could do not to raise my eight-gauge and blow his disfigured head off, but the idea of Mrs. Opelka having more of a mess to deal with than what was already being left behind by this disregard tempered my resolve.

"Why?" I said.

"Ain't going back to being locked up. Not now, not ever."

"What's your story?" Virgil said.

He looked back and forth between Virgil and me.

"What?" I said.

"I broke out a while back."

Virgil glanced to me, then looked back to the bleeding man.

"Yuma?" Virgil said.

He looked at Virgil for a long bit, then nodded.

"What's your name?" I said. "Your real name, and don't lie."

"Ricky," he said. "Ravenfield."

"You're one of the five that escaped a few months back?" Virgil said.

He stared at Virgil for a long moment, then nodded.

"Where are the others?"

"I don't know," he said. "Went our separate ways. All I know is I ain't going back there. Not now, not ever . . . You'll have to kill me."

"We don't have to do anything," Virgil said.

"I was in that goddamn place since I was sixteen," he said.

"For?" I said.

"Killing a man that tried to kill me."

He lowered his head and shook it back and forth. Then he looked up to the ceiling and cried.

"Oh, God, I hurt . . . fuck."

"How was it you and Truitt come to team up with Black?" Virgil said.

He breathed and breathed, then looked to Virgil with bloodshot eyes. He was having a hard time keeping his head up.

"Truitt . . . knew him . . ."

"What were you doing with Bill, for Bill?" I said.

He shook his head.

"Truitt said we'd get a good wage, I . . . I was trying to stay out of trouble, I was, I swear to God."

"Good wage for what?"

"I don't know," he said.

"You don't know?" I said.

"They talked with each other and not to me."

"Why," I said.

Ricky leaned over in pain and coughed blood.

"Why did you ride to Benson City?"

"Money . . ."

"What money?"

"We left in a hurry, and Bill knew this lady he could get money from."

Virgil looked to me, then back to Ricky.

"How'd you know Truitt?"

He spit before he spoke.

"He come to Yuma a spell for thieving. I goddamn protected him and now this shit . . . Truitt acted all tough in front of Bill, but got jumpy, Truitt got jumpy and shot a goddamn lawman."

Ricky turned his head to the side and spit again.

"Oh . . . hell. Oh," he said, wincing in pain. "The next thing you know we are on the run and . . . Truitt don't think shit about me. Said he didn't need me, said he was the gun hand. Fuck. Then I get sick as hell and now they goddamn leave me."

"Where we gonna find them?" Virgil said.

He tilted his head a little to look at us. Then he looked to me with a pleading expression.

"I'll tell you," he said. "If you can do me a favor."

"You ain't in a very good position to be asking for favors, Ricky," Virgil said.

Ricky moaned and tears welled up as his eyes looked back and forth between Virgil and me.

"Finish me . . ." he said. "I do not want to live no more."

Virgil glanced over to me, then looked back to Ricky.

"I don't got nothing now," Ricky said. "And all I done was wrong and I'd hate like hell to live like this and I damn sure don't want my life to be the last life I take . . . Please?"

Virgil looked to me.

I nodded.

"Sure," I said. "Talk."

"They're headed for Socorro," he said.

Virgil looked to me.

"Lying, Ricky?" I said.

"I ain't," he said.

"They gone to La Verne?" I said.

"No," he said. "Socorro."

Ricky lowered his chin again and was still.

"Ricky?" I said.

He did not move.

"Ricky?"

He looked up.

"We know about La Verne," I said.

Ricky shook his head ever so slightly.

"Socorro," he said. "That is where you will find Truitt . . . bet your ass."

"What makes you so sure?" Virgil said.

"Truitt has a bunch of shitheads he runs with from there," he said. "His gang, he says."

Virgil looked at me and shook his head.

"You telling the truth?" I said.

"Mark my words," Ricky said.

# 21.

Why should we believe you, Ricky?" I said.

"Believe what you want."

Ricky leaned over and moaned.

"We been moving fast," he said, and then spit some more blood into the patch of blood on the floor in front of the chair. "You can catch the shit. The threat of you or any other law . . . was . . . fading from his sight, Bill's, too."

"Didn't fade from yours," I said.

He grimaced and shook his swollen head a little.

"They ain't as smart as me," he said. "They ain't spent half their born days locked up in no prison. And they weren't left behind in the middle of the night, neither."

He leaned forward with his elbows to his knees and spit more blood on the floor, then looked back up at us.

"All he fucking talked about," he said. "Once he's down Socorro way, that any law better look out."

Virgil looked at me, then back to him.

"And Black?" Virgil said.

"Fucking left with him," he said.

"Where in Socorro?" I said.

He shook his head.

"Shouldn't be too hard to find . . . There's a cantina in the square there, north side of the plaza, a lively place with pretty whores. Saturday night, the place is famous for good times and there is nothing that would make me happier than to see the two of you spoil his good times."

Virgil stared at Ricky.

"It's his birthday," Ricky said with a bloody smile.

Virgil looked to me, then back to Ricky.

"No bullshit," he said. "Swear on Grandma Ravenfield's Bible. You get there by Saturday night, that's where he'll be, with all of his no good friends."

"You know something about Black you ain't telling us?" Virgil said.

"I don't," he said. "I'd fucking tell you if I did, 'cause I don't give a rat's ass about him. He never really said shit to me about nothing."

Virgil stared at Ricky for a bit.

"All Truitt talked about for fucking days now. Truitt's got two cousins there, too, big boys, Walt and Douglas. Assholes, the both of 'em. They think they are tough shit. Truitt and his fucking bullshit. He's just full of shit. Even Bill told him to shut the fuck up."

"What else ain't you telling us?" I said.

"Nothing, not a fucking thing . . ."

Ricky leaned over and spit again.

"Don't think Black would be party to a party," Virgil said.

"Hard to say about him," Ricky said. "I think he's planning to get as far away as he can."

Virgil looked at me and shook his head a little.

"Goddamn all I know. When you find Truitt, and Bill, for that matter, you can tell them it was me, Ricky fucking Ravenfield, that sent you."

Ricky leaned his head back and looked to the ceiling. A bubble of blood swelled again, then popped.

"All I know," he said quietly.

"Why'd you kill the fella here that run this station?"

Ricky tilted his head a little, making his neck pop.

"He was gonna warn you, when you come," he said. "I could not let him do that, you see."

Ricky leveled a look at me as more tears welled up in his eyes. He lowered his chin to his chest.

"Let's get this over with."

Virgil looked at me for a long moment, then nodded. He looked to Ricky for a second, but Ricky didn't meet his eye and Virgil walked out the front door.

I collected the Winchester Ricky dropped by the window, then removed his pistol I'd snugged behind my belt.

"Ricky," I said. "I am most comfortable with one of a few choices that will decide your fate."

"What?" he said.

"Take you with us back to Appaloosa where you can face a judge, who will decide your fate for all that you have done and will not continue to do."

"You said you'd finish me."

"I changed my mind."

I removed all but one bullet from his revolver and placed the wood-handled pistol on the counter near the front door. I looked back to Ricky. He looked at the pistol, then at me.

I left out the front door, walked across the road and up the embankment toward our horses, and when I got to the other side of the rise I heard the report of Ricky's pistol from inside the way station.

I stopped for a moment and looked back toward the building. I could only see the roof of the place and the thin trickle of smoke coming from the chimney of the wood-burning stove inside.

I thought about Ricky and what he'd been through, his time in prison and his broken life. Then I thought about Skinny Jack and all he'd been through. He was as good-hearted as they come and all I could readily allow was how some people just have a better shot than others.

# 22.

Virgil was gathering our horses near Mrs. Opelka when I got back to the wash.

"That it?" Virgil said.

"Is."

Virgil nodded a little.

"You believe him?" I said. "'Bout Socorro?"

"No real reason not to," Virgil said.

"He didn't seem none too happy with Truitt or Boston Bill," I said.

"Don't seem like a story he'd make up while he's sitting there with his nose shot off," Virgil said.

"No," I said. "It does not."

Mrs. Opelka got to her feet and brushed the dirt from her dress.

"That's what I heard," she said. "That skinny blond fella was going on about going to Socorro, about turning thirty, about his friends and his gals. The sniveling piece of shit; I only wish my boys would have been here to give him the proper goddamn whipping he deserves."

"What about the big fella?" I said. "He's the main one we are after. You hear anything? You pick up anything that might help us find him?"

"No, he did not talk much," she said. "He wanted food and quiet. He wanted to rest his horse and that was it. He was mad that we had no fresh horses, but that was all the anger he showed other than when he told the blond fella to shut up . . ."

She stared to the ground, then looked off in the direction of the way station.

"I'd like to get my husband out of the field and prepare him proper before my boys get back. I want their daddy to look as good as he can look."

Virgil nodded, then handed me the reins of my horse.

"Everett, why don't you find Skinny Jack's horse and gather Skinny. And I will help Mrs. Opelka here."

I took the reins and swung up.

"Best I can remember, Socorro is a near full day's ride past where you turn back west to go on to La Verne," I said.

"Sounds about right," Virgil said.

"We're going to need to stay after it if we are going to get in there by Saturday," I said.

"We will," Virgil said.

Then I moved on up the wash and rode off back toward where Skinny Jack lay dead.

By late into the afternoon, Mrs. Opelka's boys arrived, and after a display of shock, tears, and anger upon hearing the news of what had happened to their father, the sturdy young men helped bury the dead. We buried Skinny Jack in a shallow grave with some plank boards covering him so as to exhume him at a future time and bury him next to his mother.

That night, Virgil and I rested up a little in Opelka's barn, but we were on our way to Socorro hours before sunrise.

We figured we had a full two days' ride to get to Socorro by Saturday night, so we maintained a steady pace. The next night we rested near an old mission, and again we were up and riding long before seeing the rising sun.

Socorro was fifty miles past La Verne, this side of the border. We had planned on arriving Saturday afternoon, but it took us longer to get there than we anticipated and it was good and dark by the time we arrived.

As we approached Socorro there was a cemetery on the left side of the road. Crosses towering crookedly above the graves within the low rock wall bordering the graveyard showed dark against the evening sky. Beyond the many and different-sized crosses, a hint of a golden light from within and the silver quarter-moon from above gave us a clear outline of the city.

"Here we go," I said.

"Yep," Virgil said.

"Don't suspect it's a good idea to ride in with our shoulders back and badges showing."

"No."

"Ricky said the cantina was on the north side," I said.

"Did," Virgil said. "East end."

"Don't think we been in it."

"No," Virgil said. "Don't think we have."

It'd been some time since Virgil and I were in Plaza Socorro, but we knew the town. We'd passed through there time and again in the last few years and we knew how it was laid out.

Virgil slowed a little and looked back to me.

"What do you figure it is?" Virgil said.

"Sun has been down for two hours, and from our last stop it seems we've been on the road for at least five hours, right? I'd say it's about eight, maybe nine o'clock."

"Sounds about right."

"Good timing," I said.

"We'll know soon enough."

We rode on a bit more. We were riding into the city with a slight breeze in our faces, and there was a faint smell of smoke and livestock.

"Let's go this side, on the south, and get a look at this cantina from across the plaza."

It was dark, but Virgil and I did not risk riding through Plaza Socorro. That would not be smart. The quarter moon provided us with enough light to show our way. We turned off the road and moved around a fenced hilltop cemetery. We rode downhill and passed a large stockyard, cut between a few houses, crossed a dry brook, and entered Socorro from the back side of town.

We rode behind a row of two-story buildings that faced the south side of the plaza. To our left was a number of adobes, but it was late enough in the evening that there was only a scant light or two burning. We rode on past the big church and a few alleys among the buildings. I slowed when we got close to the end of the row of buildings and the last alley leading to the plaza.

"I'll be goddamn," I said. "Hear 'em?"

Virgil didn't say anything, but I could see the whites of his eyes when he turned in his saddle and looked at me.

"Sounds like a party to me," I said.

# 23.

D oes," Virgil said.

I pulled my eight-gauge from the scabbard as we entered the back side of the dark alley.

Singing, laughter, and piano and fiddle music mixed together and cut through the otherwise peaceful evening like noisy unwanted guests.

"Sounds like they're having a lively time," I said.

"For the moment," Virgil said.

I nudged my bay and followed Virgil on his muscled stud. We moved slowly through the narrow passage between two single-story buildings toward the street. Loud laughter roared and echoed from the cantina across the open town square, as if someone had told a joke.

"Sounds like more than a few, too," I said.

"Damn sure does," Virgil said.

"Got some liquor flowing," I said.

"They do at that."

The laughter, hooting, and hollering made it sound like the rabble-rousers were right there with us in the alley.

We set our horses in the shadows and watched the cantina across the way. The windows and open door offered about the only substantial light in the small triangle-shaped plaza.

"If it is him, looks like Truitt has a few more than a handful of friends here," I said.

"By God," Virgil said.

"Could be Ricky wasn't lying."

"Could be," Virgil said.

"What do you think about Boston Bill?" I said.

Virgil shook his head.

"We'll know directly."

We watched and listened some.

"Best I can tell, there's what? Twelve horses?"

Virgil nodded.

"What do you want to do?" I said.

Virgil didn't reply as he watched the cantina across the way, thinking about our options.

"Could let them carry on," I said. "Then see if we see Truitt or Black leave the place."

Virgil nodded a bit.

"Could," he said.

"Then again," I said. "We risk them going separate ways. Might lose Truitt and Black in the dark."

"If there is a party," Virgil said. "And even though we're not invited, I believe we best pay our respects."

He stepped down from his saddle and tied off on a post of a side overhang.

I moved my horse to the opposite side of the alley and dismounted.

"We know Truitt's not afraid to pull," I said.

"We do."

"Ricky said there's the two others that most likely aren't afraid of a fight."

"He did," Virgil said. "Walt and . . ."

"Douglas . . . Douglas," I said.

Virgil nodded.

Another fiddle and piano tune started up. It was a lively, knee-slapping tune. I recognized it, "Carve Dat Possum." A female with a squeaky voice was singing the song and the crowd was chiming in out of key on the chorus.

"Once we know," I said, "that it is for sure Truitt and Black, I suspect we'll ask them polite-like if they want to go peaceful with us back to Appaloosa. Go from there."

My tall bay worked the hell out of the bit in his mouth, then lowered his head, shook it hard and let out a loud snort.

"Hush," I said, and pushed his butt up to the wall.

Virgil took a few steps out of the alley. He looked to the left, then right. I moved up next to him.

"Be best to not walk directly across, don't you think?"

"I do," Virgil said.

We stepped up on the porch of a feed store, stayed under the plaza's awnings, and worked our way around the town square toward the cantina.

I slid back the hammers of the eight-gauge as we neared and Virgil pulled his bone-handled Colt.

It was late enough that nobody was out on the plaza moving about. We came up on the twelve dozy horses hitched in front of a cantina with no name, no sign. Virgil edged up and peeked in the window.

Another spirited song started up, and with it some foot stomping and vigorous yelps.

Virgil looked to me and nodded.

I nodded back.

He tilted his head and I followed him into the saloon.

The barroom was small and full of happy-faced drunk men and a few unsightly equally drunk women having a festive time. A fat rosy-faced fella with a red scruffy beard was pounding on the piano. He was accompanied by a skinny kid sawing on the fiddle and a short, round woman dancing around and laughing as she showed the partiers the underside of her frilly dress.

Boston Bill was nowhere to be seen, but Truitt saw Virgil and me right away. He got to his feet, not real fast but not real slow, and took a step backward.

"Happy Birthday, Truitt," Virgil said.

# 24.

The piano player, fiddler, and dancer stopped their performance and turned their attention to Virgil and me standing in the doorway, holding weapons pointed in their direction. Looking down the bores of a double-barrel eight-gauge always altered the atmosphere in a room. For the moment, Truitt was like everyone else in the room, completely unsure what to do, so Virgil spelled it out for him.

"You're under arrest, Truitt."

Truitt stood slack-jawed, looking at Virgil. He was lankier and his blond hair was longer than it had been when we last laid eyes on him. He turned his head slightly to the side, eyeing Virgil with a testing look.

"I'll be damned," he said.

"That'd be your choice."

Truitt smiled a little.

"But there are better choices to make," Virgil said.

Truitt shook his head slowly.

"Virgil Cole."

"It is . . . And Everett Hitch. You remember Everett, don't you, Truitt?"

Truitt glared at me but didn't say anything. Then he looked back to Virgil.

"Under arrest for what?" he said.

"Right now it is attempted murder," Virgil said. "There is a good chance, though, the man you shot will die, and if that happens you will be charged with murder."

Truitt didn't say anything.

"Fella you shot was a policeman," Virgil said.

"He pulled and I shot him in self-defense."

"Plenty of witnesses that will testify otherwise," Virgil said, "so that will be for the judge to decide."

"That's bullshit," Truitt said.

"It's not," Virgil said. "You also been helping a wanted man."

Virgil glanced about the room a little.

"Where is he?" Virgil said.

"Who?"

"No reason to start acting like you are more of a dumbass than you are, Truitt," Virgil said.

Truitt's eyes narrowed.

"Who's the dumbass?" Truitt said.

"What do you think, Everett?" Virgil said.

"I think the more you help us out, Truitt, the better your chances will be."

"You been with him since you left Appaloosa, Truitt. You show some cooperation here, and I will be sure and let the judge know how helpful you were when we take you in."

Truitt shook his head and looked around the room at his friends.

"Just two of you," Truitt said.

"Oh, we have help," Virgil said. "Wouldn't undervalue your lack of sense or judgment."

Truitt looked to the window and leaned a little, looking out the front door. He smiled, then looked around the room at his friends. His teeth were white and straight, and he had a charming, boyish smile. He looked back to Virgil and stopped smiling.

"This is my town, my people," he said. "You really think the two of you can arrest me?"

"I don't think."

Truitt looked around the room at his friends again.

"I guess not," Truitt said. "Guess you don't think . . . Not a good idea coming in here, throwing claims around in front of my friends."

"Speaking of friends, what's the young fella's name, Everett, that swore on his granny's Bible we'd find Truitt here, at this cantina, Ricky what?"

"Ravenfield."

"That's right," Virgil said. "Ricky Ravenfield."

"He also said you got jumpy and shot the policeman," I said.

Truitt stared at me.

"Ricky was not too happy you left him."

"Fuck him," Truitt said.

"No need," Virgil said. "Ricky's dead."

Truitt stared at Virgil.

"Shot himself," Virgil said.

"Bullshit."

"Not," Virgil said. "Before he did, though, he swore on his granny's Bible you'd be here, and, well, sure enough, he was right."

Truitt looked around the room at everyone looking at him, then looked to Virgil.

"You planning on taking on everybody in this room?"

"Not planning on taking on anybody, Truitt," Virgil said. "But like

I said, whether you go to hell or not is your call. You should just let the judge handle this, go from there."

Sweat was beading up on Truitt's face.

"So let's get on with it, Truitt," Virgil said.

A big, angular-looking man that was sitting next to Truitt got slowly out of his chair.

"You ain't taking nobody nowhere," the man said.

"You must be one of the two Ricky said he didn't care for so much," Virgil said.

"Fuck you and fuck Ricky," the man said.

"You Walt or Douglas?" I said.

The man glanced at me, then looked back to Virgil.

"Truitt," Virgil said. "Let's not waste any more of my and Everett's time."

"Get on," the big man said. "We got you outnumbered so you two better get the fuck on down the road or you'll not live to talk about what will happen here if you don't."

Virgil took one step toward the big man.

"There is only one thing for certain, one very sure thing that will happen here tonight if you choose to pull on me," Virgil said. "And that is you will be dead, no matter."

A heavyset man to my right had been slowly inching his way more to my side the whole time we'd been in the room. I was watching him, just like Virgil had been watching him out of the corner of his eye. Virgil saw everything.

"Far enough," Virgil said, without looking directly at the heavy-set man.

The heavyset man scoffed a little, and because he was to our side he thought he had the speed, the snap. He reached, but Virgil shot him in the chest before he could get his revolver out.

The big man next to Truitt thought this was his chance, too. He moved fast, flipping the table in front of him, and pulled his revolver. But just as he went down behind the wooden tabletop, Virgil's second shot hit him in the forehead and blood splattered across Truitt's face.

"Goddamn," Truitt said.

Truitt stood with his hands up a bit and away from his sides, making sure we didn't suspect he was going to go for his sidearm.

Virgil stood steady, and for the moment the only thing in the room that moved was the lingering gun smoke.

Virgil nodded slightly.

"Anybody else?"

# 25.

Nobody else dared to move.

"Where is he?" Virgil said.

"Hotel," Truitt said, nodded in that direction. "Just across the square here."

"Had to hear the shots," I said.

We quickly disarmed Truitt, hustled him with us across the plaza to the hotel.

The hotel was a small two-story place with a narrow room on the first floor with a desk, a few dining tables, and a door to a back room.

A heavyset Mexican man was standing at the front window watching us, then looked over to us when we entered. He stared at us with a startled expression, then raised his arms a bit at the sight of my eight-gauge. He knew right away what we were doing there, even before Virgil showed his badge. He pointed out the rear door.

"He's gone," he said. "I come out when I heard the gunshots, and in a second he was down the steps here and gone."

We moved quickly out the back side of the hotel and found nothing but a small empty corral with a feed shed and an open gate.

"Where to, Truitt?"

"How would I know?"

I grabbed a handful of Truitt's collar and shoved him five full steps back until his head hit the adobe wall of the hotel.

"You remember Skinny Jack Newton don't you?"

"What?"

I slapped him.

"You know him?"

"Newton? Fuck. Yeah, I know Skinny Jack. Not seen him, though, in years. Shit, why?"

I slammed his head again against the wall.

"He was shot and killed by Ricky Ravenfield is why."

"What?"

I slammed him again.

"That's right, Truitt, Ricky shot and killed him, and for that you are equally responsible."

"Me?"

I slapped him hard a few times before Virgil got his hand on my shoulder and eased me back from Truitt.

Normally when push came to shove it was me that was the one who took the temper out of Virgil. The memory of Skinny Jack looking up at me as he took his last breath, however, was a memory that was not welcome, one I could not forget, and one that had left me boiling mad.

"Truitt," Virgil said. "We been after you and Bill Black for a good while, you know that. And so far, besides the lawman you shot, you've got five men killed, so you better cooperate before we are forced to see you become the sixth."

"I really don't know where he went, or where he's planning on going."

"Bullshit," I said.

He shook his head hard from side to side.

"I got no idea," he said.

"You came here with intention," Virgil said.

"Nothing other than I didn't know where else to go."

"And he just came with you?" Virgil said.

"He did."

"Truitt," Virgil said, "I'm gonna ask you a few simple questions and I want you to give me a few simple answers."

He looked back and forth between us.

"How is it you was with Bill in the first place?"

"We been friends for a while and he hired me to work with him."

"Friends from where?" Virgil said.

"New Mex," he said. "Las Vegas."

"What's in Vegas?"

"What ain't in Vegas?" he said. "I mean, I been there for a while, was living there, and I met him there at the Double Nickel next to the Harvey House. We played cards when he come through and, hell, I got to know him and, well, we was friends, that's all."

"But why Appaloosa?"

"I hadn't seen him in a while and he came in and offered me a job, well, me and Ricky. He met Ricky and he said he could use a few hands."

"When was this?"

"Three weeks back."

"Why?"

"Well, shit, Bill was always normally in the money and I'm always normally in need of money, so I come along to Appaloosa."

"With Ricky?" Virgil said.

"Yeah, Ricky was the reason he wanted to hire me in the first place."

"Why's that?"

"'Cause Ricky is . . . was . . . was a gun hand and Bill needed a gun hand."

"What do you know about Black being a wanted man?"

"All he told me was there was a good chance someone would be looking for him and he was not about being caught."

"So the two of you were Black's bodyguards?" I said.

He nodded.

"From what?" I said.

"Black . . . got wind a bounty was on his head and that there would be bounty hunters coming."

"How did he get wind there was a bounty on his head?"

"Don't know."

# 26.

The two men that Virgil killed in the Socorro cantina were in fact the men Ricky had warned us about. That night we locked up Truitt in the Socorro jail and we spent the following morning seeing if we could get some kind of idea as to the whereabouts of Bill Black. But by noon we came up with nothing, so we collected Truitt from the jail and we set out for Appaloosa.

It was a three-day ride back. The journey was without incident or much in the way of conversation with Truitt. He was quiet and sullen, and damn sure not interested in being in the situation he was in.

We arrived just after midnight and I slept on the bunk in the cell next to Truitt. In the morning, as the sun was coming up, I found Virgil waiting on me to tell Chastain, Book, and the rest of the deputies the story of Skinny Jack's murder.

"Not gonna be easy," I said.

"No," Virgil said, "it's not."

We sat quietly on the porch and drank coffee as Appaloosa started coming to life, and within an hour, Chastain, Book, and the remaining deputies had heard the story of Skinny Jack's demise.

After Book and three deputies left Appaloosa with a buckboard to collect Skinny Jack from the shallow grave behind Ray Opelka's place, Virgil and I sat on the porch with Chastain and he got us caught up on what had taken place since we'd been on the hunt.

"I'll be damned," I said. "Messenger is still with it?"

"Still hanging on, but he ain't with it, not at all," Chastain said.

"Figured he'd be dead," I said.

"Doc said considering the amount of blood he's lost that if he does come back he's likely to not be right in the head."

"What about the Denver police?"

Chastain nodded.

"Oh . . . they showed."

"The unit," I said.

"Two detectives. One older fella, Claude . . . Lieutenant Banes is his name. He's a senior with the department, nice enough, but the one that did all the talking was a younger fella . . . A little smart kind of guy, his name is King, kind of full of shit. Made a point of introducing himself as a detective . . . *Detective Sergeant* King."

"What'd they have to allow?" Virgil said.

"Questions about Roger Messenger."

"Like what?" Virgil said.

"Wanted to know if we talked with him, how long he was here, if he was alone, who he came in contact with, what happened. The details 'bout the shooting and so on.

"When I started asking questions, the young fella said that this case, the details about it were . . . confidential."

"Confidential?" Virgil said.

Chastain nodded.

"That's what the smart-ass shit, the young *detective* told me . . . confidential."

Virgil looked at me and shook his head.

"Maybe Messenger was acting on his own, without the department's knowledge," I said.

"Might be," Virgil said.

"So you don't know anything about the murder of Ruth Ann Messenger? How or when it happened or the evidence that was found?" I said.

"No. They shared nothing, really. All I can really say is they had more goddamn questions than they did answers."

"When did they arrive?" I said.

"Afternoon train, yesterday . . . Soon as they got off the train they stopped to see me."

"What other questions?" Virgil said.

"'Bout Bill Black, of course."

"What did they want to know?" Virgil said.

"Same thing everybody wants to know."

"Where is he?" I said.

"Yep," Chastain said. "Now there is three thousand dollars on his head. Where the hell is he."

"What did you tell them?" Virgil said.

"I told them you were after him but had no idea where you were or if you'd caught up with him."

"I don't guess you know anything about who put the money on Black's head?" I said.

"Don't know, they didn't say . . ."

"They say anything else about Messenger and how he was related to the victim?"

"No, but they was anxious to get to him, to see him. I pointed them to the hospital, so they could go see him."

"And?" I said.

"Well, hell," Chastain said as he got the coffeepot and topped off our cups. "I told them that all they could do was see him, have a look at him. I told them he was in bad shape, but they wanted to see him anyway . . . They might as well have been looking at drying hay."

"Now what?" I said.

"Got no idea," he said.

"They say what they were planning on doing here?" I said. "By staying here?"

"No, but I suspect they're interested in seeing how the two of you fared."

Chastain walked to the edge of the porch and poured his cold coffee in the street, then filled his cup with some hot coffee from the pot. He stood with his back to us, looking out at the street with his cup in one hand and the coffeepot in the other. He stood silently for a moment, then spoke to Virgil and me without turning to face us.

"Gonna miss that boy . . ." Chastain said. "He was like a son to me. I'm sure gonna miss him."

# 27.

Chastain had one of his young deputies fetch the Denver police-men and bring them to the office to talk with Virgil and me. We closed the door between the front office and the cells, separating us from Truitt.

Detective Lieutenant Claude Banes, the larger and older one of the two, had broad shoulders and large hands. He had that look of a man that likely drank too much whiskey.

After the introductions Lieutenant Banes dropped in a chair, un-buttoned his jacket, and leaned back with his hat in his hand. Every-thing about his demeanor suggested he was tired, had seen it all before, and was less than interested in his job.

The younger one, Detective Sergeant Sherman King, was a lean, clean-shaven man with a bowler pulled down just above his eyebrows. His manner was precise and rigid, and as Chastain had said, he was certainly full of himself and every gesture he made let us know he took his job seriously.

Chastain, Virgil, and I sat across from Lieutenant Banes, but Ser-geant King remained standing as if he were an officer at attention.

King looked to Banes and the lieutenant nodded a little, as if to give the young sergeant permission to speak. King quickly weighed in with some brazenness that would be short-lived.

"Where did you lose him?" King said.

"Lose who?" Virgil said.

"Bill Black, of course."

Virgil glanced at me before he answered King.

"We didn't lose Bill Black," Virgil said.

"The deputy that called on us said there was an apprehension of someone."

He nodded to the back cell room.

"Someone that had been with Bill Black, but that Black got away."

"Let's start with something a bit easier," Virgil said.

"What's that?"

"Why are you here?"

King looked to Banes, then back to Virgil.

"Official business of the Denver Department of Law Enforcement."

"What sort of official business?"

The young sergeant stood straight-backed with his jaw clenched.

"We are here to investigate."

"Investigate what?"

"I don't have to tell you this is serious business involving a member of our department."

"Tell us about this murder," Virgil said.

"I can tell you what is within my purview to be shared."

Virgil glanced to me again, then looked back to the sergeant and smiled.

"Tell us all you know, within your purview."

"I can answer the questions I feel are appropriate for me to answer, Marshal."

Virgil looked to Banes, and Banes averted his eyes to me.

"Roger Messenger a member of the Denver Department of Law Enforcement?" Virgil said.

"Was," King said.

"He's not anymore?"

"He is on leave, pending investigation," he said.

"Providing he lives," Virgil said.

The young detective sergeant stared at Virgil.

"Who is Ruth Ann, and how is she related to Roger?"

"I'm afraid I cannot answer that."

"There is really nothing for you to be afraid of, Detective Sergeant King," Virgil said.

King blinked a few times.

"The case is confidential, Marshal."

Virgil glanced to me.

"We heard something about that," Virgil said.

"There is a warrant and there is a bounty," I said. "Not much confidential about that."

"Nonetheless . . ." he said.

"Messenger come here by himself," Virgil said, "or as a member of the Denver Department of Law Enforcement to serve the warrant?"

Detective Sergeant King pulled his shoulders back and looked at Virgil without answering the question.

"Guess that means confidential," Virgil said.

"I cannot answer that."

"How is it that Boston Bill Black ends up being charged with this murder?"

"I told you this is confident—"

"Shut up, Sherman," Banes said. "Goddamn it, son, just shut the hell up."

King looked to Banes like his feelings were hurt.

"Ruth Ann was Roger Messenger's wife," Banes said. "Maybe you figured that part out already? Nothing goddamn confidential about that."

"How is it that Boston Bill is wanted for her murder?" Virgil said.

"Ruth Ann was fucking Boston Bill Black," Banes said.

# 28.

Detective Sergeant King raised a rigid finger and said, "That is unauthorized and—"

"I said, shut up," Banes said, looking sternly at the young man. "And I mean it. These fellas have lost one of their men trying to sort this shit out, and I'll be goddamned if I'm gonna just sit here and listen to you avoiding what they need to know so they can do their job."

Banes looked back to Virgil.

"If I said Ruth Ann was promiscuous, that would be a pound-and-a-half understatement. She was as wild as a March hare. She had a hard time keeping her legs together, you see . . . and Bill Black was not the first. Roger was no match for her, not from the damn beginning. Not sure how she even ended up with Roger or how he ended up with her, but when Black was in Denver, working on the gambling house there, he was giving it to her on a regular basis."

King shook his head back and forth with a disappointed look on his face. Banes ignored him.

"Everybody knew about it," Banes said. "Apparently, Ruth Ann had her hooks in Boston Bill bad."

"Roger knew about it, too?" I said.

Banes nodded.

"Yeah," he said. "Poor sonofabitch . . ."

"When it started up with Bill she flaunted it and shit. That was hard on Roger, you can imagine."

King looked to Banes and said harshly under his breath, "Sir . . ."

Banes continued without acknowledging King.

"Rumor is Boston Bill tried to break it off with Ruth Ann, but she had different ideas. She wanted to leave Roger. Anyway, she leaves Roger, so the story goes, and Roger starts to drinking and then he gets his ass kicked off of the force."

"And Ruth Ann?" Virgil said. "What happened to her?"

"Next thing you know, Ruth Ann ends up missing. Then two weeks go by, then Ruth Ann is found down by the South Platte behind the inn where Bill Black was staying, facedown in a foot of water. She'd been beaten, brutally murdered."

"Any witnesses?"

Banes nodded.

"Folks, the owners of the inn, heard him, Boston Bill, and Ruth Ann arguing in the middle of the night, the night before Bill left Denver."

"But no eyewitness?"

"Not directly, but all indicators point to . . . Black," he said. "There was blood found on the back steps."

"Who found her?" I said.

"Some kids who were fishing," he said.

"How could you tell after that long a time what had happened to her?" I said. "That she had been beaten? Hard to believe no coyotes and other varmint got to her."

"She was in shallow water, a bunch of green river weed wrapped around her, when the kid found her. When the officers got there to the riverbank and pulled her from the water she was still intact. She was brought in, looked at carefully."

"And?" I said.

"She had a number of cuts on her body," Banes said. "Looked like a blow to the head is what did her in. Hard to say, she could have been held down in the shallow water and drowned, for all we know. But it was her, it was Ruth Ann, and she was killed."

Detective Sergeant King lowered his head as if he'd been defeated.

"You and Roger friends?" Virgil said.

Banes sat stoic as he looked at Virgil a bit, then nodded.

"Yes."

"What he ever say to you about any of this?"

"Nothing."

"Roger ever a suspect in Ruth Ann's murder?" I said.

Banes looked at me.

"It was discussed," he said.

"By who?" I said.

"All of us."

"What do you think?"

Banes stared at me for a long moment.

"Maybe."

"Maybe?"

"He had to be mad as hell at her. Fact, he even said to me he'd like to see her dead for making a fool out of him like she did . . . I suppose I would not have put it past him."

"So what do you figure?" Virgil said.

Banes nodded a little, then shook his head. He glanced to his detective partner before he spoke.

"I'd most likely put my money on Roger as the killer of his wife, Ruth Ann."

The young detective reacted liked he'd been shot and said with volume and precise, sharp, emphatic words, "Bill Black is the murderer of Ruth Ann Messenger . . . and he is a wanted man. He is on the run. And his warrant is supported by evidence and not hearsay. And not you or anyone else outside of the court of law can hypothetically go putting money on it."

"I can hypothetically do what the sam-hell I want to do," Banes said, looking sternly at his partner, but then he nodded a little. "But I can also say . . . you might be right."

"There is no doubt," King said.

"Oh, there is always doubt in this line of work," Banes said. "Always . . . even when it involves friends, family, and loved ones. Always. It's just how it is."

"But if Roger did do it," I said, "why would he come here and see to it that Bill be arrested?"

"Retribution, maybe, get back at him for the humiliation, hell, I don't know."

Banes shook his head.

"Roger was a good policeman. Honest, fair, and he believed in the law and that every man deserved his day in court, including Boston Bill, I guess . . . He did everything by the book . . . but a man can be pushed only so far."

Chastain had been working on a plug the whole conversation, and now spit it into a spittoon by his desk and said, "Then you got to ask yourself, Why would Bill take off like he did if he didn't do it?"

"Don't know," Banes said.

Chastain worked the plug a bit.

"Men do get jumpy," he said, "when they are wanted."

Banes nodded.

"Also," he said, "I think at some point Bill realized, maybe not until Roger come upon him, maybe before, that he stepped into a big pile of shit when he started up with Ruth Ann. She was really something to look at, but, well, Ruth Ann brought with her a damn rat's nest full of trouble."

"What about the warrant?" Virgil said.

"Not sure of all the particulars, but it was standard. Once information came in, all of it pointing to Black, the chief issued the warrant."

"Chief suspect Roger, too?"

Banes was quiet for a moment, then . . .

"I can't say . . . but the warrant was drawn up for Bill Black."

Banes looked to King, then back to Virgil.

"There you have it," Banes said.

"What about the reward money?" Virgil said.

Banes glanced to King again, then back to me.

"That was offered by the chief, too."

Virgil looked at me and squinted a little.

"Why all the fuss about confidential," I said.

"Roger Messenger," Banes said. "Is the son . . . of our beloved chief of police."

# 29.

Within a few days Roger Messenger died of the gunshot wound he received from Truitt Shirley, and Truitt was subsequently charged with his murder.

The day after Messenger died, Detectives Banes and King returned to Denver with his body. The fact that it was anyone's guess as to the whereabouts of Boston Bill at this point in time left the two officers no real choice other than to move along and wait and see if a law official or bounty hunter was lucky enough to apprehend him.

Skinny Jack, too, had a proper funeral. He was buried alongside his mother, who he had taken care of during a long, drawn-out illness and had passed away one year to the day Skinny Jack was killed.

After the funeral, Allie, Virgil, and I sat at a table near the bar, where Virgil and I were drinking mugs of cool beer and Allie was sipping on a glass of Irish whiskey.

"Just awful," Allie said.

"Nice funeral, though," Virgil said.

"Was," I said.

"I am just so sick about it, though," Allie said.

"Me, too, Allie," I said. "Me, too."

"And to think he was killed exactly a year after his poor, sick ol' momma's passing away is just, well, it's just as sad as can be. He was so young and sweet. He had no business being a deputy lawperson, none whatsoever."

"It was his job, Allie."

"I don't care, it is sad and wrong."

"He was a good man, Allie, and I share your deepest sympathy, but he liked the job he did and he was good at it."

"Well, it is just terrible, and to think that skinny young boy took such care of his poor, sick ol' momma like he did for as long as he did and now this. Just is not fair."

Virgil nodded.

"Not much is fair, Allie."

"That could have been you," Allie said.

"It wasn't," Virgil said.

"And then what on earth would have become of me, can you tell me that?"

"Well, we don't have to think about that, Allie."

"We do have to think about it, Virgil."

We'd been through this before with Allie. Many times. It was like a burr under her saddle. She would be doing fine until there was an incident that got her imagination churned up and she imagined things she had no control over.

"You don't have to dwell on it," Virgil said.

"Not dwelling, Virgil. It could happen."

"Well, hell, Allie, everybody has to face such things, whether they are lawmen or law-abiding citizens or criminals or whoever, everybody has to think about it."

"I just don't like what you do."

"Without men like me, you, the people, are not protected."

"Don't mean it has to be you being the one that is the protector."

"Can we just enjoy this beer?" Virgil said.

"Absolutely," she said as she took a sip of her whiskey. "Everett, you will look after me, won't you?"

"Well . . . sure, Allie."

"I'm right here, Allie," Virgil said.

"For now," she said. "And thank God for Everett."

"What about Everett?" Virgil said.

"What about him?" she said.

"What gives Everett this good fortune that you ain't pointing in my direction?"

"Don't be silly, Virgil. I'm not saying that, not pointing good fortune in Everett's direction at all. Though I do wish you all the good fortune God has available to grant you, Everett, I do. I'm just concerned about having a contingency plan is all, Virgil. You have to understand that. Everett understands that, don't you, Everett?"

"A contingency plan?" Virgil said.

"Yes," she said. "A contingency plan. You want me to be taken care of, don't you?"

Virgil looked at me for a second, then looked at Allie.

"Well, of course I do, Allie."

"Well, good, then, I'm glad to know that you agree with me and Everett."

Allie turned in her chair and held up her empty glass for Wallis to see.

"Wallis," she said as she wiggled her glass a little. "Would you be so kind?"

"Right away, Mrs. French," Wallis said.

# 30.

Two weeks after burying Skinny Jack, there was still no sign of
Boston Bill. Old Man Pritchard stayed in town and continued
with the duties required for his gambling parlor's July Fourth grand
opening, which was less then a month away.

With the expansion of the silver mining north of town, the parlor
was already being rumored as a popular destination, mainly because
Pritchard was quite the salesman. He let it be known the opening of
the casino would be the grandest, most spectacular event to happen
west of the Mississippi. Nothing the likes of Appaloosa had ever seen,
complete with fireworks, a lively orchestra, spinning roulette wheels,
and dancing girls.

It was cloudy when the sun first came up, but the day turned out
to be a warm one. I'd spent the morning cleaning out the stable and
working with a new horse I'd recently purchased. He was a big ornery
black geld named Ajax, and I saddled him up and rode to S. Q. Johnson's Grocery near the depot to buy Ajax and me some refreshment.

S. Q. Johnson was almost eighty and was one of the original men
that started Appaloosa when the first mine opened up thirty-five

years back. He was spry for his age, but slow, and with each passing day was becoming more forgetful.

After I placed my order with S.Q. and he moved off to the back room, a bright flash of light caught my eye. It shot through the dimly lit store, ricocheting off a mirror behind the counter for a brief instant, then was gone. I looked back.

It was glaring sunlight reflecting off a silky white parasol carried by a slender woman. She was passing by on the boardwalk, and I moved a bit toward the window for a closer look.

I couldn't see her face under the dome of fabric as she walked on, but she was a graceful creature, and there was something damn sure arresting about the way she carried herself.

"Here you go, Everett," S.Q. said.

I watched her for a moment. She stopped and walked back and looked in the window. For a brief second I thought she was looking at me, but she looked down at the display of fruit S.Q. had laid out. I could not see her face clearly, but well enough to see she was pretty. She twirled her parasol a little, turned, and then walked on.

"She was in here the other day," S.Q. said.

I moved back to the counter where S.Q. had my goods laid out.

"Who is she?"

"Don't know, but she's a flower. Smelled like one, too . . . Every now and again a little nice comes to town, an element that brings value and beauty. But that is only now and again. Damn place is getting bigger every day, Everett. I don't have to tell you most of what is populating Appaloosa these days is nothing but riffraff."

"No, S.Q. You don't have to tell me."

"I don't, but I am telling you anyway . . . riffraff, like that gambler you and Virgil were after."

"Well, it's a growing place, I'll give you that."

"You ever catch that murderer?"

"No, sir."

"Shame," S.Q. said. "I remember that fella that got shot 'cause of him. He came in here and bought a can of beans . . . Oh . . . I forgot your ice."

S.Q. turned and walked slowly to the back room.

"Yeah," S.Q. said, "that fella came in here just before it happened. I visited with him for quite a while, nice man."

"That so?"

S.Q. said nothing else, but I could hear him chopping some ice. After a moment he walked back slowly from the rear of the store.

"What did you visit with him about?" I said.

"Who?" S.Q. said.

"The man that got shot in front of the gambling place."

"He came in here."

"Yeah. You said. He bought a can of beans."

"He did."

"You talked to him?"

S.Q. nodded.

"He came in here just before he got shot, poor fella."

"What'd you talk about?"

"He sat there on the porch and ate his beans," S.Q. said. "Nice morning. I sat there with him and we visited."

"What did you visit about?"

"Oh . . . a little bit of everything."

"Like what?"

"Think he was feeling the effects of a bit too much of the good stuff, Everett."

"Do you remember what you talked about?"

"Oh, let's see . . . He told me he was a policeman."

"Anything else you remember?"

S.Q. leaned in closer.

"Said that he had come to town to arrest the man responsible for murdering his wife. Was gonna take him in single-handed."

"He said that to you?"

"He did," S.Q. said. "Said he had nightmares 'bout it, it was haunting him. Poor fella. Guess it didn't turn out like he had planned."

"You remember anything else?"

"About what?"

"Anything else he said?"

"Who?" S.Q. said.

# 31.

When I walked out of S. Q. Johnson's Grocery it was even hotter than it had been when I entered not fifteen minutes earlier, and there was not so much as a hint of moving air.

I gave Ajax a chunk of apple. He gobbled it up, then I gave him the rest and untied him from the hitch. He was clearly not too happy about standing saddled in the blazing sun.

"I know, it's hot . . . We're moving, we're moving . . ."

I draped the gunnysack with the beer and ice on the horn and mounted up. The saddle was so damn hot I had to stand in my stirrups. I moved off without sitting and let my seat cool as I rode down 2nd Street.

When I turned onto Main Street, I saw the woman with the parasol again.

She was ahead of me a ways on the busy boardwalk. I slowed, sat back in the saddle, and followed her as she walked.

The silk wheel was casually spinning above her head as she strolled leisurely. She paused, looking in the window of a barbershop. As I got closer I could see she was watching a small boy getting a haircut.

I angled a little toward the boardwalk to have a better look at her, and when I slowed, she turned, looked right at me.

This time she was looking at me.

She had dark, almost black hair, rosy cheeks, and big brown eyes. I tipped my hat and she smiled as I rode past. I looked back to her, she gave her parasol an extra spin, smiled a slight more, then slid effortlessly through the open door of a fabric shop.

"She smiled at me, Ajax, not at you . . ."

I rode on up the busy street and there were a lot of people moving about for such a hot day.

Like S.Q. was saying, the place just gets bigger every day. It was hard to keep up with all the comings and goings, but there was most certainly more coming than going.

There was always something new happening, some new business opening, but mostly the growth—no doubt—brought a mischievous lot.

There were not any new churches, but there were plenty new saloons and whoring establishments.

Pritchard's gambling hall was opening soon, and it had already caused a good deal of trouble with its own brand of mischief, like Boston Bill Black, Truitt Shirley, and Ricky Ravenfield.

When I rode past the place, prominently located on the corner of Main and 3rd Street, there were a slew of onlookers watching workers on tall ladders hoisting a huge colorfully painted canvas banner above the entrance.

I slowed to a stop next to Juniper Jones. Juniper was an amusing little man with a round body and red face. He sported a tall dark green flattop hat, was always sharply dressed, and was without exception the best attorney in Appaloosa. He was Harvard educated and wealthy, but he was also most assuredly gaining a reputation as the town drunk.

Juniper was perched on the edge of a water trough with a newspaper tucked under his arm, looking up at the sign being strung up across the street. He glanced up, squinting at me.

"Everett," he said.

"Juniper."

He looked back to the sign being hoisted.

"What's this place coming to?" Juniper said.

"Good question."

"I'm not talking about this godforsaken place, not Appaloosa. I'm talking about this country. What is it coming to?"

"Another good question."

"Gambling has this motherland by the short hairs, Everett."

"'Spose it does, Juniper."

"Oh, it does . . . It's an insidious kaleidoscope, offering the illusion of chance as a contender, a competitor to hard work and discipline. Not to mention it is a catastrophe for meaningful relationships."

"Everything is a gamble," I said. "This motherland was a gamble coupled with hard work."

Juniper looked at me.

"Yes, but it has become an addiction for many, you see. Even when the gambler knows the odds are against him, when he can't afford to lose, he still rolls the dice."

Juniper got to his feet and brushed the back side of his trousers as he looked at the sign.

"Believe that's French, Everett?" Juniper said. "Maison de Daphne?"

"Believe it might be," I said.

Juniper laughed.

"Might?" Juniper said. "Besides me, you are the smartest person in this goddamn godforsaken town. You know French when you see it."

"I do."

"Of course you do."

The workmen got the banner where they wanted it and tied it in place. Then I saw her again: the smooth-walking woman with the parasol. She came through the gathered crowd, waited as a buggy passed, then crossed the dry street and stopped, looking up at the sign. She watched the workers for a moment, then turned and looked at the onlookers. After a few seconds she walked between the ladders, up the steps, and entered Maison de Daphne.

# 32.

Allie was working in the garden when I rode up. She was draping bed linens over the top of her plants so they didn't fry in the hot sun. She looked up, seeing me as I tied off Ajax under one of the two oak trees that had grown tall enough in the past year to provide a little shade.

"Hey, Everett," Allie said.

She stood from being bent over and pushed her hips forward, arching her lower back. Her hands were dirty and her blousy shirt was sweated through, but she looked pretty with strands of hair falling across her flushed cheeks.

"Hot enough for you?" I said.

"Nice day for a lizard," she said, shielding her eyes from the sun.

"Where's your bonnet?"

"I know. I hadn't planned on being out here, but you know how it goes, one thing leads to another."

"I do."

"How are you?" she said.

"I'm not working in the garden in the hot sun."

"I had to do this before the whole thing burnt up."

"You need some help?"

"No, I'm done for now, it's quitting time."

"Guess I timed it just right."

"You did."

I opened the gate onto the stone walk leading to the house and made my way toward where Allie stood in the garden. I thought about how I laid every stone of that path with Virgil on a day that was as hot as today.

"I should have gotten out here earlier, but I piddled around until it got to boiling, silly me."

Allie pulled back the strands of hair hanging in front of her eyes.

"What kind of no good are you up to?"

"Thought I'd just pay my respects."

"Well, I'm glad to know that I am owed."

"Always, Allie."

"Virgil's not here," she said.

"Who's Virgil?" I said.

She cleaned the dirt off her hands with the front of the apron as she turned, appraising her garden.

"Would you just look at this?" she said. "This is a full-time job."

"Tomatoes look good," I said.

"Fat and juicy. Problem is keeping enough water on 'em."

Allie took off her apron and shook it free of dirt.

"Yeah, well, it's been hot, that's for sure."

"What you got in the bag?"

I held up the dripping gunnysack.

"Beer, ice."

"What?" she said.

"Yep."

"What's the occasion?"

"Wednesday."

"Is it?"

"It is."

She looked down at herself and her blouse was soaked with sweat and clinging to her chest.

"Aren't I a sight?"

She pinched the fabric of her blouse and gave it a few pulls away from her chest so as to give her breasts a little air.

"You look just fine to me, Allie."

"Why, Everett, you are a flatterer if I have ever heard one."

"I'm sure you have heard plenty."

"Oh, Everett."

I smiled.

"Why don't you let me freshen up a little and I will meet you on the back porch for a taste of some of what you have there."

"Sounds good, Allie."

I put the bottles of beer into a bucket with the ice and sat on the back porch, listening to the meadowlarks, as I waited on Allie. A welcome breeze picked up and under the shade of the porch was beginning to feel comfortable.

I thought of the conversation I had with S.Q., about what he said about Roger Messenger, and then I wondered about what really happened, about who really did kill Ruth Ann Messenger.

I heard Allie call from the house.

"Be right there, Everett."

I looked back and could see Allie through the curtains of the open bedroom window. She had her back to the window and for a moment she was without covering, but then she slipped a dress on over her head.

After a few moments Allie came out. She was wearing a loose-fitting white cotton dress with her wet hair wrapped atop her head and held in place with an ivory hair comb.

"Forgive me, I had to water myself a little," she said.

"By all means," I said. "I waited on you."

I got a bottle of beer and poured us each a glass.

"You are a gentleman, Everett Hitch."

I handed Allie a glass.

"Look at the foam."

"Cheers," I said.

"Cheers to you," Allie said.

We touched glasses and drank.

"Oh, my," she said.

Allie licked the foam from her top lip.

"My goodness. Is that refreshing."

"It is."

"Thank you."

We sat and sipped our beer, and for the moment we didn't say anything. It was comfortable with Allie, and she was, after all we had been through, a friend and I had grown to enjoy her company.

We heard Virgil come through the gate, then open the front door.

"Back here, Virgil," Allie said.

Virgil made his way down the hall and out the back door, and when he did Allie held up her beer.

"Look what Everett brought."

Virgil looked back and forth between Allie and me.

"Sit, I'll get you a glass."

Allie was up and into the house before Virgil had a chance to take his hat off.

"See you got a saddle on that black."

"Good to know he's still out there."

"He is."

Virgil took off his hat and wiped his brow with a handkerchief he pulled from his pocket as Allie came back out the door with a glass. She poured Virgil a beer and handed it to him, then kissed him on the cheek.

"What have you been doing, Virgil Cole?"

Before Virgil answered he took a long pull of the beer, then held it up in the light and looked at its color.

"That's damn good," he said.

Allie smiled.

"S.Q. got that from Saint Louis," I said.

"Glad for it," Virgil said, then looked to Allie.

"I been over at the Western Union office."

"What's happening?" Allie said.

Virgil looked to me.

"Boston Bill Black has been caught."

# 33.

W here?"

"El Paso."

"Damn, Virgil," Allie said.

"Yep," Virgil said.

"No," she said. "Is this necessary?"

"What?"

"You sure do know how to spoil a good time," she said.

"How's that?"

"Everett and I have been doing just fine, drinking this lovely beer that come all the way from Saint Louis, and now this business of being caught."

"Hell, Allie," Virgil said. "Everett and me spent a good goddamn amount of time searching for him, and the fact he has been caught has significant meaning here."

"That does not mean we have to bring it up on a pleasant Wednesday afternoon, does it?"

"I know I don't need to tell you this, Allie, but in the process of chasing that sonofabitch, we lost one of our friends, a friend of yours, too."

"No, you do not need to tell me, I know," she said. "I miss Skinny Jack, too, I do."

"I know you do," he said.

"But I still don't think this is right," Allie said.

"What?" Virgil said.

"That Boston Bill Black did this heinous crime he is accused of," she said. "I told you that before."

"And like I said before, Allie. That will be up to the judge to decide."

"Oh, the judge. There is always a judge. I thought it was a foregone conclusion the other man, the fella from Denver, was the one that was the murderer."

"There is still a warrant and a bounty on Black's head, Allie."

Allie got up out of her chair and filled her glass with beer.

"I'm gonna go make supper."

She looked at me.

"Thank you, Everett," she said. "It was so lovely to spend some pleasant time with you."

"You too, Allie."

"I'll leave you two to it," she said.

Then she went into the house. I watched after her as she walked back into the house and rounded the corner into the kitchen.

"Heard something from S.Q. just before I came over here today," I said. "We know S.Q. is going around the bend, getting more forgetful and a bit slower every day, but he told me Messenger spoke to him the day he was shot and that Messenger told him in a sober moment that he had come to town to arrest the man that killed his wife."

Virgil looked at me for a long bit, then shook his head a little.

"The Denver detective that come here, Banes. He thought differently," Virgil said. "Thought it could have been Roger Messenger that murdered his wife."

"I know," I said.

"Guess we'll find out soon enough," Virgil said.

"Who caught Black?" I said.

"A bounty hunter," Virgil said.

"They sure it's him?"

"So it seems."

"I'll be damned," I said.

"Yup."

"When did this happen?"

"Today, I think," Virgil said.

"Now what?"

"He's being brought back here."

"To Appaloosa?"

"Yep."

"Not Denver?"

"No," Virgil said. "He's gonna be tried here."

"But the murder was in Denver."

"According to the Denver DA, Black was here, hired a gunman here, fled from here, and was involved in a crime here that left a Denver policeman dead."

"He's not charged with that shooting, Truitt is."

Virgil shook his head.

"I know, but Denver DA said since Judge Callison is coming through, dealing with Truitt, and this crime happened here, they'd deal with Boston Bill then, too."

"How will they do that, the fact that Ruth Ann Messenger's murder happened in Denver and the potential witnesses and such are in Denver, you'd think they would want him, need him back there to stand trial?"

"Could be the profile of the case gives Denver an opportunity to get it out of their backyard. Maybe it has to do with the fact of what this is all about, the nature of it."

"You mean, seeing how this has to do with the fact the son of the police chief was married to a woman running around flaunting her goods with an itinerant gambler, they don't want to make this any more public than they have to?"

"Don't know," Virgil said, "but I would suspect that is right. They are taking this opportunity to keep Black out of the chief's path . . . All this business was happening over the wire between El Paso, Appaloosa, and Denver these last few hours, and I think suppertime crept up and nipped it. Anyway, that was that."

"I'll be damned," I said. "And if he's convicted, what then?"

"Don't know. Figured they'd let him get shipped here and go from there, let Black fend for himself," Virgil said. "Last bit back from Denver said they are sending in a reception team to deal with this."

"Another unit?"

"Sounds like it," Virgil said. "Bounty hunter left a demand, too, that stated if the three thousand was not available with the return of Boston Bill Black, he would let Black go free."

"When will Black get here?"

"According to the El Paso sheriff's office, he would have already been here, but Mr. Black needed a day to heal up."

"What happened?"

"Seems there was some altercation that happened and Black was knocked around a bit. Office said they'd be here within a few days."

"Who's bringing him in, who's the bounty hunter?"

"Don't know," Virgil said.

# 34.

After two days there was no sign yet of Boston Bill Black or the bounty hunter, but both the Denver authorities and Judge Callison had arrived and were awaiting Black's arrival.

Early evening, as the sun was going down, Virgil and I walked over to the Colcord Hotel to have a talk with the Denver authorities.

We met them in the dining room as they were getting up from a table near the back door. They were the Denver district attorney, Eldon Payne, and the captain of police, G. W. McPherson.

Both men looked to be in their mid-sixties. Payne was a slender, solid-looking man with deep-set eyes and dark skin. He wore a dark gray suit with his bowler tilted back on his forehead. McPherson was a big, rough-looking, ruddy-faced Irishman with silver-red hair and wearing a blue police uniform with gold buttons and tall boots in need of polishing.

After our introductions, Virgil and I walked out on the back porch with them, where they lit cigars.

"It will be about time to put an end to this," McPherson said.

"Yes," Payne said. "Good he was apprehended."

"We don't have to tell you two why we are here and why we are not bringing Bill Black to Denver," McPherson said.

Virgil glanced at me, then looked back to Payne.

"You don't have to," Virgil said.

"Yeah," McPherson said. "The sensitive damn nature of this, the political backlash, you understand? So the fact that Black was involved in an altercation that put him on the run with other criminals was in some ways a blessing in disguise."

Virgil nodded.

"It would be harmful for the chief and his family," Payne said. "Newspapers have already brought a great deal of grief to the chief and his wife."

"And the department," McPherson said.

Virgil nodded a little as he puffed on his cigar.

"I take it you have plenty of evidence that supports this warrant on Bill Black?" he said.

"We do," McPherson said.

Payne looked to McPherson.

"Enough for this to go to trial?" I said.

"We do," McPherson said.

"You think?" Virgil said.

"Why do you ask?"

"Callison is a fair judge," I said.

Payne nodded.

"I know," he said.

"You don't have it, he's likely to call bullshit on it," Virgil said. "He's not one for hearsay."

"From what we heard, there were no eyewitnesses," I said. "That correct?"

Payne looked to McPherson, then back to us, and nodded.

"That is correct," Payne said. "But Ruth Ann Messenger was killed in the Platte River woods, where Black was boarding. There was blood found on the back steps."

"The owners of the inn heard them arguing," McPherson said.

"This much we heard," I said.

"Then," McPherson said, "the next thing you know, she's gone missing . . ."

"That might be enough for a warrant," Virgil said.

"And to squeeze out a bounty," I said.

"But you are gonna be hard-pressed to get a conviction with that," Virgil said.

I looked to Payne.

"You'd have to figure that, don't you?" I said. "You know better than we do, that is your business, but you are going to have to spin a silky web with that."

"Black taking off, on the run, does not bode well for his defense," McPherson said.

"Might not bode well for him, but it damn sure don't hinder him, either," Virgil said.

I nodded.

"He hired gunmen when there was money on his head," McPherson said.

"That don't hinder him, either," Virgil said. "If anything, that helps him."

"How's that?" McPherson said.

"He was in fear for his life," Virgil said. "Three thousand dollars dead or alive is one shot away from dying."

"And what about Black's defense?" I said.

"He'll have to hire a lawyer here or have the court appoint him a lawyer."

"If it is a conviction you are after," Virgil said, "you just might want to take this back to Denver and face whatever backlash comes about as a result."

"We will remain here, Marshal Cole, and see to it justice is served," Payne said. "At least for now."

Virgil puffed on his cigar for a moment, then said, "What about the money?"

"The reward, you mean?" McPherson said.

"I do."

"Once we have him in custody and safely behind bars we will have the money wired to the First Appaloosa Bank and Trust."

"That's a lot of money," Virgil said.

"Fair amount," Payne said.

"And then some," Virgil said.

Virgil looked out over the porch railing to a tall lamp at the bottom of the steps that was being lit by a young black fella wearing a dark suit that was too short for his long legs. He puffed on his cigar for a bit, then turned back to Payne and McPherson.

"What about other suspects?" Virgil said.

"Like who?" McPherson said.

"Roger Messenger," Virgil said.

Payne looked to McPherson, McPherson looked to Payne, and they both shook their heads.

"What about him?" McPherson said.

"What are you alluding to?" Payne said.

"Not alluding to anything at all," Virgil said. "I have no alluding to offer whatsoever, but your fellow officer, Lieutenant Detective Banes, had suspicion Roger Messenger might be the killer."

Payne and McPherson shared a look with each other, then McPherson shook his head.

"Well, Banes does not know what he's talking about," McPherson said.

"So you don't think Roger could have done it?"

"No," McPherson said. "I do not and he did not."

"You know that for a fact?" Virgil said.

"I do."

"So there is other evidence?" Virgil said.

"Bill Black murdered Ruth Ann Messenger, and that will be proven in court."

"What makes you so sure?" Virgil said. "From what you have told us, it's no coffin nail."

"We *feel* certain we have the evidence for a conviction, Marshal," Payne said.

Virgil nodded a little with the cigar wedged in the corner of his mouth. Then he removed his cigar and looked at it in his hand. He rolled it between his fingers and thumb.

"One thing you can be guaranteed about Judge Callison . . ." Virgil said.

"What's that?" McPherson said.

"He will take the feeling out of it," Virgil said.

# 35.

When Virgil and I were leaving the hotel, the door opened and Hollis Pritchard entered, followed by the pretty woman I saw on the street with the parasol.

"Marshal, Deputy," Pritchard said. "I just heard—"

"Why, Mr. Pritchard," the woman said, interrupting him as she moved up beside him like an assured chess move and looked at Virgil, then at me.

"Please don't forget your manners, sir," she said.

She was not as young as I thought when I saw her on the street, but now, seeing her close up, she was even prettier. She had sharp, high cheekbones and large, brown knowing and soulful eyes.

I removed my hat. Virgil tipped his.

Pritchard looked to her and introduced her to us as a courtesy, but it was obvious he was not completely accommodating to the gesture.

"This is . . . Miss Angel," Pritchard said, "our company . . . book-keeper."

She moved a little closer and curtseyed a little. Her skin had a porcelain depth to it, unblemished of freckles, and her lips were full.

Her neck was long and slender and the satin dress she wore was open and revealed just a hint of her collarbones.

"It is a pleasure to meet you," she said.

Virgil grinned a little.

"Likewise," I said.

"I have heard about the two of you."

"All good, I imagine?" I said.

She smiled, and it was a warm smile full of confidence and assurance.

"And it's Daphne," she said, glancing back to Pritchard. "Daphne Angel."

"Daphne," Virgil said with a bashful-like smile.

"Daphne," I said.

I nodded to Pritchard.

"The name of your new establishment."

"And I'm flattered," she said.

"Yes, saw the sign," I said. "I believe I saw you as well the other day out on the boardwalk."

"I believe you most certainly did," she said. "It was a hot one that day."

"It was," I said. "I think I lost ten pounds from all the sweat that day."

She laughed, and it pricked Pritchard's impatience.

"Welcome to Appaloosa," I said.

Pritchard was clearly annoyed and anxious, but she didn't seem to care and neither did Virgil or me, especially me.

"Thank you," she said.

"So I just heard," Pritchard said, interrupting in a huff. "Tell me, is it true?"

"What's that?" Virgil said.

"I understand Bill Black has been arrested?"

Virgil glanced to me.

"Where'd you get that understanding?" Virgil said.

"Charles told me. He said he overheard two Western Union operators talking about it. Is it true?"

"No."

"But why would Charles overhear such a thing?"

"Bill Black has been apprehended," Virgil said. "Not arrested."

"Arrested, apprehended, my God," Pritchard said. "Where is he, for God's sake?"

"Mr. Pritchard would like to see him," Daphne said.

Virgil looked to her.

"He's not here," Virgil said.

"Where?" Pritchard asked.

"He's en route."

"We'd like to help," she said. "I know Mr. Pritchard is seriously concerned for him and, well, me, too. I know him very well. We know him as a good man. I have worked with him for some time . . . he's our friend and we'd like to do what we can . . . Do you have any idea when he will arrive?"

"We are expecting him anytime now," Virgil said. "Providing there are no hiccups."

"Hiccups?" Daphne said. "Is he all right?"

"I believe he is," Virgil said.

"What will happen now?" Pritchard said.

"Well, he'll be arrested."

"Then what?" Daphne said.

"Then there will be a preliminary hearing . . . He'll face the judge for the charges the warrant was issued for," Virgil said. "And, providing the judge feels the evidence is substantial enough, he will stand trial for the charges of the murder."

Pritchard shook his head.

"What can we do to help him?" Daphne said.

"Don't know there is anything you can do," Virgil said.

"He's going to need an attorney," Daphne said. "Correct?"

Virgil nodded.

"That be a good idea," Virgil said. "Not mandatory, but a good idea."

"When will his hearing to face the judge take place?"

Virgil said, "The judge is here now, so like I said, providing there are no hiccups, it will take place as soon as he arrives."

"Who is the best attorney in Appaloosa?" she said.

Virgil looked to me.

"Dickie Simmons?" Virgil said. "Or Juniper?"

"Juniper Jones," I said. "When he's sober."

"Where would we find them?" Pritchard said.

"They are not hard to find," Virgil said.

"They both have offices here in town," I said. "Like Virgil said, this will happen quick, so you might want to find that lawyer right away."

Pritchard nodded.

"Good," he said, then looked to Daphne.

"Shall we?" Pritchard said. "I'm starving."

Daphne smiled at Virgil and me.

"Thank you," she said. "And it was certainly nice to meet the two of you."

"Same," we said.

They moved on and Virgil walked out the front door. I turned, watching her as she walked with Pritchard to the dining room. Just before she got through the dining room door she looked back at me and smiled.

# 36.

"S he doesn't look like any bookkeeper I ever saw," I said as I walked down the steps and caught up with Virgil.

"You questioning her skills?" Virgil said.

"No, she just doesn't seem like the adding and subtracting type."

"You saying a fella might think of something else?" Virgil said.

"No might to it," I said.

Virgil and I rounded the corner just as Chastain came riding up and reined to a stop when he saw us.

"By God," Chastain said.

"Black?" Virgil said.

"Yep," Chastain said. "Been looking for you for an hour."

"Locked up?" Virgil said.

"He is."

"I'll be damn," Virgil said.

"What kind of shape is he in?" I said.

"Looks pretty exhausted. I think he's thinner, and he's got a few cuts and bruises, but he's here, and he's locked up."

"Anything said?"

"Nope, not to me," Chastain said. "Book gave him some food. He was hungry. Don't think the bounty hunter cared too well for him while he was getting him over here. He was locked in a prison wagon."

"Where is the bounty hunter?"

"Think he went for some grub and such. I didn't see him at all. I was at the house when they got to the office. Book came and got me after he got him locked up."

Virgil and I went to the office to see for ourselves that Boston Bill Black was in fact behind bars. When we got there Book opened the door to the cells, but Boston Bill was dead asleep, lying facedown on the bunk. Truitt was in the cell next to him. He looked up when we entered. We stood there for a moment, but Black didn't stir, and we didn't wake him. Fact was we really had nothing to say to him other than welcome back to Appaloosa.

Truitt stood looking at us dejectedly, but we walked out before he could let us know how bad it was being locked up. Book closed and locked the metal door and put the key in the desk drawer and locked the desk drawer.

"Bounty hunter say where or how he found Black?" I said.

"No," Book said. "I posed to him that very question, but he didn't say much, really, other than he was hungry and thirsty."

"Where is he?" Virgil said.

"Think at the Boston House," Book said. "He did say he was wanting to see you. Said he was an old friend of yours. Said he was looking forward to seeing you."

"What's his name?"

"He didn't say. Not from around here, though, never seen him before, that's for sure. He was nice, friendly like, but was . . . I don't know, unusual, I guess you could say. He just asked me where he could get a steak, some good wine, maybe play some tall dollar cards. I told him at the Boston House he could do all three and that it'd be busy with some good gambling because tonight was faro night and such. He thought that was funny."

"What?" I said.

"Said Appaloosa was lousy with Bostons. Boston this and Boston that, a place called the Boston House and a missing man that was now caught named Boston Bill. He laughed as he walked out the door."

Virgil stubbed out what was left of his cigar in the ashtray and looked at Book for a long moment.

"What'd he look like?" Virgil said.

"A real colorful character, that's for sure. Big, strong-looking, older, along in his fifties, I'd say, short-cropped hair on the sides, thick, full beard. Wore a brim with a flipped-back front."

Book pinched his earlobe.

"He had one of those silver loops in one of his ears."

Virgil squinted his eyes a little, looking at Book.

"Flashy dresser?" Virgil said.

Book nodded.

"As a matter of fact, he was," Book said. "Long frock coat, striped trousers tucked inside tall fancy boots and Mex silver spurs with huge rowels."

Virgil shook his head.

"Cutlass on his hip?" Virgil said.

Book looked to me, then Virgil, then nodded.

"Damn sure did," Book said. "That's him."

Virgil looked at me.

"Guess you know who that is," I said.

He nodded.

"By all accounts I do."

Virgil walked to the door and looked out to the street as if the man in question might be in sight. He stood quiet for a moment, looking off. He nodded to himself, then shook his head a little as if he did not believe what he believed.

"Been a long damn time," Virgil said. "But that sounds like Valentine Pell."

"I think I heard about him," Book said.

Chastain nodded.

"Pell," he said. "Was he a marshal at one point in time, too?"

Virgil looked at Chastain and nodded a little.

"Among other things," Virgil said.

# 37.

The streets were crowded with people moving about and enjoying the pleasant evening air as Virgil and I made our way up the block and a half to the Boston House. Virgil did not say anything as we walked, but I could tell there was something on his mind, there was something about Valentine Pell that bothered him.

"He really a friend of yours?"

Virgil walked a bit before he answered.

"I wouldn't say that," he said.

"If it is him, if it is Valentine Pell," I said, "you think he's gonna be a problem of some sorts?"

"If it is him," Virgil said, "he already is a problem."

"Boston Bill Black has caused quite the stir."

"Has."

We got to the porch of the Boston House and started up the steps.

"Valentine a gun hand?" I said.

"He is."

"Can he shoot?"

"He's deadly," Virgil said as he opened the door to the hotel.

There were three significant hotels now in Appaloosa, the Windsor being the quietest, the Colcord the plushest, and the Boston House the liveliest. It was the oldest hotel, too, and though it had changed hands a few times it still remained the most popular. The back room off the bar was still the only place in town where high-stakes gamblers of Appaloosa plied their trade, and with the growing city industry, the place was always full.

It was also the very reason Hollis Pritchard and Company had decided to build a gambling hall in Appaloosa. Pritchard was not shortsighted when it came to making money, and with the number of businesses cropping up in Appaloosa and the people needed to operate them, he knew a good bet when it presented itself and how to profit from investment.

The back room of the Boston House still consisted of ten poker tables, a billiard table, and a three-sided table used for throwing dice, and when Virgil and I walked in every table was in use and the cigar smoke was so thick the far wall was just slightly visible.

We stood looking around the room until Virgil spotted at the far corner table the big fella with the beard and wide hat with the flipped-back brim that Book described.

"That him?" I said.

Virgil nodded.

"By God," he said.

Virgil started walking toward the table and I followed. When we got close, Valentine looked up, seeing Virgil. He leaned back in his chair and smiled wide. His flashy blue eyes had that flair of being friendly and menacing at the same time.

"Well, Lord have mercy, as I live and breathe, if it's not Virgil," he said. "Virgil, Virgil, Virgil."

"It is," Virgil said.

Valentine was a handsome man, and like Book had said, he was strong-looking, especially for his age. He was rugged but well groomed, and his beard revealed only a small hint of gray.

"Yes, it is," Valentine said. "Yes, it goddamn sure is. Look at you, you have not changed a bit, not aged a day since I last saw you. I'll be goddamn. Been what, twenty years?"

"You looking for me, Valentine?"

"Inadvertently," he said. "Inadvertently."

Valentine looked to the six men sitting around the table. A few of them Virgil and I were acquaintances of, but the rest were strangers.

"Gentlemen," Valentine said. "I'm going to have to remove myself from this game of chance, and I know because of my good fortune, none of you will mind my self styled elimination thereof."

Valentine held up his cards.

"Would you mind, Virgil," he said. "Soon as I pocket this last go-around, I'll be right with you."

Virgil nodded.

"We'll be at the bar."

Virgil and I walked back into the main barroom. We sat at the far end of the bar and ordered two beers from Wallis.

"Coming right up," Wallis said.

"Well?" I said.

Virgil shook his head a little.

"Something tells me Valentine's jovial demeanor is just a show," I said.

"Something's telling you right," Virgil said.

"What's his story?"

Virgil leaned with his elbows resting on the bar and looked to the back room where Valentine sat at the poker table.

"Crooked as a dog's hind leg," Virgil said.

I followed Virgil's look into the back room.

"What do you know about him?"

Virgil shook his head.

"A thief, turned snake-oil salesman, turned liquor peddler to Indians, turned Navy deserter, turned preacher, turned lawman, turned safe cracking outlaw, turned goddamn bounty hunter. He's . . . He's a liar, a thief, a coward . . . but he can be a brave sonofabitch, too."

"And by his looks . . . a pirate," I said.

"He is at that."

I looked back to Virgil, who was no longer looking at Valentine but staring at the mug of beer resting on the bar in front of him.

"I never heard you mention him before, but it sounds like you know him pretty well," I said.

"I do," Virgil said.

"How so?"

"He's my brother," Virgil said.

# 38.

Virgil sat up straight with his shoulders back. He took a big pull of his beer, then rested the mug on the bar in front of him. I leaned forward a little to catch his eye.

"What?" I said.

Virgil nodded.

"Bullshit," I said.

Virgil shifted his eyes to me and shook his head.

"No bullshit."

"Goddamn, Virgil."

"What?"

"*What?*"

Virgil sipped his beer but didn't look at me.

"Well . . . hell, Virgil, I never knew you had a brother, you never said a damn thing."

I looked back to Valentine, who was conversing with his poker partners.

"All these years I've ridden with you and you never mentioned you even had a brother."

"No," he said. "I did not."

"Can I ask why?"

"No reason."

"No reason?"

"Long time ago, Everett," Virgil said. "Past. Past is past."

"Well, hell."

"Some things are best forgotten."

"Until now," I said.

"That's right," Virgil said.

I shook my head and looked at Virgil for a long bit.

"Pell?" I said. "He a half-brother?"

Virgil glanced back to Valentine at the poker table and nodded slightly.

"He is."

"I'll be damn."

I looked back at Pell, then looked back to Virgil.

"You want to tell me about it?"

"Not really."

"But you will."

Virgil sat quiet for a moment.

"Blood brothers?" I said.

Virgil nodded, then looked over at him again for a moment.

"Complicated," Virgil said.

"How so?"

"His pa ran off, left my mom, she remarried, had me."

"So you grew up together?"

Virgil nodded.

"For a while. He was five years older. He was gone by sixteen."

"I'll be damn . . ." I said. "Valentine Pell."

Virgil nodded.

"Rhymes with hell," Virgil said.

"Same name as his old man . . ." Virgil said. "Valentine Pell. He was a lawman turned outlaw . . ."

"You knew his father?"

Virgil looked over to Valentine again. He stared at him for a long moment, then nodded slowly.

"Not sure anyone knew that old sonofabitch . . . after my dad died . . . I was ten, Val was fifteen; his old man, Valentine Senior, comes back around . . . Not real fond memories, Everett . . . That was when Val took off and left Mom and me there to fend for ourselves . . . After some time . . . he took off again . . . Not long after that the man got himself shot and killed."

Virgil shook his head a little, as if he still did not believe who it was, that a person from his past, a member of his family, would actually be in his presence. I, too, was having a hard time with the notion.

Nothing about Virgil had ever made me think much about his family or that he even had a family. I'm not sure why. I guess I've always felt some business is better left unsaid. I know there is not much about any of what I did before today that really amounts to much in terms of memory.

I never thought about Virgil being anything but Virgil or anything but just perfectly present in the here and now. Maybe that is why the idea of his family, or the idea of him even having a family, seemed improbable and was a subject that we never engaged in.

Maybe he discussed his history with Allie, but I seriously doubt it. For certain Virgil never discussed family matters, so I figured it was not open for discussion, but now family was here and it was in the form of a colorful and enigmatic brother with the unusual name of Valentine Pell.

"They were the same person, those two," Virgil said. "His old man and him, cut from the same cloth."

Valentine finished his hand of cards and came into the front bar and joined Virgil and me. He was big and he walked as if he were even bigger.

"Goddamn, it is good to see you, Virgil," Valentine said.

"Kind of figured it'd be you," Virgil said.

Valentine smiled a big grin and patted Virgil on the back. Then he leaned forward on the bar, reached across Virgil, and held out his hand for me to shake.

"You must be Everett Hitch," he said.

I nodded and shook his hand.

"Pleasure to meet you," he said. "I have heard all about you and the big gun you carry."

"Eight-gauge," I said.

Then he looked at Virgil and grinned again.

"Still not shaking hands, Virgil?"

Virgil didn't say anything.

"Picked that up from his old man," Valentine said.

Virgil looked at Valentine without a hint of an expression on his face.

"Well, shit," Valentine said, "I just can't get over it, as I live and breathe, Virgil. And a goddamn marshal to boot."

Valentine clapped his hands a few times. It was unwelcome applause.

"And I hear you have a fine wife and a house with a fenced-in yard," Valentine said. "Allison, right? Allison French, Allie?"

Virgil didn't say anything.

"Part of my job to know these things, Virgil," he said. "Just like you."

"We're not alike," Virgil said.

Valentine laughed, then turned to Fat Wallis, who was leaning on the back of the bar with his arms folded across his big belly, observing the room.

"Excuse me, gentleman, sir," Valentine said. "Might I have a bottle of your finest whiskey and three glasses?"

Valentine looked to Virgil.

"You will have a drink with me, won't you, Virgil?" he said.

"On me, of course, and you, too, Everett."

I looked to Virgil. Virgil stared at Valentine, then nodded slightly to Wallis.

Wallis set the glasses in front of each one of us and poured.

"Thank you, kind sir," Valentine said.

Wallis nodded, then set the bottle in front of us and moved off to the other end of the bar.

Valentine raised his glass.

"To my little brother," he said.

# 39.

Valentine smiled and drank his whiskey. Virgil looked at him for a long moment, took a sip of whiskey, and set his glass on the bar in front of him.

"Said you'd just as soon be dead as to ever cross the Mississippi again," Virgil said.

"I say that?"

Virgil stared at him for a long amount of time, then offered a sharp drop of his chin.

"Did."

"I lied," Valentine said.

"You did that, too," Virgil said.

"Well, there you have it," Valentine said. "Intentions sometimes just go awry."

"Awry?" Virgil said. "More to the fact, truth was never something you was ever too concerned with."

Valentine laughed.

"Well, now, hell, Virgil, truth is way over appreciated."

Virgil shook his head a little.

"Over appreciated?" Virgil said.

Valentine laughed, then looked to me.

"Over appreciated. 'Sides, plans are like goddamn rail tracks, they just put you places and that is it, buy a ticket and you go there. I prefer the open road as opposed to being staked in the yard like a chicken-chasing dog."

I was beginning to see some similarities between Virgil and Valentine. They were kind of like the opposite sides of a coin.

"I was in some trouble," Valentine said. "Spent a little time in jail over here for it, nothing serious. Virgil never really . . ."

"Robbery," Virgil said.

"He's a stickler for details."

"You shot a man in the process."

"He pulled on me," Valentine said.

Valentine smiled at me and continued. He was addressing me with his talk, but he was really talking to Virgil.

"Anyway," he said. "This bone-dry country was bothering the hell out of me, so I made my way back to the more civilized world. According to Virgil, I verbalized I would not come back this way, that's what Virgil is talking about. Isn't that right, Virgil?"

Virgil didn't answer him.

"So, hell, let's see . . . I been back on this side for the last ten years," he said.

"Heard rumblings of that," Virgil said.

"Was hoping I'd find you someplace along the road, that I'd get to see you, Virgil, that you'd be doing okay."

Valentine picked up the bottle and filled the glasses.

"And now, after all these years, here you are."

"Yep," Virgil said.

"My little brother," he said.

Virgil calmly stared at his whiskey.

Valentine looked at Virgil and smiled a little, but Virgil did not look at him.

"Was east there for a spell, New York, Boston. Like the wine, and the food is a hell of a lot better, but I got tired of those goddamn Yankees. They are different. Was in Chicago, too. I like Chicago. Ever been to Chicago, Everett?"

"I have," I said.

"It is a decent place," Valentine said. "But way by God cold Chicago . . . Worked my way back, was in Abilene there for a bit, then Denver for a while, then eventually made my way down to Texas. Goddamn Texas."

He smiled and nodded to me a little.

"I've been doing pretty well, Virgil," he said. "Don't have a special lady friend like you, but I get by . . ."

Virgil crossed his arms and leaned back, and Valentine leveled a look at him.

"Don't worry, Virgil, I'm here on business," he said. "Nothing for you to worry yourself about . . . but I won't be gone until I get paid for my services rendered. Money well deserved, too, I have to say. I waited on him for days before I caught him."

"Where?"

"Juárez," he said. "That is where I reside these days. Well, across the river in godforsaken El Paso, Texas, but when duty calls, I go across the river and just wait, easy pickings really. So many on the run end up there in Juárez. That is why I moved down that way in the first place, to be close to a revenue source. Just have to sit back and let them come to you, kind of like waiting on a dove to come in on a sunflower patch at sunset. Pretty stupid on Boston Bill's part, in particular."

"Why's that," I said.

"Because the big sonofabitch stood out like a black leopard in a litter of kitties down there."

"Any thought as to whether he did it?" I said.

Valentine looked to Virgil and then to me.

"He said he didn't, but you know, they always say that," he said. "But if I were a betting man, which I am, I would say no."

"What makes you say that?" I said.

Valentine thought for a moment.

"Well," he said. "Because he's a . . . well, he just doesn't have what it takes is about all I can say."

"What makes you say that?" I said.

"Just a hunch," Valentine said.

"Regardless, the judge will see to his future as he deems fit," Virgil said.

Valentine nodded, looking at Virgil.

"Denver authorities are here, too, to pay you for your service," Virgil said.

"Good," Valentine said.

"They are right across the way and up the block here, Colcord Hotel."

Valentine nodded.

"Good to know," he said.

"Then you'll be moving on," Virgil said.

"Not sure, Virgil," Valentine said with a smile. "Since the judge is here and the preliminary will be tomorrow, I thought I would at least stay around and see the outcome."

"Then you'll be moving on?" Virgil said.

"I'll be gone soon enough, little brother," he said with a smile. "Rest assured."

# 40.

I ate dinner with Virgil and Allie that night, and it was not until we finished Allie's scalded plum pudding that Virgil said anything to her about his long-lost brother. Virgil took his time and explained to her pretty much the same history he shared with me about Valentine Pell, but without the tidbits that describe the unfavorable character details.

"And he's the bounty hunter that had captured Boston Bill Black," she said. "And returned him here to Appaloosa?"

"Yep," Virgil said. "'Fraid so."

"Valentine Pell?" she said. "Well, isn't that a pretty name? I can't believe this. Your brother?"

"Half," Virgil said. "Half-brother."

"Half, yes," she said. "Well, my lands."

Virgil nodded and Allie looked at me and grinned.

"My God," she said.

She shook her head in disbelief and looked to me as if I should say something.

"How about that?" I said.

"I had no idea," she said.

She remained looking at me as if I needed to say something more.

"Tonight was the first time I ever heard of him, too, Allie," I said.

"Goodness," she said. "Well, I just can't believe it."

"Yep," I said.

"You visited with him, Everett?" she said.

"I did, well, some, he did most of the talking . . . He likes to talk."

"What did he talk about?"

"Oh," I said, "this and that."

"What'd you think about him?"

"Well, he's, um . . . an interesting sort of fella."

"He'll be moving on soon," Virgil said.

"Good Lord," she said. "And what now? What will happen with Boston Bill Black?"

"He will be arraigned in front of Judge Callison," Virgil said.

Allie's eyes were wide. They had been wide, looking back and forth between Virgil and me, since Virgil first mentioned Valentine.

She put her napkin to her mouth with both hands and dabbed at any touches of pudding that may or may not have been on her lips as she stared at Virgil. She held the napkin there to her mouth for a moment, then, in a rather dramatic fashion, let her hands go limp and fall to each side of her plate, making the dishes rattle.

"I feel like I don't even know you, Virgil," she said.

"What?"

"I don't."

Virgil looked to me, then to Allie.

"What are you talking about, Allie?" he said.

"You have a brother?"

"That's what I just said."

"And I never knew."

"We were never really that close, Allie."

Allie started to frown, then abruptly turned sideways in her chair and stared at the floor.

"But I guess that stands to reason," she said, shaking her head slightly, as if she were talking to the floor.

Virgil looked to me, then to Allie.

"What stands to reason?" he said.

"That I don't feel like I know you," she said. "Because you never feel it is necessary to share anything with me."

"Not true, Allie," he said.

"It is true, Virgil," Allie said.

I thought about what Valentine had said earlier about truth being over appreciated.

"Not intentional," Virgil said.

"Well, what is it, then, if it is not intentional?"

"Just not something I ever really felt like talking about."

"Well, obviously," she said.

"Hell, Allie, if it is any comfort to you, I was not sure Valentine was even still alive."

"It's not, Virgil," she said.

Allie got to her feet. She moved her chair back under the table to give herself room to pace between the table and the cupboard. She made a few turns, cogitating this revelation and its residual, then looked to Virgil.

"Where is he?"

"Boston House."

"Did you invite him here?"

"I have not," he said.

"Why?"

"Not necessary."

"And why not?"

"Just not a good idea, Allie," he said.

"What about me?" she said.

Virgil didn't say anything, then Allie pointed to the Boston House.

"You need to go over there and invite him over here."

"Don't really want to do that, Allie."

She put her hands on her hips.

"Virgil, I want to know your brother," she said. "I have no family to speak of, and, well, family is important, no matter."

Virgil just looked at her.

"If you don't," she said, "I will."

"He'll be gone soon."

"Even more of a reason for us to get to know one another," she said. "Everett said he was interesting, and I'd very much like to meet him, Virgil."

I could feel Virgil cut his eyes to me, but I remained looking at Allie.

"Please," she said.

"Don't think it a good idea . . ." Virgil said as he folded his napkin and dropped it on his plate. "But I will ask him to come by and visit before he leaves."

"Good," Allie said. "Tomorrow I meet with my ladies' social, but after I will make something delicious for supper and have a proper sit-down visit with the only known kin between the two of us that we know is alive."

Virgil looked to me. I could tell the notion of Valentine Pell coming over for a proper sit-down visit was not something he was looking forward to.

"Anybody else?" Allie said.

"What?" Virgil said.

"There's no one else, is there, Virgil?" Allie said.

"No, Allie."

"You sure?" Allie said. "Your sister Easter is not gonna show up here?"

# 41.

The following morning Virgil and I accompanied the Denver men, DA Eldon Payne and the captain of police, G. W. McPherson, to the First Appaloosa Bank and Trust just after it opened for business.

Valentine was waiting on the steps when we arrived.

"Good morning, good gentlemen," he said. "I certainly appreciate you coming here this time of the a.m. so we can square away the fortuitous exchange."

Payne and McPherson went about the process of transferring dollars out of their account and into Valentine's account.

After Valentine was assured the funds were successfully transferred to his bank in El Paso, he remained with us as we walked back to the courthouse. Payne and McPherson were in front of us as we walked. No one but Valentine bothered to say anything as we moved on toward the courthouse for the hearing of Truitt and Boston Bill.

"Now that we got that money squared away, I will pontificate about the saga of Boston Bill Black," Valentine said with some volume for Payne and McPherson's benefit. "I can tell you that you fellas might just be paying me again to find him after he's set free. Only maybe this time you will leave the 'alive' part off of the 'dead or alive' wording. Seems to me somebody has a personal vendetta for this sap. By no means am I saying he did or did not do the deed of murdering Ruth Ann Messenger, that will be for the judge and God Almighty to decide, but I got a suspicion there is more to this sordid yarn than meets the eye."

Valentine stopped talking as we walked up the steps to the courthouse. When we entered the courtroom we discovered—and it was no surprise to me—that the room was fairly crowded with expectant spectators.

Besides a horse race, or a good dance, or an alley fistfight, courtroom drama was always an attraction in Appaloosa, especially when it involved murder, and this was looking to be no exception.

Chastain and his deputies already had Truitt Shirley and Boston Bill Black locked up in hand and leg irons. They were sitting up front in the warm courtroom, waiting for the scheduled noontime hearing with Judge Callison.

Seated front and center in the second row were Hollis Pritchard and Daphne Angel. They were with their new attorney, Juniper Jones. Juniper was standing, looking toward the rear of the room, when we entered, and he saluted us. Daphne turned and looked at me. She had at first a serious look on her face, but when she saw me her look changed quickly to a soft smile. At least I think it was me that changed her expression. She waved a little. I tipped my hat, she smiled a little more, then she turned back forward in her seat.

Behind her and off to one side sat Allie and her group of women from the ladies' social. I pointed them out to Virgil.

"What the hell are they doing here?" Virgil said.

Allie looked back, seeing Virgil, and waved, then made her way over to us just as Valentine stepped up next to Virgil. She was wearing a dark pink gabardine dress with a black velvet collar and she was looking particularly radiant and fresh.

"Thought it was ladies' social day?" Virgil said.

"It is," she said with a beaming smile. "We're all here."

"I can see that."

"What better way to serve our community than to support the municipality, so we came to witness the proceedings and show our support."

Allie looked to Valentine, who was standing less than a foot from Virgil, looking down at her. He took off his hat and bowed a little.

"How do you do?" he said with a wide smile.

Allie smiled back.

"You . . . must be Virgil's brother?" she said.

"Half-brother," Virgil said.

Valentine looked to Virgil and grinned, then looked back to Allie.

"Valentine Pell, my dear," he said. "And don't tell me. You must be Allison French?"

"Why, yes, I am," she said. "And it's Allie, please."

"Well, it is a pleasure to meet you, Allie," he said. "Virgil has told me so much about you."

"Why, Virgil Cole," she said.

"But," Valentine said, "I can tell just by looking at you he hasn't so much as scratched the surface."

"Well, we will have a chance to scratch that surface when you show up tonight for supper," she said.

"Supper?" he said. "Well, I would be delighted."

Allie looked at Virgil, giving him a slightly brief shot of the slant-eye that said *You haven't asked him for dinner like we agreed you'd ask him to do.*

"I am so looking forward to it," Allie said. "Virgil, too . . . and Everett will be there as well."

"Very good, very good," he said. "I am looking forward to it myself."

Allie smiled a flashy, full-teeth smile, then looked back to the courtroom with a changed expression of seriousness.

"I tell you," she said under her breath, as if she were telling us a secret, "these sorts of carryings-on just make me plain old-fashion nervous."

The back door of the courtroom opened and Judge Callison came out wearing his black robe, and like always, he was all business.

Allie mouthed *Bye* to Valentine and me, kissed Virgil on the cheek, and moved back off and sat with the ladies of the social.

"All rise," the bailiff said.

# 42.

Valentine came for dinner at seven. He was wearing fancy clothes that impressed Allie, complete with his cutlass clipped onto his belt. His topcoat was burgundy velvet and his shirt was made of fine polished cotton and was open around his neck, exposing partial tattoos on his chest. He showed up with a box of gifts that included wine, an after dinner liqueur, a bouquet of flowers for Allie, and a box of cigars for Virgil.

Before supper we sat on the back porch watching the orange and red blazed sunset that prompted Valentine to wade into a Navy story about chasing a pirate ship down the coast of Mexico. It was an elaborate tale about Mexican pirates and American seamen that provoked Virgil to ask him which boat he was on. He told the story with great fervor, describing the environment—the weather, the ocean, the sailors, the captains, and the deckhands. The yarn had Allie captivated. He went on and on until the adventure led him to a final battle that was explained in dramatic detail, right up to the burning of the pirate ship at a place Allie thought sounded funny.

"Teacup?" she said crinkling her nose.

"No," Valentine said with a laugh. "Teacap-an. Boca Teacapan. The outlet of the Estero de Teacapán of the lagoons of Agua Grande in Sinaloa and Agua Brava in Nayarit to the Pacific."

"Well, that just wore me out," Allie said, fanning herself with a Chinese fan, another of the gifts from Valentine.

"How about some food, Allie?" Virgil said. "I'm sure Val is hungry, aren't you?"

"I am at your mercy," he said to Allie. "My cup already runneth over with good fortune."

"There is no need to get into the details about all that," Virgil said. "How long before we eat, Allie?"

She smiled sweetly.

"Just a bit, it's all ready," she said. "Let me go and get to work on finishing the preparations . . . won't be but a few minutes."

"You need some help, Allie?" I said.

"Oh, no, Everett," she said. "You boys just stay out here and enjoy yourselves."

She put her hand on Valentine's knee.

"I'm sure you and Virgil have a lot to catch up on," she said. "And we are so glad you are here."

"Thank you, Allie," he said.

With a final pat of Valentine's knee Allie was up and through the back door. Valentine watched after her as she moved off down the hall, then looked to Virgil.

"She's lovely, Virgil . . ." he said. "Simply."

Virgil was quiet for a bit. Then . . .

"She is," he said.

Valentine smiled and did not say anything else. He looked off, watching the sunset, and after a moment of extended silence he got out of his chair and walked down the few steps. He walked away from the porch a little. He looked down at the sandy soil with the occasional cluster of short grass. He walked in a circle as he looked down. He kicked at the dirt a bit, thinking, then looked back toward the falling sun with his back to us.

"I am sorry, Virgil," he said.

He looked over to Virgil. Virgil was looking at him. Valentine looked away, back toward the sunset.

"I regret the day I left you and Mother."

I looked over at Virgil. He didn't look at me or say anything. He was looking at Valentine, who was looking away.

"I know I made things hard for her by leaving you two," Valentine said. "And then getting myself in trouble all the time, doing the things I did, I know . . . made her . . . ashamed of me, and that has never settled well with me, Virgil . . . never."

He looked back to Virgil. Virgil was looking down now, and he did not look up and meet Valentine's eyes.

"Not everything I did was ignoble and dishonorable," Valentine said. "I know it seemed that way."

Valentine turned and walked back to the porch. He stood at the bottom of the steps, looking at Virgil.

"I missed her . . . and you, but I knew if I stayed there he would have killed me. I think he saw so much of himself in me that it made him angry. I thought in some way if I was not there, things might be easier for her, and you . . . most likely I was wrong about that."

Valentine put a boot on the bottom step.

"I suppose I could have stayed, should have stayed to be there for her, and you. But I would have shot and killed him . . . And in hindsight that might have been the thing to do, the noble and honorable thing to do."

Allie lifted up the kitchen window and poked her head out.

"Hey, out there," she said. "It's suppertime."

# 43.

Allie had been taking some well-deserved cooking lessons from an elder woman with the ladies' social and it was paying off. Her dinner that consisted of a chicken, potatoes, carrots, and bread was nicely prepared and tasty.

After we ate I helped Allie remove the dishes and reset the table for dessert.

Valentine's fine red wine and prior reflection on the past had softened Virgil some. At least for the moment, the combination of the two allowed Virgil a bit of breathing room in respect to his forbearance that previously had been less than tolerable.

The talk during dinner was dedicated for the most part to the country and its changing times. We discussed everything from silver mining to time zones, to the ever-expanding rail system, the U.S. Mail, and the chain-stitch single-thread sewing machine.

It was not until we polished off Allie's apple pie and poured the after dinner liqueur did we discuss the courtroom proceedings we sat through earlier in the day.

"That all went so fast today," Allie said. "I hardly knew what happened."

"Callison is a no-nonsense judge," Valentine said.

"That he is," Virgil said.

"Did not take him long to decide," I said.

"No," Virgil said, "it didn't."

"I think I know what happened, but all that legal gibberish got me confused there toward the end."

"Trial is set," I said. "It, too, will happen quick, Callison will move it right along."

"Well, I can't believe that ol' Judge Callison, though," Allie said. "The ol' coot."

"Why is that?" Virgil said.

"Well," she said, "it did not seem to me, nor any of the women, smart women, I might add, from my social that were there with me today, that there was enough evidence in this case to bring Boston Bill to trial."

"I don't think he had much of a choice, Allie," Virgil said.

"No," I said. "He did not."

"It was a preliminary, Allie," Virgil said. "That supported the warrant and the fact that Boston Bill was on the run and Val apprehended him, and the fact that he is the prime suspect and there are no other suspects at this time other than her husband, who is dead, the trial will be in order."

"It does not mean he is guilty," Allie said.

"No," Virgil said. "It does not."

"Also, there have to be other suspects," Allie said. "You can't just say because they were having . . . relations . . . that Bill and her husband are the only suspects."

"I don't disagree with you, Allie," Valentine said. "I was saying that before."

"Thank you, Valentine," she said.

"Does seem like the prosecution has some ace up their sleeve," I said.

"A vendetta in the making," Valentine said.

"They are confident, it seems," Virgil said.

"Callison," I said, "was not about to let them get what they want without the prosecution bringing in the witnesses and material evidence."

"The promise to provide witnesses with testimony that they felt would seal the deal," Valentine said, "is what most certainly persuaded the good judge."

"Now what?" Allie said.

"Callison won't waste any time," Virgil said.

"Soon as the witnesses arrive, the trial will get under way," I said.

"Do you think he did it?" Allie said. "Do you think Boston Bill killed that Denver woman?"

"I don't know," I said.

"What was described sounded just awful," Allie said. "That poor, poor woman."

"It did," I said.

"I can relate to her," Allie said. "It's confusing for a woman in this country. This is a man's world, and without a man, a woman has few resources to work with, to ply her trade."

That thought settled across the table for a moment, then Valentine said with an uplifting tone, "Most assuredly, Allie."

She smiled, removed her napkin from her lap, and placed it on the table.

"Well, then," she said with a chirp in her voice that was meant to change the direction of the conversation. "Enough of that sort of rigmarole. How about a recital?"

"That would be lovely," Valentine said.

Virgil looked to me as Allie got up from the table and walked to the piano.

"Any requests?" she said.

She paused and turned back to the three of us sitting at the table.

"Valentine," she said. "I can't play that many by heart, I only know a few, but I can read music."

"Whatever your heart's desire, Allie," he said. "Whatever your heart's desire."

# 44.

Virgil was getting more and more comfortable with Valentine. I was not sure if he would ever be completely at ease with him, but there was at least a growing feeling that there was enough space for the two of them in the same room. After Allie's fifth tune, I excused myself and left Virgil, Valentine, and Allie and walked to the Colcord Hotel. Earlier in the day after the preliminary hearing I had a chat with Daphne Angel that concluded with a proposal from me that we get together after my scheduled dinner, and she agreed.

When I stepped into the lobby of the Colcord and went to the bar in the dining area, our designated meeting place, Daphne was nowhere to be seen. The place was empty except for an older couple sitting at a corner. They looked to be having a romantic moment, giggling as if they were youngsters. I bought a beer at the bar, then stepped out the door and onto the back porch. I walked over to the railing and looked off out into the darkness beyond the spilling light of the hotel, and for some reason I thought about Ruth Ann Messenger, about what really happened to her. The details that were presented during the preliminary hearing came to mind, about how she was discovered with her clothes ripped off her body and how badly she had been beaten.

*Who could have done this,* I thought, *and why?*

Boston Bill Black and Roger Messenger both had personal enough reasons to kill Ruth Ann. Her husband was obviously ashamed, embarrassed, belittled, had been made to be the fool and was drinking heavily, had basically become a mess over Ruth Ann flaunting her relationship with Black. And Black found himself in a situation with a woman that was obsessive and wanting a relationship.

*But why would either of these men do away with her in the way she was killed?*

It did not add up. Leaving blood on the steps of the inn, then ripping her clothes from her body and then beating her.

*Which one of these guys was the killer, which one of these men savagely beat her to death . . . or was it someone else?*

"Boo."

I turned to see Daphne standing behind me in the doorway.

"Sneaked up on you."

"Glad you did."

She looked stunning. She was wearing a dark gray dress with a silvery lace shawl that dropped down some, exposing her bare shoulders.

"What do you see out there?" she said, nodding out to the dark.

"Oh, I was just . . . just standing here . . . thinking."

"Penny?"

"Not worth it."

"No?" she said.

"Naw . . ."

"Maybe I should be the judge of that," she said with a smile as she moved over to me by the rail.

"You think?"

"Perhaps," she said.

She placed both of her hands on the rail and looked out.

I looked down at her hands. She followed my look, then covered up the two fingers of her right hand that were stained.

"Ink of the trade, I'm afraid," she said.

"Maybe try a pencil."

"Not good enough for permanence."

I smiled and she laughed.

"Sorry, I was running a little behind," she said.

"Better than running in front with someone chasing you."

"Depends on who's doing the chasing," she said with a smile. "And for what purpose."

I laughed. She grinned.

"Well, no apologies necessary here," I said.

"I can't believe I said that," she said, blushing.

"Well, I instigated it," I said.

"I guess I have been cooped up too long," she said.

"Well, I am glad I got you out."

"Me, too," she said. "Mr. Pritchard is fair and generous, but he can be demanding."

"Had you working this late?"

"Well, prior to the preliminary hearing we went and visited with Bill today."

"I heard about that," I said.

"Mr. Pritchard is . . . well, upset?"

"And you?"

"It's hard," she said. "I . . . well, I don't know what to say really, other than today set me back. Not to be insensitive. On the contrary, I'm very sensitive to what's happening, this is just awful . . . but I keep records for Mr. Pritchard's multiple businesses and I am always on a deadline it seems, and, well, there just is not enough time in the day."

"All work and no play," I said.

"There you go again."

I smiled.

"Believe me," she said. "I appreciate it."

I intentionally left alone the fact that she mentioned the hearing and the talk of Bill. I figured there might be an opportunity to maybe learn something about Bill and Pritchard that might be of interest, but I avoided furthering the conversation in that direction. Mainly because reminding her of the details regarding Bill's incarceration and Ruth Ann's murder was not part of my bid for good favor.

"No appreciation necessary," I said. "It's what I do."

"I can see that," she said. "But you are right, too much work leaves little time for taking care of the fun stuff."

"What you get for being good with numbers," I said.

"We all have a cross to bear, it seems," she said.

"You sure don't look like a bookkeeper."

"What do I look like?"

"Beautiful."

"Why, thank you, Mr. Hitch."

"Everett," I said.

"So what do other bookkeepers look like, Everett?"

"To be perfectly honest, you are the only official bookkeeper I have ever met."

She smiled, looked out into the dark, and took a deep breath.

"What a beautiful evening," she said.

"It damn sure is," I said.

She looked at me and smiled.

"Nice to see you," she said.

"Nice to see you," I said.

"And how are you?"

"Better now," I said.

She turned her body, looking at me in the eyes, and grinned.

"Good," she said.

I held up my mug and said, "What can I get you?"

She looked back to the bar, then back to me.

"I would love to get out of here."

"Where would you like to go?"

"Surprise me," she said. "I have been in this hotel too long. I work out of my room and I eat their food and, well, it's nice, but a little too nice, and . . ."

"'Nough said."

# 45.

We left the hotel and walked for a half-block on the boardwalk before either of us said anything. Daphne spoke up first and asked about my work. She wanted to know about my lawman history, and about how I met and began working with Virgil and how we ended up in Appaloosa. I gave her a brief version, starting with my days at West Point, through fighting Indians, then becoming an itinerant lawmen and up to being current-day marshals.

"Dangerous," she said.

"Can be."

"But danger is your business," she said.

"Not all of it," I said. "But some."

"I just can't imagine."

"It's a profession."

"Oh, it's more than that," she said. "Why, it's upholding values of good versus evil and . . . protecting the innocent."

"If you are making me out to be chivalrous," I said, "you're not going to get any argument out of me about that."

"Obviously, though, from what you told me, with your history, you have . . . ?"

"What?"

"Had to shoot people?"

"Some."

"And obviously you must be good at your job?"

"Why's that?"

"You're alive."

"Ha!" I said. "And glad of it."

"And I imagine some of those you have shot have died?"

"Yes."

"Besides the Indians, during the battles, you have killed others, too, I assume?"

"I have."

She nodded as we strolled a little.

"Fascinating," she said.

"You think?"

"I do," she said, "and I'm sorry, I will say no more, other than it's exciting."

"What's that?"

"You?"

"Me?"

She stopped walking.

"It excites me," she said. "What you do."

We were standing on the boardwalk in the dark, and she took a short step away from me and put her back to a post.

"Who you are . . . interests me."

"You interest me, too," I said.

"I'm glad," she said.

"From the moment I saw you walking with your parasol."

I moved closer to her. She pulled her shoulders back some, and the movement lifted her chest a little.

"Tell me about you," I said.

"What would you like to know?"

"How come you are not a married woman?"

"Oh, I . . . I don't hold as much stock in that notion as other women," she said.

"Why?"

"I enjoy my independence, I guess."

"So you have never been close to the altar?"

"Oh, well, I must admit there was one time, but . . . I don't know. I just decided it was not the right thing . . . And you, what about you?"

I shook my head.

"Not me," I said.

"And why not for you?"

"Guess my line of work has kept me from it, mostly."

"Mostly?"

I nodded.

"It defines you," she said. "Work. What we do."

"I guess," I said. "And how 'bout you. How does a beautiful woman like you become a mathematician?"

She laughed.

"I'm not a mathematician," she said.

"You do multiplications and such, don't you?" I said.

"I'm a bookkeeper," she said.

"How long have you been working for Pritchard?"

"A long time now," she said. "I started as an apprentice, then, after some time, one thing led to another and I got the job."

I moved a bit closer to her.

"Go on," I said.

"No," she said. "You go on . . ."

"Me go on?"

She nodded.

"Yes," she said. "Go on and kiss me."

# 46.

I kissed Daphne for a respectable amount of time there under the awnings and in the shadows of the boardwalk. Then, like a gentleman, I stopped and took a step back. After a few refined and polished words regarding refrainment, I walked her back to her hotel. We strolled slowly across the hardwood floor of the dark lobby to the bottom of the stairs. She stopped and turned to me.

"Thank you," she said, looking up at me. "This was lovely."

I kissed her again. She kissed me back, and though we'd spent some good kissing time previous to this kiss, this one instigated her to kiss me so hard it took my breath. After a solid moment she pulled away and looked in my eyes.

"You're good," she said.

"I try."

"Oh, you more than try."

She kissed me again with both of her arms pulling me tight as if she were holding on for dear life. This one felt desperate and hungry, and after another long, passionate go of it, she looked up again, and this time her eyes were moist.

"My God," she said.

I didn't say anything as she remained holding me.

"I suppose I will see you tomorrow," she said. "At the proceedings?"

"I will be there," I said.

"I'm glad for that."

She stared at me for a long moment.

"It's all so worrisome," she said.

I nodded a little.

"I know," I said.

"So I appreciate this . . . this wonderful time together, this diversion."

"That's me," I said smiling. "Diversion."

She put her hands on my shoulders and rubbed them up and down, as if she were trying to warm me. She looked at me, too, with appraising intensity, as if she were trying to see past my eyes. Then she shook her head and a concerned look came across her face.

"How do you think this will go?" she said. "Tomorrow?"

"Hard to say," I said.

"I'm concerned," she said.

"One thing about Judge Callison," I said. "He's fair."

She nodded a little.

"What do you think?" she said.

"About Bill Black?" I said.

She nodded.

"I've never really even talked to the man," I said. "Since he's been here in town I've only seen him here and there, heard things about him, so I'm just not sure."

"What sort of things have you heard?"

"Nothing to do with this trial."

"But you've heard things, things that give you some kind of indication?"

I shook my head.

"No, not really, nothing admissible, anyway," I said. "You said you've known him?"

"Yes," she said. "Since he started with Mr. Pritchard."

"And that's been a few years?" I said.

"Yes," she said.

"So you know, or would have some idea?"

"Yes," she said. "But . . ."

"But what?"

"Does anybody really ever know anyone?" she said.

"You like him?" I said.

"Enough."

"So what do you think," I said. "Do you think he murdered Ruth Ann Messenger?"

She looked down for a moment, then looked at me. She peered into my face for a period of time before she spoke.

"No," she said. "I don't think so."

"You can only hope, then, justice prevails."

"On your recommendation, I think the attorney Juniper Jones that Mr. Pritchard hired will do what he can."

"Juniper is the best in Appaloosa."

"He said we will likely be called to the stand," she said.

"He will do what he has to do."

She nodded.

"It's all so frightening," she said.

I nodded.

"I understand how you feel," I said. "But you have to know, or keep in mind, a woman was murdered and that is what this is all about, not Bill, but the fact she was murdered and Bill was reportedly the last person she was in contact with."

"Yes," she said. "I know . . ."

"Did you know her?"

"Ruth Ann?"

I nodded.

"God, no," she said. "I did hear things about her, though, things that were not so favorable, but I don't think they were unfavorable enough for him to murder her."

"Well . . ." I said. "I've been leaning that way myself, but it is up to the judge."

She pulled me close to her and she hugged me, then pulled back and nodded, then kissed me one last time.

"Good night, Everett," she said. "And thanks again."

She put her hand to my cheek, pecked me with one last touch of her lips, then turned, and I watched her walk up the stairs. When she got to the landing she looked back, smiled blissfully, then moved on and was gone from sight.

# 47.

Chastain and Book took Truitt for a stroll in cuffs while Virgil and I accompanied Juniper Jones to have a discussion with his new client, Boston Bill Black, before his trial.

Black looked exhausted. He was on his bunk, leaning over a bit, with his big hands draped across his knees. His mustache that was normally dyed black as coal was now showing half-inch roots of gray and his face was covered with long gray stubble that was beginning to look like a beard.

Juniper sat at a small table just outside of Black's cell and Virgil and I perched ourselves on a bench behind and off to the side of Juniper.

Juniper previously had a short discussion with Black prior to the preliminary hearing, but this was Black's chance to help provide Juniper with a defense, and so far Black was doing himself more harm than good. For ten minutes he had been staring at the floor in front of him as he repeated, "I did not kill her."

"You have said that," Juniper said.

Juniper dropped his notepad on the desk. He leaned back in his chair and clasped his chubby hands over his belly and looked at Black with his head tilted to the side.

"I did not kill her," Black said again.

Juniper briefly glanced over at Virgil and me, then looked back to Black and slowly shook his head back and forth.

"I can't decide whether you are trying to convince yourself or if you are losing your mind, Mr. Black," Juniper said.

Black looked up at Juniper and stared at him. Then he looked to Virgil and me.

"I don't know who did this," he said. "But I am a victim here."

"Right now you are a bit more than that," Juniper said. "You are charged with murder."

Black sat silently and shook his head.

"Look," Juniper said. "I don't feel at the moment the prosecution has that solid of a case, I don't. But with the way things are going, they just might have enough ammo to convict you. So unless you provide me with some kind of details that can help me, I'm afraid there is a very good chance you will most definitely become a victim . . . of circumstance."

Black looked up, pushed his hair back on his head, and stared at Juniper.

"Give me some details and let me figure out how best to use them, Mr. Black," Juniper said. "Gamble with me here."

Black nodded.

"What can I say?"

"Let's start with the argument that the owners of the inn over-heard."

Black looked over to Virgil and me, then back to Juniper, but didn't say anything.

"Did you have this argument with Ruth Ann Messenger the night she went missing?"

"I did," he said.

"And what did you argue about?"

"She was . . . crazy."

"Let me repeat the question," Juniper said. "And what did you argue about?"

"The same thing that has happened to many a man."

"This particular argument, involving you and Ruth Ann Messenger."

"She said she loved me and wanted to leave town with me."

"Did you love her?"

"No."

"Then what were you doing with her?"

"What do you think?"

"What I think has no bearing on what you were doing with her."

He shook his head.

"I don't know."

"Well, that is not very helpful or convincing, Mr. Black."

He got to his feet and started to pace.

"Ruth Ann was real . . . seductive. Goddamn nice to look at. So, you know, at first there she is, this very attractive and beautiful woman, and she was, I don't know, for a while, okay, and . . . we were having a good time."

"A good time? Can you elaborate?"

"Oh, hell, she'd come around and she wanted attention, you know, and, well, I gave it to her."

"In what way?"

Black's eyes squinted a bit, reflecting.

"In the obvious way," he said.

"How long had you been doing the obvious way with Ruth Ann?"

"About two weeks, I'd say."

"Then what happened?"

"She started getting very possessive of me."

"And in this two weeks' time you spent with her did you know she was married?"

"Not at first, but I learned later."

"How did you learn that later?"

"At first when I met her, when she was flaunting herself at me, when we was doing the obvious, she said she had been married but was no longer married. Then after a few times together she up and says she's only separated from her husband but was in the process of getting a divorce. And I was . . . like, oh, shit . . ."

"Did you know he was a policeman?"

"Hell, no," he said, shaking his head. "No . . . she didn't mention his line of work. That came out later, too. She started off as something delicious and worked her way into being nothing but a stick of goddamn dynamite."

"So she told you that later? About her husband being a Denver police officer?"

Black looked down and away from Juniper as if he was lost in thought.

"Yeah . . . she was manipulative . . . the . . . bitch. She doled bits and pieces. It was her way, how she churned her butter."

Juniper glanced at Virgil and me.

"You wanted her out of you life?"

"Hell, yes, I did."

"Did you kill her?"

Black smiled and looked over to Virgil and me, then looked back to Juniper.

"First, she is a divorced woman looking for someone to scratch her itch, then she's a married woman that is separated, later I discovered she was really still with him and that he was a member of the Denver police force."

"And his father?" Juniper said. "Did you also learn his father was the chief of police?"

"Yeah . . . another part of her butter batch . . . The chief has surely got me in his sights with the hammer back," Black said. "Not my fault she was the way she was and her husband and his chief father got their goddamn feelings hurt."

He nodded, then shook his head.

"Been interesting," Black said.

# 48.

And did you also learn Ruth Ann's husband knew about the two of you?"

"Oh, yeah . . . sure I did."

"How did you find that out?"

Black laughed.

"She told me."

"And how did you react?"

"Oh, I did a goddamn jig . . ." Black said.

Black's eyes narrowed.

"Listen," he said. "I was mad as hell."

"And what did you do with that madness?"

"What?" Black said, as if he were just snapped back to being present in the moment.

"Did you act out in any way?"

"What do you mean?"

"Did you tell her to leave, did you walk out, did she run off crying, did you hit her, did—"

"That is what we had the fight about at the goddamn inn that night."

Juniper made a note. Then leveled a look at Black.

"If you did not kill Ruth Ann—" Juniper said.

*"I didn't,"* he said with a snap.

Juniper nodded.

"Okay . . . Who do you think did?"

"I don't know."

"Do you have any idea, do you know anyone who would have a motive to kill her?"

"Hell, goddamn, for all I know she has a slew of men with a motive . . . I'm telling you she was crazy."

"Do you know if there were others she was doing the 'obvious way' with besides you?"

"I don't know but I damn sure would not put it past her . . . but I don't think so."

"Why?"

"'Cause she was obsessed with me."

"Do you think perhaps it could have been her husband that murdered her?"

"Well . . . ya know," Black said with a sarcastic tone, "it damn sure could have been."

"Do you know if he ever hurt her? Physically?"

"Not that I know of, no . . . But being around her for any length of time would make most men want to do something to her physically, that is how she liked it. Don't think she was comfortable unless there were chips on the table. Taller the stack the better, and now that I think about it, the more players the better. Maybe there were others like me that had anted up."

"But did she say anything, did you learn anything specifically about her husband, in respect to you?"

"She told me he was mad as hell. She played him, I'm sure, like she was playing me. She's a sharp if I ever saw one."

"What else did she tell you about him."

Black shook his head.

"Nothing, really . . . other than she said he was not the type to do anything about it."

"The following day, after her murder, you left Denver?"

"Yes."

"How do you know she was murdered, then? It was not until many days later her body was discovered."

"Well, I am just . . . I don't know, assuming."

"For your sake and mine, Mr. Black, let's avoid assumptions altogether."

Black nodded.

"When was the last time you saw Ruth Ann?"

"The night of the argument," Black said. "At the Bloom's Inn?"

"Bloom's Inn?"

"Yes," he said. "Where I was staying."

"What happened, did she just walk out? When and where exactly did you last have eyes on Ruth Ann?"

"That night, we argued. I told her to leave. She was angry as hell and she stormed out."

"What time?"

He shook his head.

"I say about eleven o'clock in the evening."

"And you never saw her again?"

"No."

"You are certain?"

"Yes."

"Did she leave out the front door or the rear door of the inn?"

"I don't know," he said. "She left my upstairs room and that was the last I saw of her."

Juniper glanced to us then looked back to Black.

"Then, the following day you departed Denver, for . . . where?"

"Here," he said. "To get ready for the opening of the new hall here."

Juniper looked at his notes.

"But you were in Las Vegas prior, were you not?"

"Well, yes, I had a few weeks in between, some time off, I had been working nonstop for a long time and I like Vegas, I have friends there, and yes, I was there."

"And that is where you met with Truitt Shirley and Ricky Ravenfield?"

"Yes."

"And you hired them?"

"I did."

"Why?"

"I felt, I knew, my life was in danger."

"Danger from whom?"

"There was a bounty on my head."

"How did you know this?"

"I received a wire from Denver that Ruth Ann had been murdered and I was the prime suspect and that the chief of police had put a bounty on my head."

Black looked to Virgil and me.

"I've been in this part of the country for a long time," Black said. "I've spent a good amount of time elsewhere, Saint Louis, Frisco, Boston, and the like, but I know these parts . . . Santa Fe, Las Cruces, New Mexico. And I know about bounty hunters and I knew I was being set up."

"Set up?"

"Yes, somebody was out to get me," he said. "Ruth Ann's husband, his father, I don't know exactly, but somebody."

"So you hired Truitt and Ricky?"

"I did."

Juniper jotted down a few notes, then nodded, looking at his note-pad for a moment. He looked back to Virgil and me, then looked back to Black.

"It would be a good idea if you spiffed up a bit for the proceedings," Juniper said. "Not too much, but some. I will see to it you have your proper clothing and grooming supplies."

Black nodded.

"Thank you . . ."

Juniper got to his feet and turned for the door, but then turned back to Black.

"One more thing . . ."

"Yes?" Black said.

"Who was it that told you you were the prime suspect in this murder and that there was a bounty on your head? How did you find that out?"

"One of Mr. Pritchard's employees sent me a wire."

"Who?"

"Ms. Angel," he said. "Daphne Angel."

# 49.

The trial for Truitt Shirley was placed on the docket behind Boston Bill's and the owners of the inn where Boston Bill had been staying in Denver at the time Ruth Ann was murdered were brought in to testify, as well as the young man that found Ruth Ann's body near the river.

Also in from Denver was Roger Messenger's father, the chief of police, Brady Messenger, and the two officers that previously had come to Appaloosa, Detectives Claude Banes and Sherman King, also arrived for the proceedings. Along with this group, there remained the police captain, G. W. McPherson, and the district attorney, Eldon Payne.

Payne introduced Virgil, Valentine, and me to Chief Messenger. He was not big like his son. The chief was a small, wiry man with an intensity that made him seem as if he were twice his size.

"Gentlemen," he said.

His voice was quivering, his eyes were shifty, and his demeanor in general was unstable. He was also obviously very angry.

"I will be glad when this is over."

He looked up to Valentine and squinted.

"Valentine?" he said. "You must be the hunter that apprehended this animal?"

"I am," Valentine said.

The chief nodded.

"I'm most appreciative," he said. "Money well spent."

He looked to me, then Virgil, and shook his head.

"We will make damn certain this execution happens without fail," he said. "I won't leave here until that happens and this degenerate dreg is dead and gone."

Then he moved on with the rest of the Denver lawmen.

"The Denver contingent," Valentine said under his breath to Virgil. "Got more goddamn Denver police here in Appaloosa than Appaloosa police in Appaloosa."

"Do," Virgil said.

"What do you figure is the reason for that, brother Marshal?" Valentine said.

Virgil shook his head.

"Not very interested in the justice system," I said. "That's a fact."

"Don't seem so," Virgil said.

"Something does not add up in all this," Valentine said.

The three of us, Virgil, Valentine, and I, sat in the back row of the packed courthouse, where we waited on Judge Callison's arrival. Callison was swift when he got to the job at hand, but he had no problem taking his time getting to the bench.

Boston Bill Black was next to Chastain and Book up front. He sat tall in his chair, looking far better than he had when we saw him previously in his cell. His mustache was now black without the gray roots and he was clean-shaven, with his salt-and-pepper hair oiled and combed back. He was wearing a dark suit with polished shoes.

Allie was sitting with the ladies of her social. She was fanning herself with the Chinese fan Valentine brought to her with all the other stuff when he came to dinner. She looked back to us then got up and came over to where we were sitting.

"It is already thirty-five minutes past the time this thing was supposed to start," Allie said. "What in the world is that ol' coot making everybody wait for."

"It's what he likes to do. Like always," I said, "likes to make people wait."

"Just his way of letting everybody know who's in charge," Virgil said.

"Well, I sure wish he'd get on with it," she said. "I'm already getting hungry."

With that, Allie sashayed away, fanning herself as she walked back to where she was previously sitting.

After another five minutes Judge Callison came out and wasted no time putting things in motion. He called the defense and prosecution to the bench and said a few things to each of them that were out of earshot, then quickly got into hearing testimony from both sides.

Because the Denver DA, Eldon Payne, was not allowed by law to practice outside of Colorado, they contracted Dickie Simmons, the other fine attorney besides Juniper practicing in Appaloosa, as the prosecuting attorney.

Simmons was a tall, narrow man with thick tangled eyebrows that had a hard time filling out his dark suit, but he was a scrappy contender when it came time to do his job, and he did it well.

The prosecution first called the young man to the stand that had found Ruth Ann Messenger's body in the shallow waters of the South Platte.

Simmons did a masterly job of making the young fella describe in horrific detail how he literally stumbled across the maggot-infested, waterlogged, and badly beaten body of Ruth Ann Messenger. Juniper

Jones objected for what seemed to be a solid hour until Callison told him to sit down and shut up.

The defense led by Juniper was thin, but he started by cross-examining the young man who found the body, only to give the jury some understanding that the boy was not an expert, and also not very bright, and before Juniper was done with the boy he was nearly in tears.

Next up were the owners of the inn where Boston Bill was staying the night Ruth Ann was murdered. They were an older married couple named Bloom and their testimony of hearing Bill Black and Ruth Ann arguing the night Ruth Ann went missing and then later finding blood on the back steps brought a gasp in the courtroom, followed by a hush.

Juniper weighed in with a volley of objections, exclaiming that none of what was being said was in any way substantial evidence. Juniper eventually got his opportunity to cross-examine the couple that owned the inn and did little to dissuade anyone from what seemed to be pointed, yet without question circumstantial, evidence.

Juniper spared calling Daphne but called Hollis Pritchard and Charles Lemley, Pritchard's construction foreman, to the stand.

Each of them had nothing but good things to say about Boston Bill Black, but both men were attacked by Simmons, who was doing everything in his power to discredit their credibility. Simmons was ineffective, however, as Pritchard and Charles Lemley proved to be in every way unflappable.

Juniper also did a good job of keeping the focus off the victim and on the prosecution's lack of evidence.

After an afternoon recess, Denver detective sergeant Sherman King entered the proceedings, stood in the center aisle, and asked Judge Callison if he could approach the bench.

After some pointed questioning, Callison granted him the request, and after King spoke with the judge, the judge called for both the prosecution and defense to approach. King, Dickie Simmons, and Juniper Jones all spoke quietly with the judge, and after a moment the judge shook his head a little.

We could not hear the conversation, but afterward Judge Callison slowly got to his feet, which prompted the bailiff to call out, "All rise."

Everyone got to their feet.

"This court is adjourned," Judge Callison said. "We will reconvene tomorrow at ten o'clock sharp . . . or thereabout."

He banged his gavel, stepped down, and exited out the door behind him.

# 50.

After the court adjourned, Chastain, Book, Virgil, and I stood with Bill Black and Juniper in the court's holding room. Black began to pace when Juniper told him there was a new development in the case. A witness had come forward and the prosecution asked that they recess until the witness could be vetted, vexed, and delivered.

Book and Chastain were next to the wall behind Black and Virgil, and I stood behind Juniper, watching Black pace. He was furious, and it was obvious this news was deeply disturbing to him. Juniper just stood there looking up, watching intently as the monstrous Black, who was twice the size of Juniper, moved to the left, then to the right. After a few turns Black stopped and looked down at Juniper.

"This is bullshit," Black said.

"Well, regardless," Juniper said. "Whether it is bullshit or not—"

"It is," Black said interrupting.

"Yes, well," Juniper said. "Unfortunately, it's bullshit in the form of a human being who is coming with damning evidence."

"Who?" Black said.

Juniper shook his head.

"The pesky young Detective King didn't, wouldn't, say," Juniper said. "And the judge did not press him on it."

Black started to pace again, moving back and forth in the small room. He jerked off his jacket and threw it over the back of a chair.

"Obviously we will know who and what will be said by whom tomorrow," Juniper said.

Black shook his head.

"So," Juniper said, "I have to ask you. Do you wish to reconsider your position here?"

"What do you mean?"

"Just that."

"You mean do I want to confess?"

Juniper did not answer. He just looked up at Black without blinking and without expression.

"I goddamn do not," Black said.

"Okay," Juniper said.

"I will not," Black said. "I will hang first."

"There is that," Juniper said.

"I cannot believe this is happening to me," Black said.

"It is," Juniper said. "So tell me . . ."

Juniper was making his push to see just what Black was really about, what he was made of.

"If this is a matter of pride, you need to let that go," Juniper said.

"Pride?" Black said. "What do you mean?"

"She was threatening you," Juniper said. "Wasn't she?"

"Goddamn right she was," Black said.

"What was she threatening about, exactly?"

"I told you she wanted to be with me."

"What else?"

Black shook his head.

"All kinds of nonsense."

"Per se?"

"I told you she was crazy."

"What else did she threaten you with?"

Black shook his head. Then he dropped onto a chair.

"I told you, at first when I met her I had no idea she was married."

Juniper nodded.

Black looked at Virgil and me.

"Go on," Juniper said.

"And we went about town doing this and doing that."

"She encouraged it, getting out, not being discreet?"

Black nodded.

"Yes, she acted as though she did not have a care in the world. Then, when I was starting to not see her as much, she got desperate."

"How so?"

Black got silent for a moment. "She wanted to cling on to me," he said. "Like I told you before."

"What did you do?"

"Nothing."

"Nothing?"

"I didn't do anything . . . I just got tired of her."

"You tell her that?"

"Not really, no, but my interest in her was less than it had been and she knew it."

"She didn't like that, I suspect."

"No," he said. "She did not."

"What did you do, Mr. Black?" Juniper said.

"I told you, nothing."

"What did she do?"

"That was when she told me she was married and not just a separated woman."

Black looked at his hands and worked them together for a moment.

"She also told me that when her husband found out about us it was because she told him she was seeing me, wanting to be with me, and that he was a lawman."

Black shook his head and stared at the floor.

"She also threatened to tell her father-in-law, the chief of the god-damn police, that I raped her, that I forced her."

"And you were angry with her?"

Black laughed.

"Wouldn't you be?"

"You were?"

"Hell yes," Black said. "But . . ."

"What?" Juniper said.

Black looked at Juniper with a stern expression on his face.

"I did not kill her."

"Then who did?"

"I told you I don't know."

Juniper did not say anything.

Black looked at Virgil. He did not look at anyone else but Virgil and pointed out to the streets.

"They, someone, is out to get me," he said. "I don't know who or why exactly, the old man or someone is covering up for her husband or somebody I don't know. Maybe Ruth Ann was just in the wrong place at the wrong time, but you have to believe me."

"No," Virgil said. "I don't have to do anything. Nobody else here does, either, but there is a jury and a judge that will most certainly have to decide your fate."

Black stared at Virgil.

# 51.

Chastain and Book left through the rear door of the courthouse and escorted Black back to the jail.

"What do you allow, Juniper?" Virgil said as we walked out through the now-empty courtroom with Juniper.

"I allow I could use a drink," he said.

"Kind of early to go waving the flag, don't you think, Juniper?" I said.

"Not to worry, Everett, my boy," Juniper said. "I know when and how I go down the rabbit hole and when I simply trot about and hunt and piddle with the hare . . . both I do by choice, so you can rest assured these litigious proceedings have my full and undivided interest and attention."

Juniper slowed to a stop and looked to Virgil.

"And if you are asking me what I allow in respect to how this will go, I'm curious, too, because I simply do not know. If you are asking me if I believe he actually did it, I don't know that, either. I will say on one hand he is convincing and on the other hand he is not. At moments he seems inward, irreverent, and regretful, the prime indicator

of guilt. Then there are those flashes of pompous and painful sple-
netic conviction, indubitably erring on innocence."

Juniper started to walk, then stopped again, looking up at Virgil.

"Nonetheless," he said, "this trial by ambush is impudent and
reckless nonsense. Judge Callison is reverting back to his early wild
and woolly frontier days, it seems. In fact, I have to say it seems in
respect to Judge Callison, there is no telling what he might do. In the
past I have had great success in his room, but now his ability to disregard and miraculously transport himself into another place in time
right before our eyes leads me to believe there is no reason to bank on
reasoning here. The fact that this witness that has come forward with
what is to be important information and he's not allowing me the appropriate disclosure is like asking me to walk a tightrope and I do not
know how to walk a tightrope."

When we stepped out into the courtroom foyer, Allie was sitting
on a bench.

"There you are," Allie said as she stood. "Everett, look who I have
had the pleasure of visiting with."

Across the foyer from Allie sat Daphne. She smiled and got to
her feet.

"Marshal," she said. "Everett."

"Ms. Angel," Virgil said.

"Hello," she said. "Everett, I thought I would wait for you. I hope
that is okay?"

"Of course," I said.

"Ah . . . ladies," Juniper said with a tip of his hat and a click of his
heels. "If you all will excuse me . . ." Then he looked to Virgil and me.
"I have business to attend to, an appointment with an unsuspecting
Lagomorph . . . Good day."

Juniper tipped his hat once more, then walked out.

Allie grinned and reached out, taking Daphne's hand.

"We have been getting to know each other," Allie said, holding Daphne's hand in both of her hands.

Daphne nodded and smiled.

"We have," she said.

"That's good," I said.

"It's not every day," Allie said, "that we have someone as smart and as beautiful as this lovely lady here in Appaloosa."

"Thank you, Allie," Daphne said.

"Mostly," Allie said, "the new women that show up here are whores, don't you know."

"Well, I . . ."

Daphne blushed.

"I was also thrilled as can be," Allie said, "to find out that she works for Mr. Pritchard . . . and the new casino and, well, we have a lot in common."

"That's good, Allie," Virgil said.

"We also, of course," Allie said, "have had the unfortunate discussion about all this carryings-on, about all this awful matter regarding this trial."

"Which implores me," Daphne said, "to ask what has happened. Why were the proceedings cut short today?"

I looked to Virgil.

"Seems there has been some new discovery by the prosecution," Virgil said.

"My God," she said.

"Oh, no," Allie said. "What sort of discovery?"

"Court business, Allie," Virgil said.

"What kind of court business?" Allie said.

"Don't know."

"You don't know or you aren't saying," Allie said.

# 52.

I walked with Daphne as she spun the white silk parasol above her head, keeping the hot afternoon sun off her face. We strolled on for a long time without talking. Then she laced her arm around mine and we walked a while longer without talking.

"She's something else," Daphne said.

"Allie?"

"Yes."

"That's one way to put it."

"She likes you, you know?" Daphne said.

"What's not to like?"

"No, I mean she likes you."

"She likes you, too," I said.

"No," Daphne said. "I'm a woman, I know."

I laughed.

"No," I said.

I looked to her as we walked. She looked to me from under her parasol.

"You like her, too?" she said.

"Of course I like her."

"Yes," she said. "That is evident."

"She's my friend."

We walked for a moment.

"Allie and I have a special friendship," I said.

"I know . . ."

"No . . . not like that," I said.

"How is it?"

"We have a certain kinship because we are both partners with Virgil."

"You have known her a long time."

"Long enough."

"I can tell."

"But she belongs to Virgil."

"You say that like she is his possession."

"She belongs to Virgil and Virgil belongs to her."

Daphne shook her head a little.

"What?" I said.

"You don't have to get defensive, Everett."

"I'm not."

"I like her, too," she said.

"Good."

"And she likes me."

"She does," I said.

"What's not to like?" she said, then looked at me and offered a delayed smile.

"I have to agree," I said.

"You don't have to," she said. "But I'm glad you do."

"Pleasure is all mine," I said.

"Not entirely," she said. "But thank you for walking with me."

"It's quite difficult."

She looked down as she walked. She kept looking down, then . . .

"Can I tell you something, Everett?"

"Sure."

"It's a confession of sorts."

"I'm right here."

"I'm very . . . concerned with what is happening with this trial . . ."

"I can understand."

"Yes," she said. "Well, not fully. I'm not sure you do understand, not completely, anyway."

We walked a bit, and she waited until she spoke again.

"Before, when we talked," she said, "I was not fully honest with you."

"About?"

"Well, let me rephrase that, I was not dishonest, but I was not forthcoming."

"Go ahead."

"You know when you asked me previously if I were ever married?"

"So you have been?" I said.

"No," she said, shaking her head. "That's not it, and no, I have never been married."

"Okay."

"When I told you before that I was engaged, I left out that it was . . . Bill Black that I was engaged to."

I stopped walking, and then she stopped and turned back to me, staring at me from under the silk of her parasol.

"Not that you owe me any details of your diary," I said. "Or need any kind of explanation or accounting of your past, but under the circumstances, that's, well . . . I'm not sure what that is."

"I know," she said. "That's precisely why I felt I should confess this to you."

"Glad you did."

"It was a long time ago," she said.

"And you changed your mind," I said.

"Yes," she said.

"Why?" I said.

"Because . . . he frightened me," she said.

"How so?"

"Not by one particular action," she said. "But there was something about him that was ultimately frightening."

"Why did you warn him?"

"What?"

"You let him know," I said. "He said it was you that told him he was being accused of the murder."

"How did you know that?"

"Just part of his baring up . . ."

She nodded.

"I care for him," she said.

"Obviously."

"No," she said, "not like that, not anymore."

I didn't say anything.

"How could I not?" she said.

"I don't know," I said. "And I'm not judging you for doing so."

"In many ways he is like a little boy."

"Far from little."

"No, he is," she said. "He's a child, really."

"Do you think he killed her?"

She thought for a brief moment, then shook her head.

"No," she said.

# 53.

The following day in the courtroom was a hot one. By ten in the morning it was sweltering. After Judge Callison got settled and the trial got under way, the prosecutor, Dickie Simmons, wasted no time. He called a man by the name of Lawrence LaCroix to the stand.

LaCroix was a medium-build fellow in his forties. He was fairly nice-looking, with a strong face and wide bright blue eyes. He was lean and muscular, and his skin was tanned from the sun. His clothes were British military, made of khaki, and he carried a straw hat in one hand and a flat object covered with a cloth in the other. After he took the stand and was sworn in, Dickie Simmons went after him like a thirsty dog.

"Mr. LaCroix, do you know that man over there?"

Dickie pointed to Boston Bill.

"I do not," LaCroix said.

LaCroix was, in fact, a Brit, but his manner did not in any way give him the air of affluence. There was nothing smug or superior about him. In fact, he seemed completely pleasant and unassuming.

"Have you seen him before?"

"I have."

"Where did you see him?"

"At the Bloom's Inn near the South Platte River in Denver, Colorado."

"Bullshit," Black said as he rose from his chair until Juniper pulled him back into his seat.

Judge Callison banged his gavel and Juniper stood quickly before Callison said anything.

"Won't happen again, Your Honor," Juniper said, and then sat back and looked at Black, shaking his head.

"See that it doesn't," Callison said.

Black was red-faced and his eyes were steaming mad as he leaned in close to Juniper and mouthed *Bullshit* as he shook his head. *Bullshit.*

Callison turned in his chair and looked behind him, then looked to the bailiff.

"What is that noise?" he said.

"Your Honor?"

"What?" Judge Callison said.

"I . . . I don't hear anything, Your Honor."

Callison turned back and looked out at the courtroom, staring blankly. He was very calm looking out as everyone remained looking at him, waiting for him to say something. Then Callison turned in his chair and looked out the window to his right. Everyone in the room followed his look, as if he were focused on something that we should see, but there was only the side of the adjoining building across the way. Callison remained looking, as if he were lost in thought. Whispering conversations could be heard, but Callison did not respond to them, he just kept looking toward the window.

"What in the hell is the ol' boy up to?" Valentine said quietly to Virgil and me.

Virgil didn't answer Valentine as he watched the judge.

"Your Honor?" Simmons said.

Callison tuned and looked to Simmons.

"Yes," Callison said.

"May I proceed?" Simmons said.

Callison looked at him for a moment, then, as if he were back in the room after a brief journey beyond, he nodded.

"You may proceed, Mr. Simmons."

There were murmurs in the room.

Callison rapped his gavel a bit.

"Quiet," he said, then nodded to Simmons.

"Thank you, Your Honor," Simmons said, then turned his attention to the stand.

"When did you see him?" Simmons said to LaCroix.

"I saw him there, at Bloom's Inn a few times."

Black shook his head dramatically from side to side and wanted desperately to get to his feet again, but Juniper kept him seated.

"Were you staying at the inn?" Simmons said.

"No," he said.

"Why did you see him? Let me phrase that differently. How was it that you had seen him there at Bloom's Inn on numerous occasions?"

"I'm a painter," LaCroix said.

"You were there painting the Bloom's Inn building?"

"No," he said with a smile. "Well . . . yes, I was, in part, painting the building."

"Objection, Your Honor," Juniper said. "Let's get to it . . . either he was painting the inn or he was not painting the inn. Obviously Mr. LaCroix has no clue."

"Sit down, Mr. Jones," Judge Callison said to Juniper with a stern expression on his face. Then he looked back to Dickie. "You may continue, Mr. Simmons."

Dickie smiled, and for dramatic purposes he looked to the ground and paced a bit before he spoke. Then he said, "Go on, Mr. LaCroix. Please explain for the court what you were doing there at Bloom's Inn, where Mr. Black was residing."

"As I said, I was painting . . . I paint landscapes."

"You paint landscapes?"

"Objection," Juniper said.

"Overruled," the judge said. "Continue, Mr. Simmons, and Mr. Jones, let's let him get on with this business here."

The judge nodded to Dickie.

"Please," Dickie said. "You were saying?"

LaCroix nodded.

"Bloom's Inn," LaCroix said, "was the subject of one of my paintings."

"Your Honor," Dickie said. "I would like to place into evidence the painting of which Mr. LaCroix is referencing here."

"Objection," Juniper said.

"Overruled," Callison said.

Dickie turned back to LaCroix. "May I?"

"Oh, sure," LaCroix said, and unwrapped the covering from a painting.

"Is this the painting?" Dickie said. "The painting of Bloom's Inn, the residence of Bill Black?"

"Yes," LaCroix said.

Dickie showed the painting to the jurors. He walked slowly by each one of the jurors, letting them have a good look at the painting. Then he presented it out to us in the courtroom. It was a side-angle-view painting of Bloom's Inn with the South Platt River in the background. The sign in front of the Inn clearly spelled out *Bloom's Inn*.

"I call this painting *Bloom Where You Are Planted*," LaCroix said proudly.

The courtroom reacted with laughter.

"Objection," Juniper said. "The name of this painting has no significance, no credibility to—"

"Oh, on the contrary," Dickie said, interrupting Juniper. "The very fact this painting says *Bloom's Inn*, right here." Dickie pointed to the sign in the painting. "Gives this painting credibility as to Mr. LaCroix's whereabouts the evening Ruth Ann Messenger was brutally murdered by Bill Black."

"Objection," Juniper said. "Mr. Simmons is trying to lead the jury and the people of this court to believe this painting has bearing on the fate on my client's future. Well, it has no credence in this case whatsoever. This painting could be any number of inns. And though I am not at all suggesting that, I will give Mr. LaCroix his due, but there is nothing substantial—"

"Overruled, Mr. Jones," the judge said. "Continue, Mr. Simmons, but get to the point."

Dickie smiled, then took his time as he homed in on Lawrence LaCroix.

"Tell the jurors and this court the last time you saw this man, Bill Black," Dickie said, pointing over to Black without looking at him.

"Well, as you can see, the painting is an evening rendition and I painted this painting, *Bloom Where You Are Planted*," he said, "over a number of evenings and . . . well, I set up my easel at the same spot every evening, and on this particular evening I saw Mr. Black . . ."

LaCroix stopped and looked to the judge.

"Go on," Judge Callison said.

"I saw Bill Black dragging Ruth Ann Messenger down the path directly in front of me toward the South Platte River."

# 54.

T*hat's a goddamn lie!"* Black shouted as he towered up out of his chair, knocking over the table in front of him.

Callison banged his gavel.

*"A goddamn lie!"* Black said.

A boisterous eruption of gasps and shouts echoed loudly in the courtroom as Callison continued to bang his gavel over and over.

*"Quiet,"* he said. *"Silence . . . Sit down, Mr. Black . . . Quiet. Sit down, Mr. Black!"*

*"It's a goddamn lie,"* Black said as he pointed a rigid finger at Lawrence LaCroix and moved toward him. *"A goddamn lie!"*

Chastain and Book were quick to get in front of Black. They got ahold of Black and moved him back away from the stand.

*"A goddamn lie!"*

"Mr. Jones," Callison said. "Sit him down and shut him up. Right now!"

Juniper practically climbed aboard Black, trying to get him down in his chair with the help of Chastain and Book.

The noise in the courtroom was still at a loud level, and Callison banged and banged his gavel until everyone stopped clamoring.

"Enough," Callison said.

Chastain and Book helped Juniper get Black back in his chair. Juniper nodded to Chastain and Book.

"Thank you," he said. "We'll be okay."

Chastain and Book backed away and Juniper stood between Black and LaCroix, blocking Black's view of LaCroix.

Valentine leaned in to Virgil and me.

"How about that?" he said in a whisper. "Damn sure didn't see that one coming."

"Nope," I said. "Me, neither."

"Don't think ol' Juniper saw that in his orbit, either," Valentine said.

Juniper was in Black's face, talking a blue streak to Black, trying to calm him. Black continued to try to get a look at LaCroix, but Juniper kept moving, stepping from side to side, blocking Black's view. Finally Black looked down, like a little boy taking his medicine, but he was fuming.

By the time Callison got the room quieted, Juniper had Black settled, but Black was now beyond seething rage.

"He's fit to be tied," Valentine said with a hush.

Black had turned inward and it was obvious that his fury continued to mount. His neck was bulging, brimming above the collar of his shirt. The veins in his dark red face looked as if they would explode and he was close to foaming at the mouth. His eyes were bored in, locked solid, staring downward as if he were trying to burn a hole in the floor with his bloodshot, angry eyes.

"You may continue, Mr. Simmons."

"And what did you do then, Mr. LaCroix?" Dickie said.

"Well, I was confused," LaCroix said.

"How so?"

"I did not know what to do," LaCroix said as he looked out to the courtroom, seeking some kind of kinship with everyone that was looking at him.

"Go on," Dickie said.

"I just watched, I'm afraid," LaCroix said. "At first I thought I should do something, but then I thought I should not. I should mind my own business. He, of course, is an intimidating man. I made some sort of judgment, some assumption that what I was witnessing was most likely a lovers' quarrel, you see, and I should simply stay out of it."

The crowd half agreed and half disagreed.

"So you did nothing?" Dickie said.

LaCroix shook his head.

"I . . . I did not, I'm mortified to admit. And now, now that we know the heinous outcome of this . . . I am frankly ashamed of myself."

"No further questions at this time, Your Honor," Dickie said.

"He's going to leave it at that?" Valentine said under his breath. "Not ask what, if anything else, he witnessed?"

Callison nodded and looked to Juniper.

"Mr. Jones?"

"Dickie is smart," I said. "He's setting Juniper up, he's making it where Juniper will be the one dropping the blade."

Juniper looked to Black, who was still about to explode. Juniper whispered something to Black as he stared at the floor. Juniper whispered to him again, and Black's eyes looked up at Juniper, then shifted to LaCroix. Juniper said something to Black and Black nodded slightly.

"Mr. Jones," Callison said. "You may cross-examine, and if you do not wish to do so, say so."

"I do, Your Honor," Juniper said, and he got to his feet and moved away from Black.

"Juniper is smart, and he knows the trap Dickie has left for him," I said. "How he gets around it is another story."

# 55.

Juniper glanced back to Black, then turned his attention to La-Croix. Juniper, for the first time in the proceedings, looked uncertain as he approached LaCroix. He stopped in front of the stand and paced for a moment.

"The worm, it turns," Valentine said quietly.

"Does," I said.

"Looks like Black's goose has just been stuffed proper and over-cooked," Valentine said.

Virgil did not say anything, but he shook his head a little.

"Wonder what in the hell is this little attorney fella gonna do," Valentine said. "Poor bastard's got himself a battleship to row upstream with a sapling stick."

"Mr. LaCroix," Juniper said. "You said you saw Mr. Black on more than one occasion?"

"Yes."

"Where did you see him prior to the day in question, when you allegedly say you saw Mr. Black?"

Dickie offered an objection, but Callison overruled.

"I allege nothing, I saw . . ."

"Answer the question," Juniper said. "Where did you see him prior?"

"Why, at Bloom's Inn, like I said."

"Where did you physically see him at the Inn?"

"What?"

"Where?"

"I'm not certain what you mean."

"This is not difficult questioning here, Mr. LaCroix. Did you see him in the parlor, in the hall, on the front porch, on the roof, swinging from the eaves . . . where did you see him?"

"Oh, well . . . I saw him, let's see, coming and going. He's rather hard to miss."

"When?"

"At different times during the day."

Juniper looked at the painting. He studied it for a moment.

"You said you painted in the evening and you set up in the evening."

LaCroix nodded and smiled.

"Um," he said. "Yes, but . . ."

"*But?*" Juniper said. "*But?* . . . Why are you lying?"

"Objection," Dickie said.

"You said you painted in the evenings," Juniper said, then turned to Callison. "Your Honor, I am trying to establish some basic timeline here that Mr. LaCroix seems to be lying about, and I want to know why he is lying under oath."

Dickie shouted, "Objection, Your Honor."

"Sustained," Callison said. "Let him answer, Mr. Jones."

"I came there to the inn at various times during the day for a while, just sketching, getting my framework down," LaCroix said. "And during those times, a few times, I saw Mr. Black."

Juniper looked at LaCroix for a long moment, then he moved to the painting. He picked it up and looked at it, smelled it, and touched it with his little finger. He rubbed his little finger with his thumb and looked at the residue of paint on his fingers.

"Still wet," Juniper said.

LaCroix nodded.

"Takes a while to dry thoroughly," he said.

"When did you finish this painting?" Juniper said.

"I'm not sure I ever finish a painting," LaCroix said with a proud boyish smile as he looked to the audience.

"Yes," Juniper said. "By the look of this, I can certainly see your point."

The comment brought a few chuckles from the crowd.

LaCroix sat with his shoulders back and acted as though the comment didn't have an effect on him.

Juniper looked closely at the painting again.

"Looks like this painting was just only recently done, and just barely dry."

"No, it's been done awhile," he said.

"It's a rather crude and uninspired piece," Juniper said. "Is this your first painting?"

LaCroix's face flushed. Dickie objected, but Callison quieted him.

"First painting or no?" Juniper said.

"It is not my first painting," LaCroix said.

"So you have other paintings?"

"Objection, Your Honor," Dickie said. "I do not see how any other paintings that have been painted by Mr. LaCroix have any bearing on this—"

"On the contrary, Your Honor," Juniper said, interrupting Dickie. "I am only attempting to substantiate this man Mr. LaCroix is the painter he claims he is."

"Oh, I am," LaCroix said defensively.

"So you say."

"Objection overruled," Callison said. "Continue, Mr. Jones, but get to your point."

"Again," Juniper said. "You have other paintings?"

"Why, of course," he said.

"Where are they?"

"Well . . . they are at my home."

"And where is it you call home?"

"In Denver," he said.

"So, Your Honor, I would just like to point out to the jury, that unless this court were able to obtain those said paintings and had the opportunity to view them, or if we were able to gather witnesses that have witnessed Mr. LaCroix painting the said paintings, we have no real evidence to show this jury that confirms Mr. LaCroix is even a painter at all. Much less any evidence that proves he was where he said he was during the painting of this"—Juniper looked at the painting—"*Bloom Where You Are Planted* concoction."

"Objection," Dickie said. "This is ridiculous. Mr. Jones is hanging on by a thread and he knows it."

"Point taken," Callison said. "The jury can decide on this painterly matter based on the evidence presented in this court . . . I'm going to have to agree with Mr. Simmons here, Mr. Jones . . . Continue, Mr. Jones, but get to the point, and in doing so, let's choose a direct line of questioning that is without the unnecessary subversive commentary."

Juniper nodded, then paced for a moment.

"Did you get paid to come here today?"

"No."

"Why are you here?"

"I felt it was my responsibility to be here."

"Do you know anyone in this courtroom?" Juniper said.

LaCroix looked out to the room and scanned the faces.

"I do not."

"Are you certain?"

"Yes," he said. "Well . . . I met those here with the Denver law enforcement when I arrived here in Appaloosa, but then and only then."

"Did you pay for your travel here?"

"No."

"Who did?"

"They did, the Denver Department of Law Enforcement."

"How is it that you are just coming forward with this information?"

"I read about this in the Denver paper, about Ruth Ann's body being found, and I contacted the authorities."

"That is not the only reason, is it?"

LaCroix was silent for a long moment.

"No."

"Oh?" Juniper said. "What was the other reason or reasons?"

"Oh, no," Valentine said under his breath. "Juniper might have just belayed the wrong yard lift."

"I saw more," LaCroix said. "More of what Mr. Black did . . ."

Juniper turned away from LaCroix so quickly he looked like a calf hitting the end of a dallied rope.

"That will be all, Your Honor," Juniper said loudly. "No further questions."

Juniper hurried back to his table.

"I saw him . . . not just drag her, but I saw him beat her," LaCroix said. "Beat her to her death."

Black bolted from his chair and charged LaCroix. This time he was way too fast for anyone to stop him. LaCroix scrambled back, trying to stay out of Black's rapacious reach, but he was not fast enough.

# 56.

Prior to Black being sentenced to hang for the murder of Ruth Ann Messenger, he managed to injure Lawrence LaCroix pretty good that day. Black was quick on his attack of LaCroix. His first contact took LaCroix off his feet and slammed him so hard into the back of the courtroom the plaster caved in and fell from the wall and ceiling. By the time Chastain, Book, the bailiff, Virgil, and I could get to Black, he had broke LaCroix's nose and jaw, knocked out some teeth, cracked ribs, and fractured both his painting arm and right leg. LaCroix ended up unconscious and had to be carried out on a stretcher and hauled off to the hospital.

Now, however, the whole dramatic event was over and gallows were already under construction. The alderman of Appaloosa did not appreciate the idea of the town having a permanent structure for hanging people. So instead of having standing gallows, there was pre-cut lumber ready for reassembly when it was time for it to be used again, and according to Judge Callison, this was the time for it to be put to use.

The site where the gallows were erected was on the far outskirts of town, past a makeshift little saloon that was neatly christened as the Gallows Door Cantina. It was nothing more than a three-sided lean-to with a cluster of tables and chairs under a stand of hackberry and mimosa. The place was open only when it was warm or when there was a hanging about to take place, and currently the reasoning criteria of both were in effect.

Virgil and I sat in the shade, drinking beer and watching the workers putting the gallows structure together when Valentine came walking up behind us.

"Lovely day for a hanging," he said.

Virgil looked back.

"Not yet," Virgil said.

"Next week," I said.

"Yeah," Valentine said as he stopped and looked at the construction workers a moment. "I heard . . . Ironic, it's the goddamn day before Independence Day. The day before he was supposed to open the damn gambling joint."

"It is," I said.

"Who thought of that?" Valentine said.

"That was the good judge," I said.

"Some kind of sick joke?"

"Judge wanted to be out on the afternoon train for Yaqui so he could be home for the Fourth."

"Isn't that thoughtful?"

He shook his head, removed his hat, and took a seat. He pushed back his thick hair with both of his hands and smiled at Virgil.

"Not seen you around for a while," Virgil said.

"You been looking for me?"

"No," Virgil said.

"You need something?"

"No."

"You miss me?" Valentine said.

"Did not," Virgil said.

"I've been enjoying the good life," Valentine said.

"That so?" Virgil said.

"Made me a short trip over to the hot springs."

Virgil looked at him with his head tilted a bit.

"You should try it," Valentine said. "Take Allie. Cures what ails you."

Valentine looked to the gallows.

"'Sides," he said. "There's only so much of this kind of shit a fellow can tolerate."

"It's been expected," Virgil said.

"Understand the good judge heard the case against Truitt Shirley?"

Virgil nodded.

"Heard there was testimony that supported some self-defense, Truitt thought Roger Messenger was pulling on him, but the good judge found him guilty."

"Ten years for second-degree murder," I said. "We'll be hauling him off after the hanging."

"The old judge is on a roll," Valentine said.

Eloise came out from the lean-to. Eloise was a local barmaid in Appaloosa. She was in her forties and was a bit plump but pretty as a peach. She was a sprightly and spirited woman with pounds of curly red hair and was never without a sassy smile on her face.

"Beer?" she said to Valentine. "That's all we got."

Valentine looked her up and down.

"Well, I by God beg to differ," he said with a smile.

She put her hands on her hips.

"Well, aren't you a charmer," she said.

"I have been called worse," he said.

"I'm sure you have," she said.

"Beer it will be, my dear," he said.

Valentine watched her as she walked back to the lean-to, then looked back to the gallows again. After an extended moment he said, "Poor bastard."

"Black?" I said.

"Yep," Valentine said.

"We were just ruminating on that very thing," I said.

"And?" he said.

"Up to the painter LaCroix's last statement about what he saw, it could have been a different decision, is all."

"That *all* is a hell of a lot," Valentine said.

"Damn sure is," I said.

"His life," Valentine said. "Painter was convincing, though."

Virgil nodded.

"He was," he said.

"But you been edging on the speculation that Black just might have been railroaded?" Valentine said.

Virgil didn't say anything, but his lack of response answered the question.

"He was goddamn fit to be tied, that's for sure," Valentine said. "He was on that goddamn painter like a riled black bear."

"He was," I said.

"Well, I sure as hell knew firsthand he had that kind of goddamn fury in him," Valentine said. "I thought I had him good when I first caught him. I come up behind him there at the cactus garden just off the city square. I put my sawed-off to the back of his head and had one of my helpers, Sanchez, get the cuffs on him. I could tell the whole time this was happening Boston Bill's temperature was climbing like a hot poker. No sooner did we get the cuffs on him and went to put him in the wagon than the sonofabitch kicked Sanchez off the side of this lil' ol' bridge like an empty fruit can, spun around on me, got both hands on my neck, that I realized I just might have saddled more of a horse than I could ride. I was able to pop him a few hard fucking rights, but it didn't faze him. He picked me up off the ground and slammed me so hard up against the bars of the wagon I was seeing fireflies, and the simple fact I managed to pull my cutlass and put the tip of it to his throat is the only thing that saved me from a handmade wood box. After that I slapped him hard a few times and he showed no more effrontery . . . but up until then he kind of put the fear of goddamn Mohammed in me."

Eloise came with Valentine's beer. He leaned back as she set it on the table in front of him. He looked up at her and grinned.

"Thank you," he said.

"Are you flirting with me?" she said.

"What gives you that impression?"

"You," she said.

Valentine laughed.

"Well, as a matter of fact, I am," he said.

"That's what I thought," she said.

She walked off and looked back over her shoulder. "Keep it up," she said.

Valentine looked at his beer and smiled.

"I'm beginning to kind of like this town," he said.

"Don't get too used to it," Virgil said.

Valentine winked at me.

# 57.

To say the least, it was damn sure interesting for me to witness Virgil and Valentine together. *Blood is thicker than water,* I thought. In some ways I was relieved that Valentine was here in Appaloosa and present in Virgil's life. Though Virgil had both Allie and me as partners, I always felt Virgil was really without anyone. In most ways I know that was what he preferred, but in other ways as time marched on, I think Virgil found some comfort in having some distractions from that consuming world that was, in every respect, *the consuming world of Virgil Cole.*

Virgil pulled a few of the cigars from his pocket. He held up one for Valentine.

"Don't mind if I do," he said, taking a cigar from Virgil.

"They come from you," Virgil said, holding up the cigar.

"Damn good ones, too," Valentine said.

Virgil nodded as he struck a match and cupped it for Valentine.

"Where'd you steal 'em?" Virgil said.

"I bought those with hard-earned money," Valentine said as he puffed on the cigar until it was going good. "I chased and caught a couple of Mescaleros for the Army that used to ride for Victorio. Chased them for a hundred miles down the Rio Grande before I caught the savages, and I was given these cigars by the colonel himself."

Virgil looked to me, flicked the match, fished another from his pocket, then dragged the tip across the underside of table and lit his cigar. After he got the cigar going good he waved the flame from the match and looked at the gallows. He puffed on his cigar as he watched the men putting the structure together. We watched for a bit without talking.

"The whole town is anxious," I said.

Virgil nodded a little and Valentine shook his head.

"Juniper hit the jug," I said.

Valentine looked at me for a moment, then said, "He just got boxed in."

Virgil nodded.

"Black did not help," I said.

"No," Valentine said. "But I doubt that would have changed the good judge's decision."

"No," Virgil said. "Me, neither."

We sat for a moment, watching the workers.

"Taking the position this was the Denver contingent's plan," Valentine said as he puffed on his cigar, "have you fellas given much thought as to why the prosecution waited until the second day to bring in the Brit painter?"

"Maybe it wasn't the plan?" I said.

"If I were a betting man, which I am, I would stack chips it was," Valentine said.

"Why?" I said.

"Don't know," Valentine said. "Just my gut."

Virgil nodded a little.

"Don't make good sense," Virgil said.

"I have said all along there seems to be a Denver conspiracy of sorts," Valentine said. "But with the Brit painter and his *Bloom Where You Are Planted* painting, it goddamn sure painted Boston Bill Black into a corner, and up those hangman steps, no matter."

Valentine nodded to the gallows.

"It did at that," Virgil said.

"DA Payne had told us there was no eyewitness."

"And then there was," Valentine said.

We sat silent for a moment, thinking about that.

"I did some asking around," Valentine said.

Virgil looked at him, but Valentine just puffed on his cigar, looking at the gallows.

"What kind of asking around?" I said.

"Oh, in Denver," he said. "I got some good friends in Denver."

"What were you asking around about?" Virgil said.

"Just was curious, wanted to get the angle, what was at the apex," he said. "Had some wiring back and forth with an amigo who talked to another amigo, what they knew about this."

"And?" I said.

"Nothing much, really, only that the daughter-in-law was a dark stain on the family's reputation. The scrawny police chief's been the laughingstock because of his daughter-in-law. From what was relayed, she liked to hike her tail . . . a good bit . . . and was good at it . . . And I'd just have to bet a dollar to a dime that Black was not the only one swabbing those tonsils."

"Yeah, we got that from the Denver captain, that they wanted this over," I said.

"Chief and his wife are tighter than goddamn squeaking oak branches with the Church. He's an elder, she sings in the church choir."

"And that goddamn judge," Valentine said. "I know he's got a reputation and is a good hand, but I don't know, it seems to me he's holding on to a greased rope."

Virgil looked at me and nodded a little.

"He wavered," I said.

"Wavered?" Valentine said. "Why, he should be doing something else . . . like crocheting or carving wooden toys for his great-grandchildren."

"He's no spring chicken," Virgil said.

"I have always thought Callison the best and most reliable judge we got," I said. "But . . ."

"Nothing lasts forever, Everett," Valentine said. "Comes a time for every sanctimonious scallywag and do-gooder to get their ass dry docked."

Virgil looked down. He kept the cigar wedged in the corner of his mouth and reluctantly nodded in agreement.

"And though," I said, "this case got Black on the downslope with the testimony from the Bloom couple that owned the inn, saying they heard Black and Ruth Ann arguing and finding blood on the back porch, to LaCroix offering up his testimony, it still seemed . . . I don't know, suspect."

Virgil looked up at me. He did not say anything, but his look told me he agreed with the comment.

"The Coloradoans still here loitering about in Appaloosa?" Valentine said.

"They are," I said. "They said they would remain here to watch the ball drop."

"That's kind of them," Valentine said.

Valentine took a sip of beer and gazed off for a moment, watching the workers on the gallows, then shook his head and looked to Virgil.

"You think he's innocent?" Valentine said.

I looked to Virgil.

"Callison heard it and he pulled the trigger and there ain't nothing we can do about that," Virgil said.

"That's not what I asked."

"I know," Virgil said.

We sipped our beer, thinking about that, as the worker raised the top rope beam above the gallows floor.

"I went to Callison after the trial," Virgil said.

"For?" Valentine said.

Virgil puffed on his cigar for a moment as he thought.

"For the very thing we are talking about here," he said.

"You wanted to make sure he was looking down the cue?" Valentine said.

Virgil nodded.

"Yep," Virgil said. "Just wanted to make sure he heard enough and saw enough. And I wanted to have a look in his eyes."

"What did you see?" Valentine said.

Virgil thought for a moment and shook his head.

"He was convinced," Virgil said.

Valentine said, "Stands by the jury's decision, that sort of thing?"

Virgil nodded.

"Don't mean he's right," Valentine said.

"Or the jury made the right decision," I said.

"Just because a bunch of goddamn geese go south don't mean the meadowlark needs to follow."

"No," Virgil said. "It don't."

"Well," Valentine said. "Like I said, it was told to me Roger's wife had more than one chucker in the woodshed, so no telling."

# 58.

I had yet to speak with Daphne after the verdict. I stopped by the hotel a few times and tried to visit with her, but I was told she was not accepting any visitors.

After the sentencing she was visibly upset and had hurried from the courtroom with Pritchard, who was also in shock and disbelief. This was an obvious blow to them, as they had previously believed Black was not guilty of killing Ruth Ann Messenger.

Two days later and four days before Black's hanging I was inside the round corral behind the livery, working Ajax, when I saw Valentine walking from the livery pulling two big bay mules.

"Fine looking animal you got there, Everett."

"When he's asleep," I said.

"This here is Magellan and Columbus," he said, nodding to the mules.

"Going someplace?" I said.

"I am," he said, then pointed to his prison wagon parked behind the corral.

It was a standard sturdily built prisoner transport wagon with bars on four sides and lantern headlamps for night travel.

"Duty calls," he said.

"You got somebody you're going after?"

He laughed.

"Oh, there is always somebody in particular to be going after."

"You don't have to worry about me, Valentine."

"Now, why would I worry about you, Everett?"

I smiled and walked toward the corral rail.

"I'm not your competition, Valentine," I said. "Besides, I receive my regular government salary that precludes me from such monetary pursuits."

Valentine came close to the corral and put a boot on the rail.

"Fact is," he said, "time to move on."

I nodded.

"'Sides, I don't need to stick around for no by-God hanging, Everett."

"Not so interested in that myself," I said.

He shook his head a little.

"You headed back to El Paso?"

He looked off with a contemplative thought.

"Nope," he said. "I've had plenty enough of that goddamn dusty place . . ."

"Figure you will try someplace new?"

He nodded.

"Where you thinking?" I said.

"Oh, I will stay on the border somewhere. I can't move out of my honey hole, and I do like the sonorities . . ."

"Whole border is dusty," I said.

"That it is," he said. "But different dust, I'm thinking, is a good idea . . . Nuevo Laredo, maybe, Piedras Negras perhaps . . . I'm kind of undecided at this point, maybe even Corpus . . . Always been fond of the water."

"When you riding out?"

"No reason to dally."

"You talk to Virgil?"

"Have not."

"You gonna?"

He looked off again and smiled, then shook his head.

"No."

"No?"

"No," he said with a smile.

"You want me to tell him anything?"

He shook his head.

"Nothing else to say, Everett."

"Think he'd might want you to say something," I said.

"Like what?"

"Hell, I don't know, he's not my brother."

"Oh, you're a brother to Virgil, Everett," he said. "No doubt about that."

"In some ways," I said.

"Besides, as Virgil likes to point out, he's my half-brother," he said with a smile.

"Allie would appreciate it," I said.

"Do me a favor," Valentine said.

"What's that?"

"Tell the both of them that I enjoyed their company and hospitality immensely."

"Anything else?"

He shook his head and said, "Nope."

"Well," I said. "Think you might be missed."

"That's a nice thought, Everett," he said. "I appreciate it."

I pulled off my glove and reached over the fence.

"Safe travels," I said.

# 59.

That evening I ate a steak at Hal's Café before I paid Virgil and Allie a visit. As I approached the dark house I could see Allie through the window, playing her piano, and for the first time I actually thought she was playing pretty well. When I entered through the front gate I noticed Virgil sitting on the porch in the dark. There was a small amount of light coming through the window that provided a slight outline on one side of Virgil's face. He was leaning back in a corner with his boots on the rail, smoking a cigar.

"Evening," Virgil said.

"Evening," I said.

"How goes it?"

"Goes," I said.

"Nudge of Kentucky?" he said.

He held up his glass and I could see the amber liquid glow a little as it caught the spilling light from the window.

"Why not," I said.

As I walked up the steps, Allie stopped playing the piano and in a moment poked her head out the door.

"Why, Everett Hitch," she said.

"Why, Allie French," I said.

"How are you?"

"Fine . . . fine . . . nice night," I said.

"Oh, it is," she said.

"Don't stop on my account, Allie. I was enjoying that."

"Me, too," Virgil said.

"Oh," she said. "You two."

"No," I said. "Really."

"Y'all just tolerate my playing," she said. "I'm done for the evening. Besides, my hands are getting tired."

"Get Everett a glass," he said. "Would you please, Allie?"

"Indeed I will," she said.

Allie turned and walked back inside as I moved over on the porch by Virgil.

"What ya doing out here alone in the dark?"

"Sitting."

"Contemplating?"

"Am."

"Black?" I said.

Virgil nodded.

"Keeps turning in me."

"What can we do?"

"Don't know there is anything we can do, Everett."

"Nothing?"

I sat on the rail opposite Virgil and thought for a brief moment about what I was getting ready to say.

"Saw your brother earlier," I said.

"Half-brother," Virgil said.

Allie came out with two glasses.

"One for you and one for me," she said.

She held them out and Virgil poured us each a glass of Kentucky whiskey.

"He left," I said.

"Who left?" Allie said as she handed me one of the glasses in her hand.

"Valentine."

Allie put both of her hands to her sides before she said anything.

"What?" she said.

"Yep."

"What do you mean 'he left'?"

"Just that."

"Well . . ." she said, and then stammered her next words with a hint of growing agitation, "is . . . he coming back?"

"Don't think so."

"Well . . . where for Heaven's sakes?"

"Don't know."

Virgil sat back in his chair and didn't say anything.

"Did he say where he was going?" she said.

"Wasn't sure."

"He left without so much as a good-bye?"

"He did."

"Well . . . I just can't believe that."

"He named a few places he might end up."

Allie shook her head.

"End up?"

"He told me to tell you both how much he appreciated your company and hospitality."

Allie shook her head in disbelief and walked over by the rail near me and looked out.

"This is just awful," she said.

I looked at Virgil. His half-lit face showed no real reaction, but he did not meet my eye. He was looking at Allie, who was looking away.

"Why?" Virgil said. "Why is it so awful?"

"Why?" she said, without turning to look at Virgil. "Why . . ."

"A man has to do what a man has to do, Allie," Virgil said.

Allie turned and looked at Virgil.

"Oh . . . don't say that. A man? A man . . . Virgil . . ."

"You got to meet him," he said. "Visit with him. Hear stories about me as a kid."

"I know, Virgil . . . I know."

Virgil looked to me.

"I just wish . . ."

"What, Allie?"

"I don't know," she said as tears began to well up in her eyes.

"He did what he had to do," Virgil said.

"That does not mean he can't show us a little respect and common decency," Allie said. "Of at least coming by here and giving us a proper good-bye."

"I think it might have been hard for him," I said.

"Hard?" Allie said. "Why?"

"Oh," I said. "You know, Allie, how it is with family."

"Well, no, Everett," she said with a quiver in her voice. "Actually, I don't know . . . I don't know anyone in my family. I never have and I never will."

"Well, I'm sorry," I said.

"Not your fault, Everett," she said. "They just left, most of them I never, ever even knew, they all just sort of petered out of my life, nobody wanted me and I was left all alone."

"Well," Virgil said. "You're not alone anymore."

"First all this horrible trial stuff . . . and now this . . ."

Allie shook her head a little and walked away to the other side of the porch and stared out into the darkness. After a moment she lowered her head and started to sob.

# 60.

It was a full moon out as I climbed the stairs to my room above the survey office. It was hot and the two windows to my small room were open, but there was little breeze.

I took off my clothes and lay back on the bed. I thought about the last few days and how it was all coming together. About the Denver contingent, as Valentine referred to them. I thought about Black and how adamant he was, how demanding he was about the fact he was not the killer.

How Juniper was upset that he did not have a chance to fully cross-examine LaCroix. Juniper pleaded with the judge, but his request was denied. I agreed with Juniper's appeal, but it would be hard to fulfill his demand, given the fact that LaCroix's jaw was broken and he was not able to even open his mouth to speak.

Juniper appealed with the judge, insisting, saying LaCroix could respond with written word, but the judge would hear no more, not after Black's outburst, and Black was headed for the gallows.

I kept wondering about all of it, the trial, about the Denver men, about Roger and Ruth Ann Messenger and Boston Bill Black, about

Daphne actually being engaged to Black in the past, and I thought about the painter, Lawrence LaCroix, and what he testified he saw that day.

I sat up, wondered if sleep was going to happen. At half midnight I got tired of lying there so I got up. I put on my trousers, poured a whiskey, then opened the door and stepped out on the balcony. From somewhere in the evening I heard some music from one of the saloons on 5th Street. Then I looked down at the bottom of the steps and saw a figure in the dark.

"Everett?" she said. "It's me . . ."

"Daphne?"

"Yes. May I come up?"

"Sure."

I thought for a moment how she found me, then I remembered we walked by and I pointed the place out to her the night we were out on our walk. When she got to the top of the steps she practically fell into my arms.

"Oh, Everett."

"Come in."

I closed the door behind her and she reached up and pulled my head down and kissed me.

She kissed me hard. Then she kissed me on my cheeks and neck as if she were starving. I was without my shirt and she kissed my chest over and over, then looked up to me.

"I was sorry not to take you in when you came," she said.

"That's all right," I said.

"For the most part," she said, "I have been consoling Mr. Pritchard."

"I understand."

"Oh my God, Everett," she said.

"I know this is difficult," I said.

"What is so alarming for us is to learn that he . . . he . . . actually did this," she said. "That he in fact actually murdered that woman, that he is a murderer."

"I know."

"Is there anything we can do for him?" she said.

"Not that I can see," I said. "No."

She shook her head and turned away from me.

"It's like . . . like this is just a bad dream," she said. "But it is not, it's just a living nightmare."

She turned back to me.

"Do you have anything to drink?" she said. "Any alcohol, whiskey or something?"

"I do."

"Please, thank you," she said. "I have been nothing but a ball of nerves."

I poured her some whiskey and she drank it down in one gulp. She held out her glass and I poured her another one.

"Easy," I said.

She sipped the whiskey a little, then looked to my bed.

"May I sit, please?"

"Yes, of course."

I removed my shirt from the bed and she sat. She looked down at the glass clutched in her hand, then she drank the whiskey as if she were trying to kill something inside.

I started to put on my shirt, but she reached out and stopped me.

"No," she said. "Please . . ."

She removed the shirt from my grip, tossed it on the floor, and pulled me close to her. She kissed my stomach gently, from one side to the other. Then she looked up to me and undid the buttons on my trousers.

# 61.

I rode Ajax by the Gallows Door Cantina and Eloise stepped out from the shadows of the three-sided lean-to and waved to me as I passed. I continued on toward the gallows where the crowd was gathered to watch the hanging of Boston Bill Black. I did not see Virgil, Valentine, or Allie, or Chastain or Book, but the Denver contingent was there: Detective Lieutenant Banes, Detective Sergeant King, Captain McPherson, District Attorney Payne, and Roger Messenger's father, Chief Brady. They were all present, expectant, and waiting.

Everyone watched me as I rode up, dismounted, tied off Ajax, and climbed the gallows steps. The executioner was atop the structure, wearing a black hood along with two local ministers. Both I recognized, but I didn't know either one's name. We all said our how-do-you-dos and I stepped up to the noose and gave it a tug. I looked up to the rope draped over the gallows' top beam and turned to the executioner.

"Let's get this over with," I said.

The executioner nodded his head slowly, walked over to me, and put the noose around my neck. I looked into his eyes; all I could see were his eyes. He slipped the noose around my neck, then walked to the lever and pulled it. But it did not work. He kept working the lever back and forth, then . . . the rhythm of the lever was replaced by a knock on my door . . . followed by . . .

"Everett?"

I sat up in my bed . . .

"Everett?"

I looked around and could tell by the light it was the earliest part of daybreak. Daphne was sound asleep under my arm, and I eased myself out of the bed so as not to wake her and opened the door.

It was Deputy Book. He saw Daphne behind me in the bed and kind of lowered his head and took a step back.

"Sorry," he said with a whisper.

"Give me a sec," I said.

I put on my trousers, then stepped out the door.

"What is it?" I said, closing the door behind me.

"Bill Black," he said. "He escaped and took Truitt Shirley with him."

"Are you . . . what?"

"They are out, Everett," Book said.

"Anybody hurt?"

"No," Book said.

"How the hell did this happen?" I said.

"Looks like Black pried the bars from the window," Book said.

"What?"

Book nodded sharply.

"The strong sonofabitch pulled up the iron railings of his bunk that were bolted to the floor."

"You sure he didn't have help?" I said.

"Don't know for a fact, but it does not seem like it, Everett," Book said. "You just have to see for yourself."

"I'll be goddamn."

"I know," Book said. "I could not believe it. Just up and gone like that."

"Chastain and Virgil know?" I said.

"I came to get you first," Book said.

"When was this?"

"Well, I just this minute found out, so I'm not sure, no idea, really," Book said. "When I got in they were gone."

"How the hell did Truitt get out?"

"Looks like the bars were bent out on the backside of Truitt's, Black helping him, after he was free . . . Did the same thing but from the backside. Both are gone."

"What about the damn night watch?" I said. "Can't tell me they didn't hear anything."

Book shook his head.

"They did not hear a damn thing. We even had four guards on last night," Book said. "Two outside on the porch just in case of any shenanigans, someone trying to break Bill out, and two deputies inside. With the thickness of the door separating the office from the cells, they . . . well, apparently, they did not hear anything."

"Apparently," I said.

"Secure the outsides of this town. Get a man on each trail and road out of town, tell them to stay out of sight and to only try and stop them if they know for certain they can get the drop on them. Last thing we need is to lose one or some more of ours."

"What about Marshal Cole and Sheriff Chastain?"

"Send someone to get Chastain, I'll get Virgil, but get the deputies out now . . . right now, and get Virgil's horse and my horse saddled and ready. Get supplies, too, in case we are on the chase again, just need to be prepared."

Book nodded and turned to go.

"And Book," I said stopping him to look back at me, "just make sure nobody is on their heels."

"You got it," Book said, then descended the stairs.

I stepped back in the room and Daphne was still sound asleep. She looked like her namesake, an angel.

I sat on the bed next to her.

"Daphne," I said. "Daphne?"

I put a hand to each side of her shoulders.

"Daphne."

Her eyes snapped open, wide, full of fear. She reached up with both hands around my neck and choked me, staring at me in terror, as if she had no clue who I was.

# 62.

D aphne."
   I pulled her hands from my neck, but she remained tense and continued to fight with me.

"Daphne," I said, struggling with her tense arms. "Daphne, it's okay, it's me."

She stared at me for a moment, then slowly relaxed, letting go. The fearful expression on her face slowly softened when she realized she was not in danger.

"It's okay," I said. "It's me, Everett. You're just having a bad dream."

She remained staring at me then she softened some more and recessed back into the bed.

"Everett . . ."

"I'm here," I said.

She looked around and shook her head a little.

"My gosh," she said. "I'm sorry . . ."

"It's okay," I said. "You were obviously having a nightmare."

She nodded.

"You all right?" I said.

"Yes," she said. "Oh my God . . . Ugh . . . someone was after me, I don't know who . . . It was Bill, I think. I was being chased through the woods . . . and . . . I don't, can't remember everything, but . . . so awful . . . I was running, but I could not move quickly, you know, and I could not get away, then I was caught, he caught me, Bill caught me, and then you woke me up, thank God."

"I was right there with you," I said. "I woke in a bit of a fret myself."

She held her head.

"I drank your whiskey," she said. "I . . . I'm afraid I am not much of a drinker."

"Probably need some water?"

She sat up some and nodded, and I poured her a glass of water.

"Thank you," she said.

"Your dream," I said, "was not without some kind of foreshadowing, it seems."

"How so, Everett?"

I put on my shirt and buttoned it as she waited for me to answer her.

"It's Bill Black," I said.

"Yes?"

"He escaped last night."

She blinked at me a few times.

"What?"

I nodded.

"My God," she said, sitting up with a shocked look on her face. "What? How on earth . . . my God."

I sat in the corner chair and slipped on my boots.

"He's out and on the loose," I said. "Got out with Truitt Shirley."

"The man he was on the run with before?"

"Yep."

"My gosh. I just can't believe it."

"It happened," I said.

"How do you— How did you find out?"

"Deputy was by here just now."

"My God . . . what now?"

"Catch him."

Daphne's eyes were wide.

"I . . . what should I do?"

"You?" I said. "You don't do anything."

"But . . . I . . . I'm frightened."

"Nothing for you to be frightened about."

"But . . . I am, I . . ."

Her eyes darted around the room, as if she was thinking intently about something or imagining how he might get in or where she might hide.

"You need not be," I said.

She looked down and stared at the floor, shaking her head.

"This is not good," she said.

"No," I said. "It's not."

"It all seems so cruel," she said, almost as if she were talking to herself.

"Murder is cruel," I said.

She pulled her knees up to her chest and looked at me as I continued to dress.

"How did he escape?"

"Not real sure," I said.

"My God . . ." she said.

"We have some kind of idea . . . but the fact is, however he got out, whenever he got out, he's out."

She gathered the sheet and sat to the edge of the bed holding the fabric in front of her nakedness.

"Everett . . . I'm . . ."

"What?"

"Just scared is all."

"Why should you be scared?"

"I . . . I don't know."

"This has nothing to do with you, Daphne," I said. "He's out and he's running."

She stared at the floor long and hard, then looked up to me. Her eyes were wet.

"You must be careful," she said.

She looked like a spooked child holding the sheet in front of her.

"You don't need to worry about anything."

"But I do . . ."

"Don't. Besides, I always am careful," I said. "Part of my job description."

Like every morning, out of habit and correctness, I checked the cylinder of my Colt, then put it back in my holster and strapped the belt around my hip.

"You saw what he did to that man that witnessed him murdering that poor woman," she said. "He almost killed him right before our eyes."

"I did."

"He's an animal," she said.

"This is what I do, Daphne," I said. "What I have to do. It's my job to enforce the law. And it is against the law for a criminal to break out of jail where they have been incarcerated for a crime they have been charged and convicted of."

"But he's different, Everett," she said. "Very different."

"I thought you and Pritchard were on his side. Thought he was an innocent man?"

"We were . . . until this witness came forward and described what he did. Now my insecurities about what I thought might be real, could be real, are very real . . . I am scared to know the man I was once engaged to be married to is a cold-blooded vicious murderer. How could I have been so blind?"

"Not about being blind," I said. "People have good in them and people have bad in them, and in some people the bad . . . takes over and wins out."

"You believe that?"

"I do," I said.

I tied my bandanna around my neck, then picked up my eight-gauge.

"I'm sorry," she said. "I don't know why, but I'm just so fearful."

"No reason to be sorry," I said. "But there is nothing for you to be concerned with, just go back and stay put in your room."

"No," she said. "I don't want to go back there, not right now."

"Stay here, then."

"I . . . I don't want to be alone," she said. "He's a dangerous man."

I broke open the double barrel, confirmed there was a shell in each cylinder as I left them, then snapped it shut.

"So am I," I said.

She got to her feet and let the sheet fall to the floor and stood naked in front of me. Then she moved to me and put her arms around my neck and kissed me.

"I like that," she said.

# 63.

When I knocked on the door Virgil was already up and dressed. He answered the door in his stocking feet and holding a cup of coffee as he looked back and forth between Daphne and me.

"Bill Black is on the loose," I said. "Truitt, too."

Virgil reacted almost as if he had expected the news, but Allie came up behind him, throwing open the door wider, with a shocked look on her face.

"What?" she said. "Are you serious?"

"I am, Allie," I said.

"Be right with you, Everett," Virgil said, then drifted back into the house, leaving Allie standing in her sleeping gown with a look of complete disbelief on her face.

"Be all right for Daphne to stay here with you, Allie, until we get this settled, until she feels safe."

"Why, of course," Allie said.

"I'm so sorry, Allie," Daphne said. "I hope this is not an inconvenience."

"My God, are you serious? Come in this house this instant," Allie said as she practically jerked Daphne over the threshold. "Of course it's no inconvenience. What kind of silly comment is that? You poor, poor dear."

When I followed Allie and Daphne into the house, Virgil was coming back up the hall, carrying his gun belt and boots.

I quickly explained to Virgil all I knew about the escape, which prompted Allie to expound.

"This is just awful," she said. "How could Sheriff Chastain and his deputies let something like this happen?"

"They did nothing," Virgil said.

"Letting the killers go is not nothing."

"They got out, Allie, they escaped, you heard Everett," Virgil said as he sat on the piano bench and put on one of his boots. "They were not let out."

"It's lackadaisical and unprofessional, to say the least."

"Before you go accusing the sheriff's department, Allie," Virgil said as he pulled on his second boot, "why not let us sort this out and do our job."

"Yes, Virgil," she said politely. "I am not insensitive, I know you will protect us."

Allie turned to Daphne.

"He will," she said. "Everett, too. That's what they do."

Daphne smiled a weak smile and nodded a little.

"Regardless, it's awful," Allie said with a twist of her brow as if she had the need to snuff out her previous admonishments. "And now the whole town is unsafe."

"Before, you were sure as all hell Boston Bill Black was innocent," Virgil said as he got to his feet.

"That was before," Allie said.

Virgil picked up his gun belt.

"Now you're condemning the law enforcement as being just awful and leaving citizens unsafe."

Virgil strapped on his gun belt.

"Well, that was before he was proven guilty, Virgil," she said. "Now all I can think about is that there are murderers on the loose."

"Well," Virgil said as he pulled his Colt from his belt, checked the rounds, then snapped closed the loading gate. "Try not to think about it, Allie."

Daphne lowered her head, stifling tears.

"Oh, you poor thing," Allie said, pushing Daphne's hair from her eyes. "I know how you feel."

Allie sat her down on the sofa and held her hand, then looked up to Virgil.

"I feel just like Ms. Daphne here, Virgil," Allie said, then looked back to Virgil. "And . . . thank you, Virgil."

"For what?"

"Well . . . I think at times the unrest of my constitution adds up and sorts its way out as being ungrateful, but you need to know that is simply just not the case. This is just unnerving."

"I know, Allie," Virgil said as he put on his hat.

Allie looked to Daphne and smiled as she rubbed her hand between hers.

"It is going to be okay, Virgil and Everett know how to handle this."

"Thank you," Daphne said.

"We will do what we can," Virgil said.

He kissed Allie on the cheek and walked out the door. I turned to follow . . .

"Everett?" Daphne said as she got to her feet and came close to me by the door. "I would feel just mortified if something were to happen to you."

"Don't think I would feel good about that proposition, either," I said.

She reached up and pulled my head down to meet hers and kissed me.

"Oh, my," Allie said softly, and almost to herself.

# 64.

The early morning was quiet and the sun was slanting in through the openings of the buildings on 3rd Street as we walked to the sheriff's office. The shafts of yellow light reflected off the storefront glass enough to make us keep our brims down. It was still early, not much was open, and the streets were sparse of folks moving about.

"Maybe it's justice," I said.

"Maybe not," Virgil said.

We walked by in front of the hotel where the Coloradoans were staying. At the moment all was quiet and there was no one going in or coming out.

"Don't imagine the Denver contingent will be too happy," I said as we passed the hotel.

"No," Virgil said glancing at the hotel's front door. "I don't, either."

When we passed, Virgil looked back a little.

"Saw them earlier," Virgil said with a shake of his head.

"Like they're waiting around for rut or harvest," I said.

"'Fraid the yield's not so good," Virgil said.

"Currently," I said.

"I had a brief visit with the chief," Virgil said.

"And?"

"He's an unfriendly hombre," Virgil said. "Remembered him, too."

"Did?"

"Yep."

"Where?"

"Long time ago. He was a young Otero County sheriff. I remembered him for certain. He was with a group of others up on the Purgatoire River, up by Bent's last place," Virgil said. "Forever ago now. I was passing through when brouhaha happened there. Him and the others found a young black kid they'd been chasing."

When we came to the end of the street we saw one of Chastain's deputies. Luce, a stout-looking fellow with a thick mustache that draped down to the bottom of his chin. He was standing back off the street, holding his rifle across his beer gut and smoking a cigarette. He dropped it and crushed it under his foot when he saw us crossing the street.

"Seen anything, Luce?" I said.

"No, sir," he said. "Nothing. I been right here so I can see both directions leading off."

"Okay," I said. "Just stay alert and alive."

"Yes, sir," he said.

We walked on a ways and Virgil continued.

"They strung up the black kid, they claimed he had stolen a horse. He was just a boy. Messenger was . . . hell, real young then, that's why I didn't recognize him, really. Don't think he recognized me, either, but I remember the name, 'cause the kid was begging not to die, pleading, Mr. Messenger, please, I didn't do it . . . That I remember."

"Well, hell," I said. "Guess he's got a soft spot in his heart for hanging."

Virgil didn't say anything.

When we got to the sheriff's office, Chastain and Book led us into the cell room to have a look at Black's escape wreckage as they informed us on what was taking place.

"We got everybody out looking," Chastain said.

"When I got here and found out they were gone," Book said. "I got everybody moving right away."

"Like you told Book, we got someone on lookout at every road trail leading out of town," Chastain said.

"What time was that?" Virgil said.

"'Bout five or so," Book said.

"If the sumbitches ain't already gone from Appaloosa, they won't get gone," Chastain said. "Not this time."

"We even sent four men down to the ford," Book said. "In case they had that on their mind again."

Chastain walked into Black's cell.

"Can't believe this shit?" Chastain said, shaking his head and looking at Black's cell window that was missing its bars. "That's what we goddamn get for having strong damn bedrails."

He picked up one of the bars that had been removed from the window.

"Look at this shit," Chastain said. "He's a big strong sumbitch, I will give him that. He managed to work those bed railings free that were bolted to the goddamn floor. Then he used them to pry the bars inside the window."

"That opening was tight for him, too," Book said. "Hard to see how he got his big frame through there."

"Well, he damn sure did. Then he got goddamn Truitt out," Chastain said, pointing to the window in Truitt's cell. "He got out and then he pried those damn bars there from the outside."

"I found these outside on the ground under Truitt's window," Book said, pointing to the rails leaning against the wall. "Been a lot of big, tough, strong men locked in these cells and, well, this is certainly a first."

"When did somebody last have eyes on them?" Virgil said.

"Neil and Matt were on night duty," Book said. "Neil said he shut the door here a little past ten o'clock."

Book looked over and picked up a Bible and set it on the small table in Black's cell.

"Neil said Black asked for this Bible," Book said as he fanned the pages. "Neil said he gave it to him and then shut the door. That was the last anyone saw of them."

Virgil looked at me.

"Black got started right away on getting this frame out of the floor," Virgil said.

"Took a while, too, I suspect," I said.

Virgil nodded.

"Don't figure they been out all that long," Virgil said.

Melvin and Luis, two of Chastain's young deputies, came quickly into the office. Melvin was a big strapping kid covered with a constellation of freckles and Luis was a small Mexican fella with deep-set eyes and a scruffy goatee.

They were both out of breath as they poked their heads in the door.

"We got something," Luis said, leaning over and breathing hard.

"What?" Chastain said.

"Found two horses and two saddles that were stolen early this morning," Melvin said.

"Where?" Virgil said as he moved toward Melvin and Luis.

The two deputies backed into the front office with Virgil. Chastain, Book, and I followed.

"They were taken from the corral behind Mankin's Mining outfit at the end of Fourth," Melvin said with a point in that direction.

"Anybody see Black or Truitt?" Chastain said.

"No, sir," Luis said. "Mr. Mankin said he found one of his three horses standing outside of his bedroom window this morning."

Melvin quickly nodded in agreement.

"Said it woke him up," Melvin said. "'Chewing on the damn sill of the window. Said he didn't think too much about it, thought the other two horses were just out, wandering around grazing someplace, then he saw the shed door was open, too, looked inside and found that two of his saddles were missing."

"What time was this?" Virgil said.

Luis looked to Melvin.

"About four this morning," Melvin said.

"You boys get back out there and check with the others," Virgil said to Melvin and Luis, "see if anybody's seen anything."

Virgil followed them out onto the boardwalk and we followed Virgil.

"Everybody," Virgil said to Melvin and Luis as they mounted up, "needs to keep their eyes open."

Melvin and Luis swung up in a hurry and rode off.

Chastain looked at his watch.

"Almost seven now," he said.

"They most likely got out and got those horses pretty close to when Mankin found them gone," I said.

"Still kind of early," Book said. "Not too many folks up and moving about just yet."

"What now?" Chastain said.

Virgil thought for a moment, then said, "Where's the painter?"

# 65.

L aCroix?" Chastain said.

"Yep," Virgil said.

Chastain shook his head and looked at me.

"Not seen him," I said.

"Me, either," Chastain said.

"Been over a week since Black put him in the hospital," I said.

"Last time I laid eyes on him," Chastain said, "was when he was carried out of the courtroom, flat on his back on a stretcher."

"Could be long gone," I said.

"I did talk with Doc Burris about him," Chastain said. "Saw him at the café. He said LaCroix was pissing blood. But that was not long after he was there in the hospital. Even then the Doc said he thought he was going to be all right, would be moving on, just needed to recover, heal up and such, thought the pissing blood business would go away . . . why?"

"There is a chance he could still be here licking his wounds," I said.

Chastain looked to me, then to Virgil.

"You think Black would go after LaCroix?" Chastain said.

"Might," Virgil said.

Chastain nodded.

"Be dumb of him, though, don't you think?" Chastain said. "To get out of jail and bother with him?"

"Maybe not," Virgil said.

"He damn sure tried to kill him in the courtroom that day. Damn near beat that poor sumbitch within an inch of his life before we could pull him off."

Virgil nodded.

"In court," he said. "He did."

Virgil looked at me.

Chastain looked back and forth between us and nodded a little.

"But now you don't think so?" Chastain said.

"Don't know," Virgil said. "Black was damn sure mad enough to kill, no doubt about that. But now could be a different story."

"Get to the crux," I said.

"It's his only chance," Virgil said.

Chastain looked back and forth between Virgil and me again and shook his head.

"That guy, LaCroix. He seemed pretty straightforward convincing to me, Virgil," Chastain said.

"He was calm," I said.

"Until he was trying to crawdad backward to save his life," Chastain said.

Virgil stood looking off down the street but didn't say anything.

"LaCroix seemed solid to me," Chastain said, "and though the judge was . . . I don't know, kind of off goddamn kilter somewhat, I believe the jury and judge made the right decision."

"There is that," Virgil said.

"Let's say he did lie about Black," Chastain said. "Why? Why would he do that?"

"Don't know," Virgil said.

Chastain looked at the ground and nodded some.

"Something personal," he said.

"Or somebody put him up to it," I said. "One of the two."

"Or not," Virgil said.

"But that is your hunch?" Chastain said.

"Could be something to it," Virgil said.

"Who?" Chastain said. "Why?"

"Cops, maybe," I said.

"Why, though?" Chastain said. "Roger is dead and gone. Damn sure too late to clear him."

I shook my head.

"Or someone just wanted to see Black fucking hang," Chastain said.

"Maybe," I said. "Though Black thought he was the only one that was having his way with Ruth Ann, there has been plenty of reason not to buy into that theory."

Virgil nodded some.

"Let's say it is the cops, I mean, it could be, I reckon," Chastain said, "but why do you think it'd be so goddamn important to hang Black, just to clear the Messenger name."

We thought about that for a moment, and then Chastain said, "You're thinking Black could be innocent? Aren't you?"

"Well, for the purposes of what I'm hunching here, it has to do with what *he* thinks," Virgil said.

"Could make sense I guess that he'd go after LaCroix to prove he lied about what he saw," Chastain said.

"Like you say, though, not sure he would go to that kind of trouble," I said.

"But he could," Chastain said with a shrug.

"An escapee always has a chance to move on, go elsewhere," Virgil said, "but in the back of his mind there is always the constant threat he's going to get caught or shot."

"Hospital?" Chastain said.

Virgil nodded.

"Proof will be in the pudding," Virgil said.

# 66.

We left Book to hold down the office and walked over to the hospital. When we walked in we found Doc Burris right away. He was bent over and in the process of trying to find the right key to unlock his office door. He glanced up at us.

"Am I under arrest?" he said.

"Morning, Doc," Virgil said.

"I suppose it is," he said, thumbing through the keys in his hand. "I can never find the right damn key, though . . . oh, hold on, there it is."

He unlocked and opened the office door, then looked over the top of his spectacles at us.

"You look like you want something."

"Looking for the Englishman," Virgil said. "Lawrence LaCroix."

"He's not here," Doc said. "He was, of course, but he is no longer here. Why?"

"Any idea where he is?"

Doc shook his head

"He might have left," he said. "Here. Appaloosa. He wanted to leave the moment he got here. He could not get out soon enough. He was, however, in a lot of pain and it hurt for him to move, so he might still be here, I don't know. He wanted to get out and I had no reason for him not to get out. Free country . . . He might be at his hotel. I don't know."

"Know what hotel?" Virgil said.

Doc shook his head

"No," he said, "sorry, I have no idea . . . He walked out of here on a pair of crutches and I've not seen him since."

"When was that?" I said.

Doc thought for a moment.

"Two days ago."

"Anyone been here looking for him?" Virgil said.

"Nobody but you," he said. "Might I ask, who or whom are you looking for?"

"Bill Black," Virgil said frankly.

Doc stood up tall and looked at us over the top of his spectacles.

"Bill Black?" Doc said.

"Yep," Virgil said. "He got out."

"He escaped?"

Virgil nodded.

"And you believe he would come here?"

"Maybe?"

"To complete what he started?"

"Could be . . ." Virgil said. "Who's been working here this morning? Anyone but you?"

Doc shook his head.

"We don't have anyone staying here at the moment in need of night care, so no."

"So nobody else?" Virgil said.

Doc shook his head.

"We have my two nurses that are here when they are needed, and they work doing this and that when not needed, but they are not here. There is Buck, though. You know Buck, he keeps the place clean . . . opens up in the morning, closes, that sort of thing, but I've not seen him yet this morning . . . He's here somewhere, though . . ."

Virgil nodded and looked to me.

"Let me see if I can find him," Doc said. "Might be hauling trash, let me see . . ."

Doc turned and walked to the back of the lobby toward the rear of the building and called out the open door leading to the back section of the hospital.

"Buck," Doc said.

He waited a few seconds and there was no answer, then Doc called out louder, *"Buck!"*

Buck answered, *"Yes, sir."*

"Come here, will you. I want to ask you something."

Doc turned and walked back toward us.

"Bill Black is out," Doc said. "That is certainly one way to get a stay of execution."

"For the moment," Virgil said.

"I would ask you how he escaped, but I won't," Doc said. "I don't imagine that is a topic worth discussing."

We heard Buck coming up the hall. He was a big jovial ex-slave we all knew from working odd jobs around town. He came through the back door with a mop in his hand and stopped in his tracks when he saw us. He had that wide-eyed look of surprise that made me think he just might have thought we were looking for him.

"What is it?"

"You see anyone this morning when you opened up?" Doc said.

Buck looked at each of us in turn, then shook his head.

"No, sir," he said. "I ain't . . ."

Doc nodded, then looked to us.

"Sorry," he said.

"But," Buck said, "I can tell you this, there sure 'nough was someone here 'fore I got here this morning."

"What?" Doc said.

"Sure 'nough," Buck said, nodding.

"How do you know, Buck?" Virgil said.

"The back door was open," he said.

"You sure you didn't leave it unlocked last night?" Doc said.

Buck nodded and said, "I'm real sure . . . Someone got in the back door . . . there was dirt on the floor."

"What?" Doc said.

"Yes, sir. When I got here, I come up the back steps back here, like I always do, and I got out my keys to open the door and it was wide open."

"Who all has a key?" I said.

"Buck, Nurse Crain, and me," Doc said.

"What about her?" Virgil said.

"She was here yesterday, but she for sure left before me," Buck said.

"You sure?" Doc said.

Buck nodded.

"Nobody was here. She was gone and I locked it, Doc. Not sure how it was unlocked, but it was wide open, and there was, like I say . . . bits of dirt on the floor and on the stairs."

"Anything missing?" Doc said.

"No, sir," Buck said. "Not that I can tell."

"Were there any windows left open?" Virgil said.

"No," Buck said. "I do my routine when I leave here. Them windows all got locks on them and I lock 'em when we are gone, no matter how hot it is out."

# 67.

We had a quick look around the hospital to see if there was some kind of sign that would give us helpful information regarding the break-in, but found nothing that stuck out.

When we left the hospital, Chastain was the first out the door. He stopped on the top step, looking off down the street.

"Oh, shit . . ." he said. "Lookie here."

"Here we go," I said.

Marching up the street came the Denver contingent. Every one of them: Payne, Banes, King, McPherson, and they were being led by the chief of police. Brady Messenger.

"I don't imagine they are none too happy," I said.

"No," Virgil said. "I don't imagine, either."

"News travels fast," I said.

"The whole unit," Chastain said.

"Damn sure is," I said.

"Only a matter of time," Virgil said.

We descended the stairs and turned in their direction. We walked toward them a ways, then stopped in the middle of the street in front of a row of mining tool shops and waited for them to get to us. It was obvious the chief was agitated and intense as he strutted purposefully toward us.

"Ain't that a sight," Chastain said under his breath. "He looks like a lit' ol' Banty rooster."

We waited as they neared, and when they were within conversation range Virgil tipped back his hat.

"Good morning," Virgil said.

Chief Messenger waved at the salutation like he was shooing a fly in front of his nose.

"We just heard the goddamn news," Chief Messenger said.

"What news?"

"How could you have let this . . . this fucking happen?" Chief Messenger said.

Virgil glanced at me, then looked back to Chief Messenger.

"What?" Virgil said.

"Don't fuck around with me, Marshal Cole," Chief Messenger said, holding up a bony finger. "I am not in the mood, nor am I ever someone you want to fuck with."

Virgil smiled just a little, but did not respond right away. If he had feathers or the inclination to ruffle them, which he had neither of, this damn sure would have done it. But Virgil Cole was not a man that engaged in another man's ignorance, disdain, or discord. Fact was, it was these kinds of ignoble instants, moments of another person's righteous, self-obsessed importance, that made Virgil the noble man that he was.

"What news?" Virgil said.

"Goddamn it," he said. "Bill Black escaping, of course."

Virgil said nothing and all I could think about was what Valentine had told us about Messenger's church life and how right now he seemed to be about as far from a pulpit pounder as you could find.

Chief Messenger looked behind us to the hospital.

"What were you doing there?" the chief said with a point. "Was he there at the . . . the hospital?"

"Why would Bill Black be at the hospital?" Virgil said.

"What?"

"Do you know?" Virgil said.

"What are you goddamn getting at?"

Virgil turned and looked to the hospital, then turned back to the chief.

"Simple question," Virgil said.

"I don't know what you mean," the chief said with his chest puffed up.

"What is it you are implying?" McPherson said.

"Not implying," Virgil said. "I can rephrase the question, make it even simpler. Do any of you know why Bill Black would pay a visit to the hospital?"

"To . . . to finish what he started, of course," Chief Messenger said. "Why else?"

"You tell me," Virgil said.

"He's a convicted murderer, Marshal," Chief Messenger said.

Virgil looked to me and smiled a bit then looked back to the chief.

"In that case," Virgil said, "it might be best you stay in your rooms and lock the doors."

"What?" Chief Messenger said with a snarl.

"I don't think Bill Black is too pleased with any of you, and if he's the killer you are convinced he is, it might be best to stay out of sight so you don't get hurt."

The chief's face turned redder than it already was.

"We will do no such thing," the chief said. "There is a killer on the loose, he got loose under your watch, and he will be fucking found this time under my watch and he will be hung."

"Under your watch?" Virgil said.

"You heard me," Chief Messenger said.

Virgil smiled.

"Be better than a good idea you don't do anything stupid," Virgil said.

"*What?*" Chief Messenger said, jerking his head back as if he'd been slapped.

"Don't want to find you or any of your men breaking the law," Virgil said. "With all that is going on here, it'd be a real shame to have to arrest you . . . or them, or all of you."

The little man moved a bit closer to Virgil.

"Don't cross me, Marshal."

"Just letting you know you don't want to find yourself in a situation where we'd have to lock you up."

"Of all the audacity," Chief Messenger said.

"That, too," Virgil said. "The main thing in all this is for you to make certain you don't break any laws and that you stay out of our way."

Virgil moved through the men. The contingent parted and Chastain and I followed Virgil.

"Who do you think you are, Marshal Cole?" the chief said with a low growl.

Virgil stopped and looked back at the chief.

"You just answered your own question."

"You better beware, Marshal Cole. I will have your badge removed so fast you won't know what hit you."

Big Captain McPherson stepped up in between the chief and Virgil.

"Marshal Cole," McPherson said, smoothing with a smile that was nothing more than an attempt to calm, "I don't need to point out the chief here has lost a son."

"No," Virgil said. "You don't."

"And we lost a colleague," McPherson said.

"Lost one of ours, too," Virgil said.

"Then you must understand our obvious disappointment about what has happened here."

Virgil didn't say anything.

McPherson tilted his head to the side and pulled up on his belt as he glanced to the other Coloradoans for support.

"So," McPherson said with his palms up and out, "I'm sure you understand there is no reason for impertinence here."

Virgil smiled. I was pretty sure he did not know the meaning of the word, but by its simple phrasing he knew the gist.

"There is room for every good man," Virgil said. "There is no room for taking the law into your own hands . . . As long as you understand that."

"Of course," McPherson said with a nod and a slight but obvious grimace.

McPherson looked to the contingent again, then back to Virgil.

"We understand," he said.

*"Muy bueno,"* Virgil said.

Virgil started to walk.

"Can you tell us what you know?" McPherson said.

Virgil moved back toward McPherson a bit.

"All we know for certain is Bill Black is out and though he claims he is innocent, we will do what we have to do and hunt him down and recapture him. That's the law and that is what we will do."

"All killers posture and claim their innocence, one way or the other," McPherson said.

"I have a real good handle on that, Captain," Virgil said.

# 68.

We left the Coloradoans standing in the street, and Virgil, Chastain, and I started back toward the office.

"They got some goddamn gall, them boys," Chastain said, looking back at them as we rounded the corner.

"They do," I said.

"Think they'll be a problem?" Chastain said.

"They already are," Virgil said.

"Showed their face card," Chastain said.

"Yes, but covered their show on the fact that Black was going after LaCroix to kill him and not as an attempt to exonerate himself."

Virgil nodded.

"What now?" Chastain said.

We walked for a moment and Virgil said nothing.

"You want me to check the hotels?" Chastain said. "See if we can find LaCroix?"

"Don't think there is any need," Virgil said.

"You think he's gone?" Chastain said.

"More than likely," Virgil said. "But let's check just the same."

We searched the hotels and bunkhouses for LaCroix but found nothing. The depot had no record of LaCroix traveling back to Denver, and no one working the ticket sales had any recollection of seeing him, either.

The search for Bill Black and Truitt Shirley yielded the same. The deputies that stood watch on the thoroughfares leading out of town throughout the day had not seen any sign of Black and Truitt, and by late in the afternoon, the whole of the Appaloosa law enforcement came up empty-handed.

After the sun went down a cool breeze came in, and with it the smell of rain. We continued to search the insides and outsides of the town, and by ten in the evening a steady rain was falling and we still had found no sign of the escapees.

"By God unbelievable," Chastain said as we walked back into the office. "I just don't see how they got out without some swinging dick seeing 'em?"

"It damn sure happened," I said.

"Damn sure did," Chastain said, taking off his slicker and hanging it on the back of his chair.

"They had to have got out and gone early."

Virgil didn't say anything as he set his Winchester in the gun rack by the door, then took off his slicker and hung it on a nail by the rack. I removed my long coat, too, and hung it next to Virgil's.

"I could have swore by now someone would have something," Chastain said.

Virgil turned back and looked out onto the street. After a second he leaned on the doorjamb.

Book walked in from the cell hall.

"Hey," he said.

"Hey, Book," Chastain said.

Virgil glanced back.

"Anything?" Book said.

Chastain shook his head.

"Nope," he said. "'Fraid not."

"Well," Book said, "I been right here, like you said for me to do. I told everybody to keep looking until midnight and not to come back here until then and we'd regroup . . ."

Chastain nodded and dropped in the chair behind his desk.

"Coffee?" Book said. "Just made it."

Virgil glanced back and nodded.

"Sure, Book," he said.

Book poured us all a cup.

"Did you see the Denver lawmen out there tonight?" Book said.

"We did not," I said. "Why?"

Virgil looked back.

"Just thought you might have seen them, they got themselves mounted, some of them, anyway. They stopped by here. There were four of them on horseback that came by, including Chief Messenger. Not sure where they procured the horses, but they have them. I believe the only one missing was the DA, Payne."

"What did they want?" Virgil said.

"Just wanted to know if Black had been apprehended," he said.

"What did you tell them?" I said.

"I told them no, and they rode off."

"So they got horses," Chastain said. "That just makes it easier for them to travel the wrong direction quicker."

"Yes, sir," Book said. "I concur, Sheriff. Wholeheartedly."

Chastain looked to Virgil.

"What do you want to do?" he said.

"Only thing we can do is be ready to ride in the morning," Virgil said. "We won't ride a wrong direction, we will scout this out from the inside out."

I nodded.

"Circle out until we find someone that has seen them, and get on their trail?" I said.

Virgil nodded.

"Can't give up," he said.

Virgil took a sip of coffee, then looked out the door to the falling rain. In the far distance there was some lightning. It was offering flashes of silver over the tops of the buildings across the street.

"Can't give up," Virgil said again. "Not till we find him."

# 69.

The rain was falling steady now as we walked back toward the house. We passed the Colcord Hotel, where the Denver contingent was boarded. This time when we passed we saw Detective Lieutenant Banes on the porch with a glass in his hand.

"Hey, there," Banes said.

He was sitting in a chair, but stood up and moved a bit closer to the rail.

"Evening," he said.

"Evening," I said.

Of the whole contingent, Banes was the only one that had shown himself as being somewhat regular and not a pain in the ass.

"Any luck?"

"Not as of yet."

"Still at it?"

"We are," I said.

"Hell of a day."

"Is," I said.

"Guess you heard the chief has us mounted to ride."

"We did," I said.

"He's hell-bent."

"That's obvious," I said.

"Like a drink?" Banes said, holding up his glass.

"No, thanks," Virgil said.

Banes looked back to see if anyone might be coming out through the door.

"Well, let me just say . . . or offer my apologies."

Virgil moved in, walked up a few steps out of the rain, and I followed.

"For?" Virgil said.

"My superiors," he said.

Virgil said nothing.

"Look," he said. "I'm not certain of anything. And I don't know of anything underhanded here. But I do know this has been a bunch of bullshit for you two."

"How so?" I said.

"Having to deal with any of this shit in the first place," he said. "Trial should have been in Denver to begin with, but because of Truitt shooting Roger here and Black involved in the crime it all spilled out here on your porch . . . bunch of bullshit."

"Where is LaCroix?" Virgil said.

Banes shook his head.

"I got no idea," he said.

"What's the story with LaCroix?" Virgil said.

"I really know nothing about him."

"Why was he not here the first day of the trial?"

"Don't know."

"What do you know?"

"All I know is he contacted the office in Denver and said he had information about the murder of Ruth Ann Messenger."

"Did you know what the information was?"

"No, not specifically. We received a wire he was an eyewitness and was on his way here to testify," Banes said. "Really, that is all I know."

"You can't tell me the chief was not thinking that Black would get out and try to find him," I said.

"I can't tell you, no. But like I say, I don't know of anything underhanded here, I don't, and also like I told you before, I was not so certain this was not Roger's doing."

"You still feel that way?"

"Look, as far as I know this LaCroix was as legit as can be, so I have to believe what was said. Seemed to be convincing and earnest, a normal kind of guy and calm as hell until he was attacked. And then Black going after him like he did gained the fella a shitload of juror sympathy."

"And you don't think the chief wants to see Black hung because it will clear his family name as well as his conscience," I said.

"There has to be truth to that. That would be what any man would want for his family," Banes said, then held up his index finger, "especially if it were in fact a valid truth."

"Was anybody else fucking Ruth Ann that you know of?" Virgil said.

"No," he said.

Virgil nodded a bit.

"If there is anything I can help you with," Banes said, "I will."

"One thing that would be helpful," Virgil said.

"What's that?"

"If you do find Black before we do, it'd be a good idea that he's not accidently strung up," Virgil said.

Banes nodded a little and held up his glass.

We backed down the stairs and moved on.

"He's straight," I said.

"Seems," Virgil said.

We walked on up the street and crossed through the alley to Virgil's place.

I was thinking about seeing Daphne as we walked. I thought about sleeping with her again tonight and feeling her warm body next to me. I thought about maybe sleeping with her for a good while, not just tonight but other nights to follow. Most of the women I had any kind of sustained relationship with had either been whores, or in my dreams, or disappearing fortune tellers.

The light was dim when we entered the house. There was but one lamp burning and it was atop Allie's piano. We figured Allie and Daphne to be asleep.

When we stepped inside, though, we knew right away something was not right. Something was most definitely wrong. The first thing that stuck out was Allie and the way she was sitting.

She was at her piano, but not facing the piano. She was sitting straight back on the bench with her back to the keys. Sitting directly across from her was Daphne. She was clutching a pillow to her chest as if it were a shield. Then I saw the problem. I saw it the same moment that Virgil did.

Sitting in the dark corner was Bill Black holding a pistol in one hand and a bottle of Virgil's Kentucky whiskey in the other. The pistol was pointed straight out between Daphne and Allie.

"We been waiting for you," he said.

# 70.

Put the gun down," Virgil said.

"No."

"Put it down," Virgil said.

He shook his head and took a swig of the Kentucky.

"No."

"You got no reason to do this," Virgil said.

Black laughed.

"Bullshit," he said.

The bottle in Black's hand was nearly empty and it was clear he was beyond drunk.

"You are not in charge here," he said.

Both Allie and Daphne sat still, rigid with fear.

"I got no choice other than this," Black said.

"Sure you do," Virgil said.

"Not really," Black said.

"Put the gun down," Virgil said.

He smiled.

"You're not in charge here," he said.

"Do like I tell you."

He shook his head.

"No. Besides, this going the wrong way here," he said, waving the gun, "has no real impact on me, because . . . because . . . you see, I'm a dead man."

"No reason to hurt someone else," I said.

He smiled.

"Everybody thinks I killed that bitch."

"Right now, all you need to do," Virgil said, "is give me the gun."

"I did not do it," he said.

"What do you want, Black?"

"I want to be free."

"Let me help you."

"How can you help me?"

"Put the gun down and let's talk about this."

"Fuck talking," he said. "Look where talking has got me."

"Why this, Black?" I said. "This can't help you."

"I'd rather hang than be on the run for something I did not do."

"Let us help you."

"How are you going to do that?"

Virgil moved a little toward him.

"Just give me the gun."

Black quickly pointed the gun at Virgil.

"Back!" he said.

Allie and Daphne jumped.

"Easy," Virgil said. "Just be easy."

"Back," he said.

"Okay," Virgil said.

Virgil moved back a bit.

"Bill," Daphne said. "Don't do this. Be reasonable."

"Reasonable? I should have married you when I had the chance," he said. "I fucked up."

"Give him the gun, Bill," she said. "Don't do this."

Virgil nodded and reached out a little.

"Just stay the fuck back."

"You're drunk," Virgil said. "You're not thinking clearly."

"The hell you say."

"Let's go about this another way," Virgil said.

"I want the goddamn truth to be told."

"Okay," Virgil said. "Good."

Black's words were slurry. He was bleary-eyed and drunk tired.

"That fucker lied."

"Okay," Virgil said

Black started to cry. He looked down a little.

Virgil moved slightly but Black raised the gun up.

"Goddamn it," he said.

Virgil backed away with his hands up and clear from his sides.

"Okay, okay, let's just settle down here . . . settle down . . ." Virgil said.

After a moment Black seemed to relax a little.

"That's it," Virgil said. "Okay . . . okay . . . so . . . where is Truitt?"

"Oh, good," he said.

"Good?"

"You did not catch him? He got out," he said. "Got away, I'm fucking glad of that. I was uncertain. I hope he can keep running and never get caught. Me on the other hand, I have no intention of running. I only got out to prove I did not do this."

Black's head lowered, and when it did Daphne threw the pillow she had clutched to her chest at him and Virgil charged on him fast and grabbed the gun. Virgil's force knocked Black from the chair, and as the two men fell the gun went off. Allie screamed as the flash kicked from the barrel out into the dark room. The noise was deafening.

# 71.

It was not Sunday, but church bells sounded out across Appaloosa. Fact was, it was Friday, the day before the July Fourth grand opening of the Maison de Daphne casino.

The bells were not for celebration, however; they were nothing other than the respectful reminder that it was execution day for Boston Bill Black, a common solemn announcement for prayer and remembrance.

Black was back behind bars, awaiting execution. There was one good cell remaining in the jail and it was now, for obvious reasons, minus the bed frame.

But Black was resolved now. He had remained quiet after the incident at Virgil and Allie's. He was now a man riddled with shame and remorse, and he had no fight.

The shot he fired hit Daphne, and though it was not fatal, it was serious enough for her to require surgery and bed rest for recovery. The bullet hit her just under her arm, where it remained until Doc Burris operated to remove it.

After the incident at Virgil's home with Black, Virgil was convinced more than ever of Black's innocence. He wanted to have Callison reopen the case and reevaluate the findings against Black, but the judge would have none of it. Especially now that Black had escaped and shot Daphne. Virgil explained to Callison the shot that hit Daphne was accidental and not intentional, but Virgil's offering fell on deaf ears and Callison closed the book.

So the long and sordid ordeal was nearly over, and as Valentine had said, the sick idea of having the execution on July 3 remained a constant.

It was a beautiful day. The air was crisp and it had cooled off some since the rain. I listened to the bells as they rang and rang while I walked to the hospital.

When I entered I saw Buck at the end of the hall pushing a broom. He stopped and looked to me as the bells continued to ring. He stood there, then nodded a little as if he were saying hello, then he went back to sweeping.

Allie was sitting next to Daphne's bed with Hollis Pritchard when I entered the hospital room.

"Everett," Allie said.

Daphne turned, looking to me.

"Oh, Everett," Daphne said as she held out her hand. "The bells?"

"I know," I said.

"So sad," she said as tears welled up in her eyes.

"Oh," Allie said, dabbing a tear from her eye with a handkerchief, "Must they, Everett?"

"Be over soon enough," I said.

"I have to say," Daphne said, "I'm thankful I am not out today, on the street. I don't think I could take it."

We listened while the bells tolled. The sound echoed hauntingly throughout the hospital. After a moment they stopped and we were all silent.

Then Pritchard said, "Doc Burris said you can get out tomorrow."

"Yes," she said. "The opening . . ."

"Forget that," he said. "This timing is . . ."

"I know," she said.

"You just rest," he said.

"The doctor said I could briefly attend," she said.

Pritchard shook his head.

"No," he said. "Not necessary."

"But it's my namesake," she said.

"Clearly enough," he said, "and if I did not need to be there I would not. This is not a time for celebration . . . I know I don't want it. It's most unfortunate."

"I'm sorry, Mr. Pritchard, I just . . ."

He shook his head and got to his feet. He walked closer to the bed.

"My God, dear, there is nothing to be sorry about," he said, shaking his head. "This is all just awful."

"I know . . ." she said.

"I would postpone this, but there is too much in motion now," he said.

He leaned in and kissed her forehead.

"I will see you tomorrow at some point."

"Okay," she said.

He smiled at Allie and me, then walked out of the room. She watched after him for a moment, then looked to me.

"I'm so glad you are here," she said.

"Me, too."

"She looks simply beautiful," Allie said, "don't you think, Everett?"

"I do."

"Oh, please," she said. "I don't know what I would have done if it weren't for the both of you."

She looked to me and smiled weakly.

"So, when is this going to happen, Everett?"

I looked at my watch.

"About an hour from now."

She nodded, then looked away, out the window.

# 72.

Thirty minutes prior to the hanging, Virgil and I walked to the gallows, and when we rounded the corner it appeared the whole town was waiting to witness the hanging of Boston Bill Black.

"Good goddamn," Virgil said. "Don't these folks have something better to do than to watch a man die?"

"Guess not."

We walked past the Gallows Door Cantina and Eloise looked up and offered a wave just like the one she gave me in my dream, but this was no dream, not this time, this time it was real and it was happening.

The Gallows Door Cantina was crowded with happy and upbeat beer drinkers. It was a celebration for people to gather for a hanging. Hangings had become as much a spectator event as horse racing and boxing.

When we got close, we could see the Denver contingent standing near the gallows.

"Looks like the Coloradoans got here good and early so they had a good spot," I said.

"Does," Virgil said shaking his head.

Sitting in a covered buggy on a rise just behind the gallows was Judge Callison. He was sitting back under the buggy's shade, smoking a cigar.

Atop the gallows stood the executioner and the two main Appaloosa ministers, one from the Methodist church and the other from the Baptist church.

Virgil and I walked around the crowd and moved up the rise and stood near the judge.

He looked over to us and waited a moment before he said anything.

"You did all you could do, fellas," he said. "You are both good lawmen."

We looked to him but didn't say anything. There was really nothing to say.

"What we do is never easy," he said.

Again, we said nothing.

"I been at this for almost fifty years now . . ."

He puffed on his cigar for a moment, looking at the gallows.

"Tried my first murder case when I was just twenty-one. I defended a man I knew was innocent. I would have bet my life on it. He convinced me of it but not the jury. I lost the case and he was sentenced to hang. I was sure heartbroken, thought I had really let him and his family down. I damn near quit right then and there. When he walked to the gallows he looked to the parents of the fellow he was accused of murdering and said, 'I would do it again if I had the chance' . . . That was my first hanging . . ."

Someone in the crowd shouted, "Here he comes."

The massive crowd turned to see him and everyone started to chatter.

Coming up the Street was Boston Bill Black. He wore shackles on his hands and feet and was being escorted by Book on one side and Chastain on the other, and for extra precaution, every deputy that Appaloosa employed flanked them.

Black stood a full foot and a half taller than Chastain, Book, and the deputies. Looking at him like this reminded me of the story of Hercules as they approached. He was walking with his head up and was looking about, making sure everyone got a good look at him.

The chatter got louder as the crowd parted, making way for them, and when they got to the gallows steps the boisterous group began to jeer.

"Here we go," I said.

Virgil nodded.

We watched as Black climbed the steps. When he got to the top, the ministers held up their hands to quiet the crowd. After a bit, the crowd simmered. The Baptist minister moved forward a bit.

"Anything you wish to impart," he said. "Any last words?"

Black looked at the people, then looked to the executioner.

"Let's get this over with," he said.

The crowd erupted with excitement as the executioner moved forward and guided Black toward the gallows door. He positioned Black where he wanted and started to put a hood over Black's head.

"No hood," Black said. "I want to see the faces."

The crowd erupted loudly and began shouting, "Hang him, hang him . . ."

The executioner tossed the hood to the side, then reached up, grabbed the noose, and placed it over Black's head. He tightened it around Black's neck, then walked over to the lever. He put his hand on the lever.

"Fuck," I said. *"Look!"*

Sliding recklessly around the corner came Valentine's prison wagon being pulled by his sweat-soaked mules, Magellan and Columbus.

Valentine was on his feet with the reins in one hand and a bull-whip in the other. He was swinging the whip around and popping above the heads of his mules.

*"Haw!"* Valentine shouted, *"HAW!"*

*"Hold up!"* Virgil called out loudly. "Hold up!"

The executioner took his hand off the lever, and within a moment Magellan and Columbus parted the crowd and Valentine pulled back on the reins, stopping the prison wagon directly in front of the gallows in a cloud of dust.

Virgil and I moved forward, and when the dust settled we saw sitting in the back of the prison wagon Lawrence LaCroix.

# 73.

The remainder of July 3 was spent in the judge's chambers with Lawrence LaCroix.

LaCroix was still hurting from the beating he received from Black. His arm was in a sling and his leg was in a splint. His eyes were dark from having a broken nose and busted jaw, and it was painful for him to speak, but he was talking fairly clearly out of the corner of his mouth.

"Let me get this straight," the judge said. "You are not British?"

"No," he said. "I'm not . . ."

Callison shook his head and looked over to Virgil, Valentine, and me.

"Where are you from, Mr. LaCroix?"

"I was born and raised in Milwaukee, Wisconsin."

"Actually, let me ask you first before we get into more insanity, what is your real name?"

"Ben Salter."

Callison nodded.

"Ben Salter?"

"Yes."

"We can believe that?"

He nodded.

"We can assume you have no reason to lie about that?"

"No reason."

Callison shook his head.

"And, according to Mr. Pell here," Callison said with a glance to Valentine, "you have no idea who paid you to lie?"

"No," he said.

Callison looked at him for a moment, then sat back in his chair.

"You are a worthless piece of shit," the judge said. "You do realize that, don't you?"

He looked at the judge and lowered his head.

"I have been a judge longer than well water, and in that time I have never come across anything as despicable and atrocious as you."

Ben Salter's chin was on his chest.

"I needed the money," he said quietly.

"Come again?"

Ben looked up, making eye contact with Callison.

"I needed the money."

The judge shook his head in disbelief.

"You testified in that room out there," the judge said with a point toward the courtroom, "to send an innocent man to hang."

Ben Salter looked to the three of us, then back to the judge.

"It was him or me," he said.

"What do you mean by that?"

"I was over my head in debt," he said.

"Go on."

"Gambling debt, to some very unsavory men that were going to kill me. They'd killed others. I knew this, but I . . . had no choice."

"Where was this?"

"Saint Louis."

"You did not come here from Denver?"

"No, I did come in from Denver, I made the trip to Denver before I came here. I went to the police in Denver and told them I was an eyewitness, that was part of what I was supposed to do and then I came here, but I'm from Saint Louis."

"Why did you not just leave Saint Louis and get away from these men instead of doing what you did?"

He shook his head and started to cry.

"I have a wife and kids."

Callison shook his head.

"How was it this . . . anonymous . . . opportunity came about for you?" Callison said.

"I received an envelope with half the money that I owed," he said.

"How much money?"

"Twelve hundred dollars."

"Continue," Callison said with a roll of his finger.

"In the envelope was a letter with instructions on how and when, if I performed convincingly, as I had performed in . . . in the play, I would receive the other half."

"An additional twelve hundred?"

"Yes."

"And what made you think that there would be the money waiting for you?"

"There was the promise of a five-hundred-dollar bonus."

"And you believed this?"

"Yes, the fact there was twelve hundred was good enough for me."

Callison looked to us and shook his head dramatically.

"For the life of another man?"

He nodded.

"I fucked up."

"Oh, yes, you did," Callison said.

Callison glared at him for a moment.

Callison turned in his chair and pointed to the painting.

"This is not yours, I presume?"

Ben looked at the painting and shook his head.

"And you are not a painter?"

He shook his head.

"No."

"So how was it you acquired the . . . this *Bloom Where You Are Planted* painting you showed here as evidence?"

"The note had instructions for me and what I was to do."

"Which was what, exactly?"

"Arrive here," he said. "Check into the hotel and I would find further instruction. If I performed convincingly, I would get the rest of the money and the bonus."

"And what was the instruction?"

"There was the painting and a note detailing what I was to do with it."

Callison shook his head again.

"What is your profession?"

"I'm an actor," he said.

Callison's eyes got big.

"My God," he said. "A thespian?"

"Yes," he said.

"In Saint Louis?"

"Yes."

"Where did you receive this letter?"

"At the theater," he said. "In Saint Louis. The Saint Louis Theater."

"Explain," Callison said.

"I was doing a play," he said. "And after an evening performance I went back to my dressing room and I found the letter, with the money."

Callison turned and looked to us and shook his head slowly from side to side, then looked back to him.

"Where did you have this gambling debt?"

"All over town, really," he said. "I would borrow money, and I just kept borrowing, and I thought I would get ahead, but I didn't. For a while I was in very good favor, but then my debt got bad and I was kicked out of most places."

"Did you gamble in the casino that was opened by Mr. Black?"

"Yes."

"Yet you did not know Mr. Black?"

"No, I never met him. He was gone from Saint Louis before I ever went into the place."

"You say you were in good favor? What do you mean by that?"

"I had a credit line, but then it was called and I was barred from going into most places, including Pritchard's place."

"And you did not go to the police, I take it?"

He stared at Callison.

"No."

"You are in serious trouble," Callison said. "You understand this, don't you?"

"Yes," he said.

# 74.

July Fourth was a day of celebration. Judge Callison sat in his office with Virgil, Bill Black, Juniper, and me, and reviewed Black's history. He listened patiently and without expression to Juniper's exceptional but long-winded oratory regarding Black's wrongful incarceration, persecution, and sufferings.

When Juniper finished, Judge Callison stared at him for a long moment, then gazed out the window. Then he looked back behind his chair as if he heard something. After a few seconds he turned back to Black. He stared at Black for an enduring amount of time before he said anything.

"To say there is a litany of wrongdoing on your part, Mr. Black, would be a gross understatement."

Black sat, stoically looking at the judge.

"What you have done," Callison said, "what you have left in your wake cannot be reversed. Though I cannot hold you directly accountable for everything that has happened in your wake, I can, of course, not dismiss the direct disregard you have shown to the law and to the sanctity of the law and of this courtroom. So I find you guilty of destroying city property and charge you with a fine in the amount of however much it will cost to replace the bars you pried from the windows of the jail and the bed frame you ripped out of the floor . . . fair enough?"

"It is, Your Honor," Juniper said.

"I was not talking to you," Callison said.

Black held his head upright, smiled, and said, "Thank you."

That afternoon, I walked with Allie to the hospital to get Daphne.

"You're smitten," Allie said.

"You think?" I said.

"I do," she said.

"I like her."

"Like her," Allie said with a grin, then elbowed me in the ribs. "You're smitten."

"Maybe a little."

"I know she likes you."

"What's not to like," I said.

"That's true," she said. "You're a pretty fair catch."

We were approaching the hotel, where the chief was sitting on the porch with Detective King.

"Good afternoon," the chief said.

"It is," I said.

"Word?" he said, then scrutinized Allie a little and offered a crooked smile.

I glanced to Allie.

"Oh . . . go ahead, Everett," she said. "I want to get some clothes for Daphne, anyway. I know she'll appreciate it."

The chief watched as Allie walked up the steps past him and into the hotel, then leveled a harsh look at me.

"So the sonofabitch got off the hook?" the chief said.

"Obviously should have never been on the hook," I said.

"It's bullshit."

"Not."

"Oh, bullshit," he said. "If he did not do it. Then who the hell did?"

"I could ask you the same question," I said.

"And you think I would have an answer?"

"I don't know," I said. "Do you?"

"He tricked you," the chief said.

I looked off down the street, smiled a bit to myself, then looked back to him, but didn't say anything.

"He can't fool me," the chief said.

"No?"

"No," he said. "I don't care what happened with the fella that lied about what he saw."

"That seems apparent."

"He won't get away with this."

"Judge commuted his sentence," I said.

"So."

"So?"

"It's bullshit."

"No," I said with a smile, "it's not."

"It goddamn sure is," he said, getting to his feet aggressively.

Detective King got quickly out of his chair and put his hand on the chief's chest as a precaution to keep the chief from physically attacking me, which he was close to doing.

"Look," I said, "I know you lost your son and daughter-in-law, and I'm sorry for your . . ."

"She was nothing but a goddamn tramp," he said with red face. "A goddamn tramp."

Allie came out the door with a suitcase in her hand, looking at me like she had just seen a ghost. She glanced to the chief briefly and came down the steps in a hurry.

She hooked her arm in mine and said, "Come on, Everett."

I moved off with Allie as she practically dragged me away from the chief and Detective King.

I looked to her as we crossed the street in a hurry and tears were running down her cheeks.

"What is it, Allie?" I said. "What's wrong?"

Allie pulled me around the corner and we walked a ways farther until we got to an alley. Then she pulled me into the alley.

"What is it, Allie?"

She let go of me and continued to walk in the alley, and when she was ten feet in front of me she turned on me and said, "She did it."

"What?"

"She killed the woman in Denver."

"What?"

"Daphne," she said. "She did it, Everett."

Allie dropped to her knees and opened the suitcase. Inside the case were tubes of oil paints, brushes, and a tintype photograph of Bloom's Inn.

# 75.

Though it was not direct proof, it was proof enough that Daphne was in part responsible for the death of Ruth Ann Messenger. Allie did not accompany me to the hospital, nor did I go with Virgil. I went alone. I wanted to go alone. When I entered her room she was sitting up in bed smiling, and sitting with her, with his back to the door, was Bill Black. He turned and smiled at me.

"Howdy," Black said.

I nodded a bit.

"Everett," she said, "I'm so happy to see you today. Happy Independence Day."

Black's big frame blocked Daphne's view of the suitcase I held in my hand.

"Guess what?" she said.

"What?"

"Bill has asked me to marry him," she said.

Black nodded and looked back to me and smiled.

"I was stupid enough to let her get away before," he said. "Not this time, though."

"And you have accepted?"

She smiled.

"I have," she said.

I moved into the room, and when I did she saw the case in my hand. She stared at it as if I were holding something dead.

"No," she said, and shook her head.

"No what?" I said.

She stared at the case for a moment longer, then looked to Black. Black looked to the case, then looked to me.

"What?" he said with a grin.

I set the suitcase on the foot of the bed and Daphne recoiled like the thing that was dead was now alive.

"Found this in your room," I said. "In your closet."

"No," she said.

"Yes," I said.

She started to shake her head back and forth like a child refusing to listen to her parents. Then tears started to fall from her eyes.

"What's . . . what's going on?" Black said.

"I won't let you do this," she said. "I won't let you do this. I won't let you do this."

"I didn't do anything, Daphne," I said.

"What?" Black said. "What is it?"

"This is your doing, Daphne," I said.

"What's going on here?" he said, and reached for the suitcase.

"*No!*" Daphne screamed, and kicked the suitcase off the foot of the bed. It hit the wall next to the bed and opened, spilling the contents across the floor.

Black stood up and moved around the footboard to see the paints and brushes. He looked to me with a confused look on his face.

I walked to the case, bent down, and picked up the tintype photograph of Bloom's Inn and handed it to Black.

"You might want to reconsider that proposal," I said.

Black shook his head in disbelief and looked to Daphne.

"You?"

She smiled.

"It's not what you think, sweetie," she said.

Black looked to me.

"I just want to know if you did this alone," I said.

"Why," she said, "I don't know what you are talking about."

"You did this?" Black said.

"No, sweetie," she said.

"You did," he said. "Didn't you?"

She stared blankly at Black but said nothing. Then she backed up, curled into a ball at the headboard, and cowered like she was about to be beat.

Black looked to me slowly and said, "My God."

I moved toward her, and her eyes were wide with fear. She turned her head to the side but remained looking at me out of the corner of her eye.

"Daphne," I said.

She cocked her head a little.

"Yes, Daddy," she said.

I moved closer and she smiled.

"Daphne?"

She looked away.

"Daphne?"

She did not respond. She stared off, looking at nothing. It was now very clear to both Black and me that she was not well.

Black stared at her, but she did not look at him. She kept looking away, staring at nothing. He shook his head and moved the chair back away from the bed and sat.

"Daphne?" he said.

She did not respond.

"Are you not listening?"

She did not respond.

Black shook his head.

"My God," he said.

I moved around to the other side of the bed, in the direction she was staring. I moved close to her and it was clear she was in some kind of shock. I looked to Black and he shook his head.

"Before," he said, "I met this beautiful woman, I never knew anyone brighter, smarter, or kinder . . . but then there was always . . . I don't know, something unusual. There were glimpses of someone other than her, within her, someone other than the bright, smart, and kind woman I got to know and love. I never was certain why I moved away from her but I knew there was something . . ."

"You left her?" I said.

He nodded and leaned over with his elbows on his knees and stared at the floor.

"I'd seen this before. Not like this, not this bad, but some. I also sensed a grave jealousy within her, but she never really, truly acknowledged it or acted out about it . . ."

"Think she's done that now," I said.

# 76.

A tiny light whistled up high into the dark night, followed by an astounding kaleidoscope of bright red, white, and blue light that exploded in the night sky.

"Oh, my," Allie said.

An enormous boom immediately followed.

"*Oh!*" Allie said, placing her hand to her chest. "That was loud."

"Sure was," Valentine said.

"So interesting how the boom happens after," she said.

"Happens at the same time, Allie," Valentine said. "Just sound travels a hell of a lot slower than light."

Virgil, Allie, Valentine, and I were sitting on the front porch of Virgil and Allie's house, watching the fireworks display that was being put on by Pritchard's grand opening of his casino.

Earlier in the day, after Daphne had rested from her confrontation with me, and her subsequent mental lapse, she came to, not really remembering everything that had happened really clearly, but remembering enough.

Black and Pritchard remained with her throughout the afternoon as we made arrangements with the Denver contingent to take her back to Denver, where she would be charged with the murder of Ruth Ann Messenger.

Another tiny light whistled up high in the sky, followed by an exploding circle of bright sizzling white light and a boom.

"A dandelion," Allie said.

"Big one," Virgil said.

"That is so beautiful," she said.

"It is," Valentine said.

Another big one exploded, sending red twinkling streamers falling from the sky.

"Oh . . . look at that," Allie said.

The fireworks kept coming.

"And that," she said. "Would you look at that?"

"Another good one," Virgil said.

"That one had some spread," Valentine said, "and some kick."

"Did," Virgil said.

We watched as the fireworks continued. A huge exploding blue one lit up the evening expanse very brightly, followed by an enormous loud boom.

"Oh, my," Allie said. "Gosh . . . that one was really loud."

I looked to Allie as she stared up at the sky. She was beaming like a little girl . . . and it made me smile some. Though none of us, particularly me, were in the mood for celebration, we were doing our best.

We watched for a while before anyone said anything else. The fireworks were, as Pritchard promised, a spectacular display. He was not wrong. It was outstanding.

Allie grinned as she looked up. Her eyes were fixed and childlike.

I thought sadly of Daphne earlier in the day and how she, too, was so childlike, but the tragic circumstances were very different.

Allie, I thought, was not at all without her own disappointments and tragedies in life. She had been through a hell of a lot.

"Look at that one," Valentine said.

Hell, in hindsight, we all had been through a lot. I looked to Virgil and Valentine and thought we all have lived somewhat desperate lives and, in some ways, many lives. The person we were before was not necessarily who we were today. But then again, it's circumstances that pretty much make us who we are.

But what Daphne had endured as a child was horrific. Pritchard was the least astonished to learn of what had happened to Ruth Ann Messenger.

Turned out he knew Daphne's father and knew he was not the mathematician she said he was. In fact, he was a drunk that Daphne had taken care of since the day her mother walked out. According to Pritchard, her father abused her in ways that were unimaginable, and before Pritchard had him arrested and sent away, Daphne attempted to beat him to death with a shovel as he slept. Since that time, Pritchard had treated and raised her like his own daughter. He loved her, and though he was dreadfully deflated to learn the news about the killing of Ruth Ann Messenger, he understood it. He said there was a rage that remained inside her that he could never help suppress, relieve, or alleviate. He also knew she was brilliant, and the scheme of how she wanted to persecute Black for breaking off their engagement was also no surprise to him.

"Look at that one," Allie said. "Who would have thought?"

"The Chinese," Valentine said. "Hell, all the way back to the Tang dynasty."

"Well, it's remarkable," she said. "Don't know how on earth they do it."

"Gunpowder," Virgil said.

"Yep . . . Some Chinaman mixed charcoal, sulfur, and saltpeter together and . . . boom," Valentine said. "Gunpowder. First invented to scare off evil spirits . . . now it is more commonly used in one form or another to kill people."

I glanced over at Virgil, and he was staring at Valentine as he watched the fireworks. He remained looking at his big brother for a moment, then Virgil looked over to me as I looked back up. I could feel Virgil looking at me, but I continued to watch the dazzling display that was taking place for the grand opening of the Maison de Daphne.

## ACKNOWLEDGMENTS

As always, "much obliged" goes out to G. P. Putnam's Sons' president, Ivan Held; my editor extraordinaire, Chris Pepe; and Helen Brann for shuffling and dealing up this newest adventure with Hitch and Cole. Like Virgil says, "This sort of work we do is always a gamble." So I appreciate those who have pulled up a chair, put their chips on the table, and anted up. Without that ante there is simply nothing to win or lose, and for this go-round I have to say *muchas gracias* to gifted mountain guide Rob Wood of Rancho Roberto, Jamie "Whatnot" Whitcomb, Rex "Double Down" Linn, Jared Moses, Genevieve Negrete, Jayne Amalia Larson, Kevin Meyer, and the shifty-eyed Mike Rose. My apologies to Alice DiGregorio, Claudia, Pete, Ingrid, and Lucy Crosen for putting up with my sequestering during our retreat. And to Julie Rose for putting up with me, period. A big hand for Ed Harris, the great and talented man who so expertly brought Virgil Cole to life on the silver screen, and the incomparable Viggo Mortensen for his voice of Everett Hitch that keeps coming around throughout. And I'd like to raise you a thousand for my riverboat steam crew: Josh Kesselman, Allison Binder, agent Steve Fisher, and the rest of the

## ACKNOWLEDGMENTS

crafty card sharps at APA. A rousing toast to my sisters—the Clog-
ging Castanets—Sandra and Karen, for dancing around the table.
And in memory of Robert and Joan Parker, a tip of the hat for reminding me of the most significant of all gambler's creeds: never sit
with your back to the door.